How to Forget Almost Everything

A novel by
Joshua James Amberson

"A portrait of a thoughtful teenage outcast, learning that just like many mysteries that have come before, the quest isn't necessarily about what to do, but rather, in figuring out exactly what one's personal quest is."
 – Liz Mason, author of the *Caboose* and *Awesome Things* zine series

"Charming, poignant, and funny, *How to Forget Almost Everything* is a wonderfully written coming-of-age tale that vibrates with truth."
 – Annie Hartnett, author of *Rabbit Cake* and *Unlikely Animals*

"Joshua James Amberson creates a character who's familiar and intimate, someone to root for, to cheer on, to be angry at, to welcome home. His book presents a world in which it might be easier to forget but ultimately you–and Elly–come to understand that our memories, fleeting and fragile and imprecise, are what make us whole."
 – Tomas Moniz, author of *Big Familia* and *All Friends Are Necessary*

"I want to tell you that *How to Forget Almost Everything* is an absolute triumph of a book, with winning characters and a fascinating plot. These things are true, yet I think the lovably flawed main character, Elly Fox, might question the use of words like "absolute" and "triumph." Through his unconventional quest to help his mom and discover the meaning of memory, he learns to question the whole notion of winners and losers, villains and heroes, and absolutism of any kind. He's the fifteen-year-old philosopher and dear friend that we all need right now, no matter our age, and I honestly can't remember a time when a character—and an entire book—made me feel so gleeful about living in our uncertain world."
 – Justin Hocking, author of *The Great Floodgates of the Wonderworld* and *PS: The Wolves*

"I fell in love with Elly and his world from the very first page of this book. His voice is the beating heart of this novel, and with Elly, Amberson has created a narrator that feels as real and authentic as my own friends. I couldn't put *How to Forget Almost Everything* down!"

    – Lauren Hobson, Founder and Editor-in-Chief of *Kithe Journal.*

"I didn't know what to expect, launching into a novel with such a seemingly whimsical, sublime title. Was it a coming of age tale, or one about the dread of watching a loved one mentally unravel? It's that and so much more. Insightful, relatable, heartbreaking...Amberson has written quite a remarkable story."

    –Jonas Cannon, author of *Especially Now* and *The Greatest Most Traveling Circus!*

Korza Books
www.KorzaBooks.com
1819 Sw 5th Ave #293
Portland, Oregon 97201

Cover collage by Fred Thomas
Cover and interior design by Andrew Barton

First Paperback Edition November 2022

ISBN: 978-1-957024-03-5
Korza Books name and logo are registered trademarks of Korza Books LLC

HOW TO

FORGET

ALMOST EVERYTHING

Formerly Known as Normal

Driving around in our tiny, aging pick-up truck, my mom, out of nowhere, said, "You and me, Elly, we have genius hair."

I looked at her, trying to determine whether this was a joke. She had her gray-streaked brown (questionably genius) hair tied back in a bun it was rebelling against. Her eyes were fixed on the road, her face neutral, making it impossible to tell if she was messing with me. "Mom, you might be a genius, but you're already well aware that I am not."

"I remember," she said, pausing a little too long. "You took that test online." She laughed. "You're still upset about that?"

"I was upset in the moment. But as they say, time heals all wounds."

"Wasn't that just last week?"

"Like I said, time heals."

"Neither of us are geniuses," she said, "and that's okay. It's probably better that way—most geniuses aren't the happiest or most socially adept people. But we both have genius hair."

Without meaning to, I ran my hands through my tangle of curls and waves, my palm landing on a patch of cheek stubble on the way back down. I winced and immediately felt silly—it shouldn't be that big of a deal. "And where does this term come from, exactly?" I asked.

"This comes courtesy of my hairdresser."

"Your coworker who gives haircuts out of her apartment?"

"That's the one."

"I don't know if that's a reliable source, Mom. I mean, this all sounds sort of ridiculous."

"It could be, but I just thought you should know there's a name for our hair and that name is genius." She said it like it was a commercial for a product called Genius Hair. She took her eyes off the road long enough to give me a wink.

I couldn't help but smile. "Okay, sell me on this."

"So—again, according to my hairdresser—geniuses have an inclination towards messy, unruly hair. This part is a biological mystery, I guess. But the important part is that when people are really smart, they don't consider their personal appearance in the same way other people do. For example, glasses on smart people is a thing because the smarties are too busy to wear contacts like a normal person." She adjusted her boxy, oversized frames. "And their clothes are always wrinkled or have holes. But hair is the big one, that's how you really know. They're thinking about the universe—geniuses don't have time to worry about their hair."

"I'm unconvinced," I said. "But not as unconvinced as I thought I would be."

"I think she was trying to tell me my hair is a disaster, while making it sound like a compliment."

The community radio station droned in the background, as we laughed about our mutual hair catastrophe, the late-summer sun trying its best to warm us through the rolled-up windows. Only later that night did I realize it was a good day—a day where she didn't forget anything, a day where I rode in a car with her and wasn't nervous. In the past I wouldn't have noticed it. I would have called it normal. But now I call it good. It was a day where I could fool myself into believing nothing was wrong.

No Beginning

The week before she told me about genius hair, my mom drove us into oncoming traffic on one of the busiest streets in Portland, Oregon. We were leaving the Goodwill when she took a turn and became one of those people from out of town, going the wrong way on a one-way street. I was reading the first page of a dollar-book I'd just bought and, even though I wasn't watching the road, I immediately got an internal sense that something was off. I looked up from the page, the opening words of a world I was deciding whether or not to enter, and saw we'd entered an actual world where everything was against us: four lanes of traffic, threatening to kill us, all at once.

I shouted, but she didn't seem to hear me—just squinted like she was trying to see through a patch of thick fog. She crossed lanes, bee-lining toward the closest side-street, while honking cars dodged around us, barely missing. We made it to the far lane and came face-to-face with a lifted white pick-up nearly twice our size, its horn creating a wall of sound into which I yelled *Mom, Mom, Mom*. Gripping my seat, I braced for the hit, wondering if this was the end and, if it was the end, the end of what. I considered the whole of existence in that blink of an eye and the moment before we slammed into the truck, she turned the wheel, drove up onto the sidewalk, stomped on the brakes, bumped a street sign, and came to a stop.

Her mouth opened and out came a loop of panicked questions, her face stark white. She was like one of those dolls where you push a button or pull a string, and it says the same lines again and again. What happened, where are we, why are we on the sidewalk. *What happened, where are we, why are we on the sidewalk*. All questions that, I quickly found out, couldn't be answered from just a single response, they need-ed to be answered over and over. Just as the answers began to sink in, the owner of the white truck that had almost killed us appeared in her window, knocking, yelling. Soon after the cops came.

I watched her walk an imaginary line and touch her nose for the police, unable to figure out what had happened to her. Unable to understand how she could turn the wrong way on a street she went the right way on all the time. I couldn't make sense out of any of it until, suddenly, I could. Suddenly everything I'd been ignoring came rushing in, becoming impossible to ignore. Forgotten names, late bills, misplaced keys, repeated conversations—all these moments I'd previously told myself were isolated incidents in the life of my otherwise organized, adamantly sober mom. In that moment, I realized they were all connected, all part of something bigger.

She convinced the cops and the angry driver it was an honest mistake, that she simply hadn't been paying attention, and everyone drove away. But I knew—from the look in her eyes as she faced the truck coming toward us, the questions she asked in the moments after—that it wasn't that simple. I knew this almost-accident was somehow an oversized, scarier form of a forgotten name, or a repeated story.

I've spent a lot of my waking hours since then trying to figure out when her forgetting began. Trying to locate the first time within all this life my mom and I have shared. Replaying so many dull, passing moments. But there doesn't seem to be a sure beginning to it, no first time, just a pile of experiences for me to sift through and decide what to do with.

Life in the Moment

Since that day, I keep asking myself, trying to imagine: What's life without the memory of life? People always say to live in the moment. Instead of obsessing over the past or future, we should experience what's happening, right now, while it's happening. So maybe forgetting everything that came before could be a good thing—a complete embrace of the moment. But without memories, wouldn't the moment just be a jumble of unfamiliar people saying words without context in mysterious settings? The moment would probably be too confusing to embrace.

Thinking about memory is, in itself, pretty confusing. I'd prefer to go back to not thinking about it and believing it was something that, for everyone, just happened. Sure, sometimes we'd forget a detail or an appointment, but it wouldn't be a big deal. Someone would remind us, we would reschedule. I just don't think it's that simple anymore.

I wish I wasn't thinking about life without memory. But as it is, I have to think about it. Or I just can't stop. One of the two.

Limitations

Before my recent preoccupation with memory, I was mostly concerned with the limitations of my experience. In brief: for my entire 15 years on this planet, my life has mostly taken place within a few-mile radius. Almost everything I've ever done has happened in or around one small box with two bedrooms, a living room, and a kitchen, all with drab green walls, in the Brooklyn neighborhood of rainy Portland. Even our neighborhood feels like it has limitations, walls that keep me trapped along this southern edge of the city—the least-safe bridge in our city of bridges, a four-lane boulevard that never stops, a set of train tracks that blocks traffic for hours each day, and a big industrial zone that looks like Mars or a city after the apocalypse. It doesn't even feel like what people say Portland is supposed to feel like. Even though on a map it doesn't look far away from some of the big tourist streets, no one mentions how long the two buses take to get to those places or how helpless it feels to be waiting on a train that's been fully stopped on the tracks for most of an hour.

I take the bus to school. I run errands with my mom. Once or twice a year I climb into the middle seat of her truck and ride with her and my uncle out to the coast, 90 uneventful miles from our apartment, to stare at the ocean and collect rocks that never look as interesting off the beach as they do on the beach. But the rest of my life is enclosed within 800 square feet.

The same week as the almost-accident, I began my second year of high school. The night before the first day of school, I read a couple chapters of a book my uncle had checked out from the library about how the world is supposed to end in 2012—the very year I'm supposed to graduate—and it freaked me out. I don't know if I believed it, but it just reminded me that life is unpredictable and out of our control and what if it ends and I have nothing to show for it except 12 years of public school?

So at lunch on that first day, I stood on the Block, a piece of concrete tucked away behind the metal-shop building—a block my friends and I have claimed, as much as a piece of concrete can be claimed, as our own—and I told my two best friends Maddy and Claudia that this was the beginning of a new me. A me who goes places. They asked where I was going, and I told them I didn't know. But somewhere, I said. Many wheres. This, I declared, was the year things would change.

My mom has cashiered at a local grocery store since I was a kid and we have zero rich relatives, so if I want to go anywhere I need a job. But since most businesses don't hire people who are younger than sixteen, I needed to get creative. So I made a flier that said, *Elly Fox: professional for hire.* I thought simply saying *professional* would leave my options open to whatever type of worker a person might need. I consider myself very adaptable and, at least, aspirationally professional. But I decided to add, in small print, *aspiring archivist, experienced counselor, potential babysitter*, just in case. Some people get overwhelmed by possibilities.

At the bottom of the flier I drew a cartoon of me looking professional—the little square grandma glasses I bought from a thrift store this summer, a mess of hair on top of my head, and my pointer finger in the air like I've just made a big discovery and am saying, *Eureka*! I put my cell phone number on it—still new enough that I almost wrote our landline number by accident—made copies on my mom's absurdly loud printer, thumb-tacked it to my apartment building's two laundry-room bulletin boards, taped two in the stairwell, set aside a pile to hang up around the neighborhood, and crossed my fingers.

The flier was perhaps a bit childish, but I didn't see a better way. It was also fun. And I don't believe in depriving myself of fun based on culturally enforced age restrictions. So it also supported my belief system.

Why Blue

Since starting sophomore year of high school, I've been reading my uncle's library books as a way to make myself smarter. I figure we only have so long on this planet and I should learn as much as I can as soon as possible. While this fact has made most people think I'm very scholarly, I'm not especially great at school. I don't really care about wars and grammar and algebra-trig, but I do care about thinking deeply. People always say this means I'm philosophical, which sounds nice and good, but whenever I try to read philosophy the philosophers always seem to be arguing about whether god exists or if something we can't ever prove could really be true or not, and that's not the sort of stuff I care about either.

In this year of Uncle-book-study, my mom has always asked me about the books. "What's new in-between the pages?" she says, often while we sit at the bar, the little kitchen counter built into the apartment, where we have stools and spend most of our free time together. At first I think she was just amused that her teen boy was reading adult books, but over time it became our thing—she asks the page question, I tell her what I think of the book, she asks something like, "but what's the book making you think *about*; where is it taking your mind?", and I tell her where it's taking my mind. Then she tells me about her mind, and we both leave feeling pretty interested in each other's minds.

But I recently realized she hasn't asked me the page question in months. Once, a few weeks ago, I told her, unprompted, about a book I was reading where an Irish guy wanders around in an illogical rural dreamworld talking to cops about bicycles, which made no sense but was really fun to read, and she didn't say much at all—no page question, no taking-my-mind question. And when I brought it up the next day she didn't remember what I was talking about, despite it being an

Irish dreamworld, which seems pretty memorable.

There's a woman who wrote a book all about the color blue. "Why blue?" people asked her, and she told them, "We don't get to choose what or whom we love."

I've wanted to ignore the daily signs, the memories of past daily signs. The ones that confirm something isn't right. But I can't ignore them. In fact, they're pretty much all I can think about.

This is something I don't understand: why we think about things we don't want to think about. Why we can't always choose where our mind goes. And I have a feeling it's something like the woman with the book about blue—we just can't decide some things. We think we're in control of our thoughts and feelings, but in reality we're not. Our feelings have their own feelings; our minds have minds of their own.

Here's what I think of when I think about memory: all the thrillers and dumb comedies about people who have amnesia, elephants, Leonardo da Vinci (I don't know why), the card game some people call Match Match or Pairs but I call Concentration, my mom, my mom.

I've figured out worrying is just thinking about something you don't want to think about more than once. Which makes it sound not so bad. But, somehow, when it's actually happening, it's really bad.

Signs

My mom walked in the door. She was in her work clothes, the right sleeve of her unflattering-on-everyone khaki polo shirt accidentally rolled up so she looked like she was trying to be a tough guy, showing off her muscles, rolling up a pack of smokes.

"I just saw your fliers while walking up the stairs," she said, her eyes adding some questions her mouth didn't say.

"I'm glad word is getting around," I said, trying to keep it light.

She didn't smile. "I didn't know you wanted a job. What's the situation there?"

"Well, I guess I just want to make some money."

"That's fair. Money is useful. But it just seems odd that you haven't mentioned this to me at all and now our whole building knows you're in need of money. I mean, are you saving to buy something in particular?"

I hadn't thought this part through, since I didn't imagine the questioning would come on so hard. I wanted to tell her the truth: that I just wanted some extra money to have some adventures. Maybe I just wanted to bus to the end of the line and take a hike in Forest Park, or bus to St. John's and hang out under the elaborate bridge that's kind of part of Portland and kind of not. I didn't really know, but my life in the apartment was feeling cramped. I wanted to say all this, but I could tell I'd already hurt her feelings by not discussing the flier with her first, and I worried I'd hurt her feelings again by telling her our life didn't feel like enough to me anymore. So I did something I almost never did: I lied.

"It's for a volunteer program," I said. "To help elderly people. Me and Maddy are doing it. We travel around to different senior centers and old folks' homes and just, you know, hang out with them. Do nice things. Play checkers or whatnot. It's like an early college transcript thing; the more volunteer hours you have, the better it looks. We just need to have money for the bus and getting food and stuff." I tried to stiffen the muscles in my face, thinking it might make me look sure of myself, but it just felt like my chin was twitching.

She seemed to think it over. My mom almost never feels like a real authority figure, but I had to admit that her long, stern pause was pretty tense and believably strict mom-esque. I wondered if this was part of my new mom—a forgetful disciplinarian mom?—or just an isolated incident. Finally she said, "And how exactly are you a professional?"

"A professional?" I tried to imitate the sounds of puzzlement, even though I knew exactly what she was referring to.

"The sign claims you're a professional."

I don't know if I'd ever admitted to myself how much I actually wanted to be a professional until that moment. Not to boss people around or have a lot of power, but just to be focused and put-together and passionate—to have some specific importance in the world. I felt my reasons so intensely in the few seconds she waited, but I knew they would sound dumb or conceited once they left my head and landed on the air, so instead I said, "It does say that. That's true. Technically I'm not a professional in any known profession. But I am very confident. Which is a professional trait."

"That still doesn't make it true," she said.

"Maybe I just thought people would think it was funny," I said, even though I very much hoped people didn't.

She sighed a little, not like she was frustrated but like she was figuring out what to do on the spot. "How about you take 'professional' off the fliers, and you can leave them up. Sound good?"

I nodded.

"And just don't lie to our neighbors, okay?"

"Of course," I said, feeling glad she didn't ask me not to lie to her.

It's a Weird Deal

My dad is dead. Which sounds horrible and sad, but is kind of just neutral and odd. It's simply a fact I know to be true. For it to be horrible and sad, I would have first had to know him. Or my mom would have had to be desperately in love with him, and her deep well of sadness would have had to rub off onto my existence. But since I didn't know him at all and she only barely knew him, it's hard to feel very emotional about it. He was just a guy my mom was starting to date and before he even knew my mom was pregnant, he slipped while working on the roof of a house and was gone.

Sometimes my mom will talk to me about my dad. She'll tell me the few pieces of information she knows about him, and I always tell her, "Stop. It's okay. I don't need to know." And she'll nod and say, "It's a weird deal," which is her go-to phrase when talking about my dad. Every time. Because it is. It is a weird deal. I don't know anyone else with a dad who's dead.

What I Have

I walked around our neighborhood, staple-gunning the remaining fliers to telephone poles and a couple fir trees that probably didn't deserve such treatment, wondering if someone who wasn't me would think my little world was special instead of stifling. I knew generally that people did—everyone talked about how people were moving here from other places, that Portland was changing, and I assumed that meant it was better than some other places. But it was hard for me to see without having been to these other, presumably less-good places. Was it strange to want to go to places that were worse than the place you started? Or was better and worse not really the point and each place was uniquely its own? I just couldn't be sure.

The houses got bigger just a half-block south of our apartment. It was the opposite of everything just north and west of it, where traffic, trains, and industrial warehouses ruled. It was all houses with porches, old but not too old, that looked iconic in a way that belonged to some named architectural style I didn't know about. There were big-leaf maples hovering over the sidewalks, just starting to lose their leaves. Somewhere close by there was the entrance to the Springwater Corridor, a trail I only ever found by accident because I don't have a good sense of direction. I tried to imagine the whole neighborhood and this combination of things from the eyes of someone who had never lived inside it all, and I couldn't.

When I got back, I opened the door to an obstacle course of books. All from the public library, all belonging to my uncle. He was digging through his bookshelf on the other side of the course, apparently working out some sort of system in piles across the floor. My uncle checks out more books than anybody I know—enough to keep a medium-sized bookshelf at capacity at any given time. The sheer amount is absurd, but without it I wouldn't have read anything interesting at all, so I can't complain.

Before I even closed the door, he said, "I think the note that kicked it off was *Look up*! I made it because my shoulder had been dislocated from above while at work. This was maybe five or six years ago, I'd guess."

My uncle has a habit of starting a conversation as if it were the middle of a conversation. Which, if you see someone every day, is not completely untrue; there are continuing conversations that just get separated by sleep or work or school. Still, it's the type of thing you get used to but also never really get used to.

"I'm guessing this is how your habit of making Post-It reminders started, Uncle?" I said, remembering a question I'd asked him last night that he didn't have the answer to. Our fridge, the bathroom mirror, the dashboard of his car—all are covered with my uncle's Post-It notes. Some are practical suggestions ("Try brushing in a circular fashion"), some are inspirational quotes ("Be as simple as you can be; you will be astonished to see how uncomplicated and happy your life can become"), and some are just one-word shopping lists ("Grain").

"Your guess is correct," he said, running his hand through his tangled shoulder-length hair. "When my shoulder was hit, I was staring at the floors—I was a change-scrounger at the time, always looking for dimes and quarters wherever I went, even while on the job. I was also new to graveyards and didn't understand how accident-prone those nocturnal hours can be—then, pow! My coworker dropped a box of replacement canning lids from a stock-picker, it landed on my right shoulder—missing my head by a matter of inches—and I was left with an arm out of its socket and a new mantra."

I might not have a dad but I have an uncle, my mom's younger brother, who goes to bed just before I get up and wakes up just before I get home from school—and often picks up his library holds immediately upon waking. He has a small car that doubles as a partial storage shed, there's a friend's house he crashes at every once in a while, but for the most part he's lived on the couch in our living room since I was a little kid. He originally moved in because of a short-lived gambling problem that left him without an apartment, owing money to his entire friend group, but I imagine now—over a decade later, with half of those years spent working graveyard inventory shifts at the same store my mom works at—he could get his own place. But he just doesn't. To other people the whole thing sounds like a less-than-ideal situation but, in my opinion, it's completely ideal. My uncle is one of my favorite people.

"Initially the note was just a reminder to stay safe at work," he said, "but in time it came to mean more. I look at it now as a reminder to pay attention in a broader sense, to not let life pass by. *Look up*! it commands. And so I do."

"I had no idea a Post-It note could have so much depth."

From his spot on the floor, he took a slight bow and went back to his stacks. In his ratty flannel with his glasses on his head, he looked like an eccentric professor from the '90s.

My mom has asked him to move in multiple times—we could put up curtains and turn the couch into his own makeshift room—but he says it would change things if he officially lived here. So he just helps with bills and groceries and continues to sleep on the un-curtained couch. He seems to fear change. And, in a way, I do too. Life in our little box might be limiting, but it's comfortable. I want to go on adventures, sure, but I also want our apartment world to stay the same.

All Our Lies

Neuroscientists claim that every time you recall a memory you change it. So the memories of how you met your closest friends, or the day you fell off the swing and broke your arm are probably less factually true because you've thought about them a lot and told stories about them. And each time you've unintentionally added very slight pieces of fiction—altered details here and there, things that made the story better or easier to tell—while the real details got worn away.

So the truest memories are the ones we haven't thought about much, or haven't told stories about. And the memories we love the most are the biggest lies, or at least the biggest half-truths. Which is pretty depressing. But not as depressing as not remembering anything.

What I Dislike About Books

When I was heading out the door for school, I saw my mom kick over the box we use for recycling in the kitchen, spilling a single empty Adams peanut butter jar onto the linoleum. I had no clue what could make my even-tempered-to-a-fault mom kick an innocent box, but I'd been trying to distract my brain from the image of it all morning. I'd been reading a novel in the brief in-between moments of my day, the downtime where my mind might not be distracted enough, but it was one where the main character just reads and reads and reads and the writer is essentially like, "Isn't reading—this thing you're doing right now, dear reader—just the best?"

I shut the book and turned to Maddy. "You know what I dislike about books?" It was the beginning of lunch, and we were waiting in the big central courtyard for Claudia so we could all make the trek to the Block together.

"I'm going to guess absolutely nothing," she answered. "Because you read more than anyone I know. Even more than my parents."

"'Absolutely nothing' is a good guess, but no, there's actually one big thing: Almost every main character in almost every book loves to read. And if they don't, or when other characters don't, it's as sad as if they had a life-threatening disease. Have you ever noticed this?"

"No, but I don't read that much."

"That's sad," I said.

"I know, I might as well have leukemia or something."

"But really you're just like most people. And that's who I'd like to see more of in books."

"People who might as well have leukemia?"

"No, people who know how to read but choose to solely read text messages and sports statistics and magazine beauty tips with this ability."

Maddy flipped open her phone, pretending to ignore me.

"Someday," I said, "I'd like to read a book where there's a main character who isn't illiterate but doesn't really like to read books." I watched her put her phone away, pull out her duct-tape wallet, and dig through what seemed to be neatly organized rows of business cards. "Because I think that's way more common."

"Sorry, were you saying something?" Maddy asked, not looking up.

"No, you must be hearing voices. You should get that checked out."

"You're right, I'll head to the doctor right now. I'm sure I have his card in here somewhere," she said as she walked away, still digging through her wallet. I thought she might turn around eventually, but she just kept going. I loved that I had a friend who would carry a joke out far enough to actually walk away and not come back.

Watching her fade into the distance with her worn, formerly bright-blue Jansport pulled tight, I thought about how Maddy had a way of being a complete nerd and inherently cool at the same time. Unexplainably cool. Any other kid with a backpack that high up on her back, a mop of home-cut hair that fell continuously into her face, who didn't smoke weed or play sports and had an unusually deep voice, would be endlessly picked on. But no one messed with Maddy. Even though she was a nice, half-Vietnamese secular Jewish kid who had never done anything violent, or even mid-level harmful. Some of the mean cheerleader girls even said hi to her in the halls. The whole thing baffled me, but also made me a little proud.

Claudia walked up. "Thanks for waiting," she said, before looking around, pursing her lips, and sliding them to the right—the face she makes anytime something she assumed would be the case isn't the case. "And Maddy is where?"

"She left," I said, still half-watching her faint shape fade into the distance. "But it's for the best."

What We Call Each Other

Fourth period I had U.S. history with the teacher who won't get my name right. He's older, a military-reserves guy who sometimes shows up to class in uniform, and always references various mysterious personal grudges he seems to think we're all involved in and grudging about too. I try to be understanding—he's from a different generation, he's just not familiar with my name, he thinks boy-names are more limited than they are or should be—but he doesn't seem to extend the same understanding to me. At this point it just seems like I have to prepare myself for a minor fight each time I go into class, since he's evidently decided to call on me every day. And there it was, before the bell even finished ringing.

"Elias, would you be kind enough to read what's on the board?"

Having glanced at what was on the board, I knew it was a quote from some military general, blabbing about some apparently significant battle I'd heard of but didn't care about. The battle and the quote felt so far away from the current moment; it was hard to imagine anyone even making a case for how fighting with muskets and cannons connected to smart phones and a recession. I didn't exactly know what history class should be about, but I knew it should be something other than this. "Of course," I said. "But it's Elly, sir."

"Well, I don't see that name on my roster," he said, running his finger down his clipboard in one big exaggerated motion. "But I do see an Elias." I didn't understand how he could say these lines to me day after day, why he'd picked this battle, how exactly this qualified as school.

"Again, sir, while that is my birth name, it's a name that neither I nor my family has ever used." The idea I've been working with is that I can formally polite him into submission, even though the technique has so far gotten me nowhere.

"These pieces of information do not matter in this classroom. All that matters is what's on my attendance." He smiled a little when he said it, victorious because of some rule he created, the little nubby military-cut hairs on his head gleaming in the terrible fluorescent lighting.

I read the stupid quote on the board from some general who was probably an awful person, but it was just a string of words that amounted to no meaning in my brain. All I could think about was the unfairness of the world. Like, how did this guy have power and I had none? Why should I accept being called by a name I'd never even used?

My mom says she named me after the inventor of the sewing machine, because the movie *Help*! is jokingly dedicated to him and she always thought it was a fun detail. "But as soon as you were born your uncle and I knew the name just didn't fit you," she's told me a thousand times. So they called me Eli, which I couldn't pronounce when I started talking and instead said something close to Elly. So everyone started saying Elly. And it stuck. When I was about to start kindergarten my mom sat me down and warned me that people at school would probably tell me that my name was a girl's name, so we could start using Eli if I wanted. "But Elly is my name," I told her.

Sometimes it feels like my name is a shirt that was put onto me at two years old, and I just continue to grow into it. Like, it fits better now than it did then and maybe when my body is full grown I'll fit into it perfectly. Or I'll outgrow it and pick up a name that can act as a new, more appropriately fitting shirt. But I think it's my choice. All I should have to do is communicate my preferred name clearly and kindly—just because it's not technically legally correct shouldn't mean it's any less real.

I watched him strutting around the classroom, harassing other people who didn't deserve to be harassed, and I wondered why he was like this, who he was outside of the classroom, what he was trying to do. I tried to think about how he might be an alright guy and maybe had reasons for being this way—his own harassers, a soft inner self he was trying to protect with a hard outer shell—but then I thought about him calling me Elias and stopped.

My Nightmare Over Coffee

After school, Maddy reappeared and we rode the bus to Southeast Grind, the only coffee place vaguely near our houses. It's a 24-hour mess of stained couches, bad psychedelic art, and even worse coffee, but it feels like home. The rare times we've made it to coffee shops in other parts of the city, they always feel so blank and sterile, like all the life had been drained out of them and replaced with a design principle.

Maddy was planning our next themed movie night, something we'd been doing for years that had gone from a rare-times-only event to an almost-every-Saturday plan ever since we did a birthday-themed movie marathon for my birthday at the end of July. Since then, movie night had come to occupy a lot of our discussions and debates. In general, I don't know as much about movies as Maddy, I don't do the research she does, but I always like talking about her ideas and coming up with innovative themes together. This time, though, I had nothing to add. In my mind was a week's worth of memory-loss research, a pile of worry over my mom, and not much else. I hadn't told Maddy about the almost-accident, the revelation it triggered, or my research—even though I told Maddy about most things. I couldn't explain why I hadn't, but there was something that, at least for the time being, felt private about it all—something I needed to figure out for myself before I could bring her into it.

In the middle of a sentence about the pitfalls of movies featuring animal actors, Maddy casually smiled and waved at someone coming through the door. I turned, then quickly turned back around, wondering what gravitational force makes it so the person you least want to run into is the one you run into the most.

My personal nightmare-human is named Rain Mallory—my secret tormentor, the only person who could truly make me feel like dirt, and my former best friend. We became friends in fourth grade and spent most waking moments together for more than a year, but in retrospect she was only friends with me because she thought I held some power position in school. She'd always tell me how confident I was and how I could use that to our advantage, but by the next year she decided that I was just too dumb to realize I had things to be ashamed of. Our friendship ended for good at the beginning of fifth grade when she publicly made fun of me because I referred to Ramona Quimby—the universally beloved, Portland-based Beverly Cleary character—as my idol. At the time, Rain read books where houses were haunted and girls got pregnant, and she thought Ramona Q was girly and childish. So she humiliated me for expressing my love for the (albeit fictional) person I held most dear. I've known Rain for twice as long as I've known Maddy and, since our friendship ended, she has perpetually spewed venom at me while looking like she just finished filming a hair commercial on a beach.

Maddy went on talking like nothing had happened. Which was, for her, probably true. She knew I'd been friends with Rain years ago and no longer was, but she seemed to think it was just a casual growing apart thing, and I'd chosen not to correct this assumption. Maddy had the image of me being, in a certain way, kind of tough—not physically, but in my principles. She saw me as someone who stood up to people, someone who said what was on his mind. Which was mostly true, for most people.

I'd missed most of what Maddy had said since Rain entered but was trying to reassure myself that Rain wouldn't approach with Maddy around when, without warning, Maddy got up to go to the bathroom. And within seconds Rain was looming over me; as usual, choosing a private moment to prod at me. She was the same height as me, five-foot-four, but she somehow had a way of blocking out all available light sources, leaving me in permanent shadow.

"So I heard you're quite the little entrepreneur," she said with mock excitement. "I hear you've got a cute little flier. With a cartoon Elly on it even?"

Around Rain, everything in me tensed. All my words came out through clenched teeth, their syllables hurried, nearly blending together into a single word. It wasn't some technique I'd developed to deal with her awfulness, but more a bodily reaction I couldn't control. "I'm just trying to find a job," I said.

"Sure, I get it. Now that summer's basically over, the lemonade stand is winding down, huh?"

I imagined her, upon learning about my flier from one of her henchmen, writing down lists of potential insults, relishing all the ways I didn't fit into her shallow definition of coolness or sophistication.

"And you're a professional, I hear? Where do you find the time for all this training?"

Internally I admitted that, put that way, it did seem like a silly flier. She was the one who looked like an actual professional—her clothes fitting in a way mine never did, every detail of her appearance attended to, looking like some purebred horse that was both majestic and dangerous. But I refused to regret it just because Rain made fun of it. "Not all of us have Dad's credit card," I said.

"Yeah, some of us don't have dads at all."

I hated how much she knew about me. I saw Maddy leave the bathroom, and I released an unintentionally audible sigh of relief.

She looked over her shoulder. "Oh good, your girlfriend's on her way to save you."

I glared. "She's not my girlfriend."

"But you wish she was," she said, shaking her head as if she pitied me. "I see the way you look at her." Then, leaning in, whispered, "She must just be smart enough not to hook up with a professional child."

"Hey Rain," Maddy said as she walked up, looking so happy-go-lucky it made me temporarily, undeservingly mad at her. "So what did I miss?" she asked.

"Just getting some pro tips from Elly here," she said, socking me on the shoulder playfully like we were old buddies. "I'll let you two get back to it."

"Pro tips?" Maddy asked me, as Rain walked away.

I considered telling her everything. All the years of feeling like a fool every time Rain appeared, the way I couldn't defend myself, the way I couldn't write her words off like I did with the boys who called me a fag. How each time she insulted me, I considered the possibility that Rain's eyes could truly be seeing the unfortunate parts of myself I refused to see—something I never even questioned when the insults came from meathead boys. But I also wanted Maddy to keep believing in my toughness, to keep holding this image of me, so it could eventually come true. So I said, "Inside joke. You didn't miss anything."

Old at Heart

In an ideal world, I'd skip being a teenager. I'd also skip all the in-between parts after being a teenager that seem unexciting and sort of predetermined by cultural expectations, and I'd just spend the rest of my life in a perpetual pre-elderly, not-yet-decrepit state of old-ish.

Some of this desire, I believe, comes from being an only child. The kids who have older siblings find out about bands and swear words and sex jokes before other kids, but only-kids find out about insurance coverage and rental contracts and important-though-dated cultural references. It's like being a peripheral adult. Even at its most boring, these conversations manage to make adult life less mysterious and make the concerns of people at school seem even more pointless.

I long for a future day where my brain slows down enough to learn to quilt or needlepoint or something equally time-consuming and uncool. I've always considered errands fun, especially groceries, so I'd also do more errands and really just take my time. Maybe it's because of my mom and uncle's workplace, but I love going to grocery stores. My definition of a meditative state is just walking around a grocery store endlessly, pushing a cart, smiling to myself about the weird canned meats and the underwhelming cartoons on the backs of cereal boxes.

The funny thing about Rain and me is that we both want to be grown-ups. We always have, even in fourth grade. It was one of the main things that connected us; one of our favorite games used to be imagining our adult lives and all the stuff we would be able to do. But her fantasy of being a grown-up has always been power suits and cocktail parties while my fantasy has always just been to stop caring what other people think.

Strange Family Fact

I came home and my uncle was standing in the kitchen, eating peanut butter out of the jar with a spoon. Before he could say anything, I asked the question I'd been wanting to ask and not wanting to ask for the last week. "Uncle, have you noticed Mom forgetting things?"

He looked up at the ceiling and bobbed his head from side to side like a metronome—the way he does when he's deciding how to say something he doesn't want to say. "She's done some things that have surprised me, yes."

"Okay, that only kind of answers my question. What's she done?"

"Well, she's been repeating herself." He paused to eat another spoonful. "Maybe fairly often," he said, through a mouth full of glue. "You know, some people just repeat themselves and don't even notice, but not your mom. She's just not that kind of person."

"Yeah, she's not," I said, both relieved and disappointed that I wasn't the only one who had been noticing her changing. "Have you noticed more things?" His head bobbed fiercely. I knew he had more. "What have you noticed?"

His right foot joined in, tapping to his internal rhythm before he blurted out, "Okay, so there was one sort of odd thing."

"How odd?"

"I don't know, it might be nothing, but a few weeks ago she walked into the living room and it was like she was lost or something. She just walked slowly around the room, not saying anything—like she was sleepwalking or hypnotized or something. She sat down next to me on the couch, but it was as if I wasn't even there. Eventually she looked at me like she'd just woken up and, without saying anything, headed back to her room."

"Did you talk to her about it?"

"No, I guess I just figured she was overworked or something. And I mean, even if I did say something, it's not like she would get it checked out."

This is a strange fact in our family: my mom doesn't go to the doctor. Not even people mildly resembling a doctor. No flu shots, no teeth cleanings, no massage therapists, no optometrists—she's worn the same pair of glasses my entire life. Though I've noticed this doctor-less existence, I'd never thought much about it until recently. It was just part of life: my uncle lives on our couch, I've never gone anywhere, my dad is dead, my mom doesn't go to the doctor. So I decided to finally ask. "What's with that, anyway?"

"What's with what?"

"Mom and doctors. It doesn't make sense."

"Well, your mom never liked going to the doctor. Even when we were little kids. But as an adult it's mostly financial. She's worried about money, and the doctor is a wild card. It's something she can't budget for, because she never knows how much it'll be."

"So she doesn't even go for a check-up?"

"I don't know why it applies to even simple stuff like that, but after your birth she ended up with some pretty hefty medical bills. She was young, didn't have friends who had kids, and just had no idea how much delivering a baby costs without insurance. There were also complications, you and her had to spend a couple nights in the hospital. Collection agencies got involved, the whole thing went on for years. It might still be going on, for all I know."

"Seriously?" I felt a little betrayed that I didn't know the apparently dramatic story of my birth. Did this explain how I was the way I was in some small or big way? "How have I never heard about any of this?"

"It's a sore spot. Your mom doesn't like to talk about it."

"But that was one time, years ago. That's no reason not to go get a check-up. I mean, she has insurance now."

"Sure, but it's not great coverage or anything. It would be better if we worked for a corporate store, but you just can't expect much from a local business that still calls itself a fruit market. So I think she feels like she needs to have the insurance just to have it. But aside from your appointments, she also thinks she needs to save it for emergencies."

"But one appointment isn't going to mean she can't use it if I break my arm or something."

"Try telling your mom that."

So I told him I would. Even though I couldn't imagine that going well.

In the Kitchen, Learning to Dance

A few months ago, I was in the kitchen with mom, learning to dance. I wasn't really learning anything and she wasn't really teaching, but that's just what she's called it since I was a kid. Dancing lessons.

It goes like this: she puts an old record on this tinny portable record player we have on the bar in the kitchen, and then approaches me with a goofy little walk-dance—sometimes jazzy finger-pointing, sometimes over-exaggerated stepping, sometimes a jerky shoulder shimmy—and says in her deepest voice, "I believe it's time for dancing lessons." Then we slide around the linoleum in our socks.

So this was what we were doing back in June: an especially enthusiastic dancing lesson to an old Stevie Wonder song. While catching our breath on the couch, I asked her why she called them dancing lessons. I'd always understood the joke of it—how the lesson isn't like a lesson at all and neither of us are actually good dancers—but I just all-of-a-sudden had a hunch there was more to it. Without hesitating she said, "We're always learning how to dance."

"How do you mean?"

"Well, the learning process can never be fully completed, for one, because there's always new music. In some small way, you have to re-learn to dance every time you dance to something you've never heard before, right? And it doesn't have to be something you've never heard; it can even be something you've heard a lot but have just never danced to before."

My mom was a drummer in a band in high school, so I think she's thought a lot about drums and what a beat can do. One time, she pulled out a cassette tape of her band and we had a dancing lesson to it. The music was like walking through mud sometimes and lying down on a carpet of damp moss other times, which I guess means it felt very regionally specific. We slo-mo folded the top halves of our bodies around the kitchen and laughed at how funny it felt. The two songs ended and the tape hiss seemed to jump up in volume, though it was probably there all along. "We freaked out a lot of people in Plateau," she said.

The tape made me want to ask a thousand questions, but I knew they would make her uncomfortable and probably ultimately go unanswered. Anytime I ask her to tell me anything about her childhood in Plateau, she just says some variation of the thing she always says: "All that people in Portland know about Plateau is the big carnival. They don't know what it's like there. They don't even know there's a big juvenile correctional facility that Portland kids get shipped to every day." Then it would become a rant about Portland people not understanding how bad the rest of the state is. I truly don't know if this is an intentional technique or some internal defense mechanism, but she somehow sidesteps whatever I ask and I only come away with bits and pieces that I've assembled over the course of my life.

While I know she would disagree with this, I actually don't know that she thinks Plateau is really all that bad, but it's where her parents are, or were, and she hates her parents. They were alcoholics who weren't around much and she was often left to raise my uncle. So, when she was 17 and my uncle was barely 15, they left for Portland. Their dad had already mysteriously moved away a few months before and their mom was only sometimes around, so she says it didn't really feel like running away. They both had money saved—my uncle from helping on construction sites, my mom from waiting tables—so they got an apartment, got jobs here, got their GEDs, and six years later I came along.

I've never met my grandparents, and I don't know if either my mom or my uncle have contacted them since they left. Sometimes my mom tells a story about some weird thing she did as a kid that she was probably too young to be doing, or some funny character she used to pour coffee for at the diner, but the only time it's one-hundred percent positive is when she talks about her band. Sometimes when she's frustrated she'll say, "I wish I could whale on some drums," and I'll say "I'd like to hear you whale on the drums" and she'll nod like she's going through some drum fill in her mind.

I don't generally love music like she does, or like Maddy and

Claudia do, but I like dancing. To me, dancing is about letting your body go and finding out things you can do with it that you didn't know you could do. So my mom is right, it is like a lesson. It doesn't mean the things you do would look cool to someone else; it's a personal, internal thing.

That dancing lesson in June was the last time I remember feeling this bodily thing. Summer was just about to begin and, even though I'm not a summer person, I can't resist the charm of a season changing. The hard-to-put-into-words feeling of a solstice or an equinox. The sense that things are somehow right in the world, that on some cosmic level everything is okay. That's where we were that day. But I can see now that it didn't last.

Nothing is Weird

"Do you ever think about nothing?" Claudia asked me the next day at lunch. We were lying on the Block, watching the clouds rush by. I thought about how many times someone had probably spilled a drink or put out a cigarette right where my head was and maybe because of that I'd smell like those things for the rest of the day. I decided I had to sit up or stop thinking about it, so instead I wondered how it was so windy up where the clouds were while it was so un-windy down here and wondered if Claudia was wondering the same thing.

"Like, intentionally?" I asked. "As in, 'I'm going to think about absolutely nothing right now'?"

"No, not really. But that's kind of interesting too. What I'm talking about is like the existence of nothing. Do you ever just think about that for a really long time? Like a void or something. A black hole where just nothing is happening. At all."

"That does sound pretty interesting," I said, looking over at her. In the sun, all the sharp angles of her face cast perfect, slight shadows. The lines of her make-up'ed eyebrows looked more perfectly sculpted than anything I'd ever created in my life. She seemed so in control of her physical presentation. Coordinated bright vintage colors, old costume jewelry, so many little accessories and details that came off casually but also seemed part of a big brilliant intentional vision of self.

I felt like so much of what I put on my body was random—things I find at the big Goodwill everyone goes to, in my mom's closet or my uncle's pile of clothes, Claudia gifting me some nail polish. I wanted to ask her if she could help me express who I am on the inside on the outside, but instead I just said, "I've definitely never thought about nothing like that."

I considered how I'd been friends with Claudia since middle school and how I thought of her as my second-closest friend, but that there was still so much I didn't know. What I know is so basic, it could go on the back of a trading card. I know she owns an impressive amount of vinyl records, her parents are from Mexico, and she watches the world in a careful and curious way that I feel I can only aspire to.

Mostly we discuss the tiny minutiae of life, so I know her wit and wisdom concerning the world's details. I know the soothing way her voice rarely changes volume or pitch. But I didn't know much big-picture stuff, or even how she thought about nothing all the time. That seemed so much more personal and revealing—the kind of thing a person should know about their second-best. Some of the clouds looked like black holes to me, but I couldn't decide if it was just because we were talking about black holes or if they really looked like that.

Claudia turned to me. "What does nothingness make you think of?"

I wanted my mind to go to the far-off places where Claudia was— somewhere in outer space or other dimensions, presumably. But instead my mind went to the research I'd done over the past week. All the people who have amnesia or Alzheimer's or medical anomalies. I thought about all the ways people can become hollow shells of their former selves. To me, that was nothingness. States of being that weren't death but weren't exactly life either.

I couldn't say any of this to Claudia. "Is this a trick question?" I finally asked.

She laughed. "Yeah, maybe. I think about nothing probably more than I should," she said. "If you think about nothing a lot, nothing becomes this really weird thing."

Constraints

Most friendships have certain places they exist. For example, both my mom and uncle have their work friends, who they only hang out with at work or work events. Nowhere else. And Claudia has her concert friends, who mostly don't go to our school but who she goes to shows with almost every weekend at a place called The Artistery that I nod knowingly about when it comes up in conversation but have never actually been to.

Aside from Maddy, all of my friends are just school friends. Which is beginning to feel like a pretty weak state of friendship. People at school talk about their camp friends, church friends, soccer friends, band friends, and all the stuff they've done with these friends is obviously better than sitting together in geometry for a year.

I've never been a part of any group. And not being in a group or club or team means I've never needed to go anywhere for an event or competition or performance, which is part of why my life has mostly only taken place within a few square miles of my apartment. I sometimes wonder how much these constraints are the result of not having much money and how much they're self-imposed. Or, maybe, how much they're just me not knowing my options.

It's Natural

In the couple hours after my mom got home from work—as if on cue—I watched her misplace her keys, her purse, her checkbook, and a book she was reading. It was painful. Each time a *now where did I put that* left her mouth, it produced a small pinprick sensation inside of my chest.

When she went to her office—which was essentially just a desk in her room with a sheet hanging around it—I waited a moment before following her in. Her office is the place she goes when she needs to figure out finances, pay bills, or do taxes, and I almost never have any reason or desire to go in. So when I stepped inside and stood at the edge of her desk, I was surprised by how it was even smaller than I remembered. It reminded me how growing feels less like growing and more like other things shrinking.

Instead of leading up to what I wanted to say, making some sort of small talk to warm her up, I just said it. "I know you're not going to like this. But I'm worried about you. I'd like you to go see a doctor. About your memory loss."

She stared up at me from her desk, her face blank, as if she was trying to catch up with the moment. I held my breath, unsure of what would follow. "I see," she finally said. "You're right, I have been forgetful. A little absent-minded, certainly. And I had a bad moment in the truck last week—which I feel so guilty about. But I don't think it's to the point of calling it memory loss."

I narrowed my eyes in an attempt to glare her out of denial.

"Elly, a doctor would just tell me that I should take vitamins and then charge me a few hundred dollars. I don't have good insurance, and I really can't pay a few hundred dollars to be told to buy supplements I already have."

"But what if it's something bad?"

"Honey, I'm too young to have dementia but old enough to admit that I don't have the memory I used to have. This is just a part of getting older. I started going gray when you were in elementary school, I started getting little lines on my face when I hit 30, and now I'm starting to forget. I just have to accept that it's part of the natural process."

"If it's so natural, why isn't Uncle going through it too?"

"Well, he's a little younger. And everyone's different. We all age at different speeds and in different ways. People are prone to different things."

I knew it was true, on some level, but it was also too easy. She was too deep in denial to see how bad things were. I wanted to tell her that the amount of things she was forgetting was not normal, but I didn't know that for sure. She might have some information I didn't know about and would prove me wrong, and I hated when my mom proved me wrong. So instead I asked, "Are you taking those supplements?"

She averted her eyes. "Well, no. Will it make you feel better if I do?"

I nodded.

"Then I will."

I gave her a stone face, knowing my stubbornness was from her stubbornness and I could throw it back in her face.

She took a deep breath. "I promise, okay? If it will make you feel better, then I promise."

"Thank you," I said, even though it wasn't what I really wanted, and I didn't actually feel better at all.

I took the short walk to my room and thought about how difficult this would be to find a solution to. My mom was too stubborn to do anything I asked her to do, and my uncle clearly wasn't going to confront his older sister. I sat down on the edge of my bed and in that moment I knew, without question, that if there was a solution to my mom's issues, I had to find it on my own.

Guesses We Pretend are Facts

Here's another thing we don't know: why Alzheimer's disease happens. Areas of brain tissue deteriorate, so that's most likely the cause of the resulting memory issues (though we're not 100% positive about this), but no one knows why the tissue deteriorates. Twenty million or so people have Alzheimer's, so it's sort of incredible that we don't have it figured out. That number is growing and, because of this, some people think it might be related to industrial pollution or prolonged exposure to toxins, and scientists theorize that it'll just keep increasing. And Alzheimer's is only one possibility: it's a type of dementia, which is just a big catch-all term for a whole slew of things that can happen to the brain and cause permanent memory loss.

Experts tell people to keep their minds lively. They suggest doing word puzzles and mind games, to read books, stay physically active. But there are people who do all these things and still get Alzheimer's and no one knows why.

For the most part, I shouldn't even be considering these unknowns. My mom's right: She's generally too young to have it. She's not even 40 and most people who get it are in their late 60s or 70s. This reassuring fact is pretty much thrown out the window, though, by the existence of early-onset Alzheimer's. And the thing about early-onset Alzheimer's is, well, it comes early. Which generally just means under 60, but, though it's extremely rare, the earliest it could begin doing its early thing is the late 30s—the very age-zone my mom is in now. And rare just means uncommon—rare doesn't mean it doesn't happen. Rare stuff happens to regular people all the time.

Habitual Nervousness and its Manifestations

When I'm uninterested in the words people are saying, I focus on the way people are saying the uninteresting words. On Monday, we had an assembly about games that involve balls and generalized school pride, of which I have none, and I quickly began to notice how much everyone used *um*. Adults and kids alike couldn't go two sentences without at least one um slipping out. Though I knew I was just as guilty, listening silently made it easy to be critical. By the end it felt like ums were the point, the thing being celebrated: an assembly of ums. *Um versus um, this Friday night! Go um*!

As I filed out with Maddy and Claudia, I couldn't not say something about it. "What was with the ums?" I asked, knowing that they—without any more context than that—would understand exactly what I meant.

Maddy thought it over for a while before responding with her own question. "Why do you think people have nervous habits?"

"No idea," I said.

"Come on, if you wondered about the ums, you've had to wonder about this. Filler words are a small version of nervous habitual actions, so it's the natural bigger question behind the ums."

"Though I agree, my mind just didn't go there. I guess I've just always assumed people need some kind of physical thing to do when there's nothing much to say."

"See, you have thought about it."

"I mean, kind of," I said. "But just kind of. It's not like a theory or anything."

As soon as it left my mouth, I thought about how, since I had been researching all this brain stuff, maybe I actually should have a theory about this thing that's obviously brain-related. But since everything is pretty much brain-related, did this imply I internally expected myself to have a theory about everything?

My train of thought was derailed when, out of nowhere, Claudia said, "Nervous habits are just small routines that become neurologically ingrained." Maddy and I stared at her like she'd magically appeared. Sometimes when the two of us get going on a conversation, we forget to ask Claudia what she thinks. Which is ridiculous because she often has a more informed opinion. Or, as in this case, the answer.

"They're the result of a pretty simple system of cues and rewards," she said in her steady monotone. "But even though the system is simple, they're generally kinda hard to break without outside help because people either don't notice them or just get so used to them that they can't imagine life without them."

"How do you know all this?" Maddy asked.

Claudia shrugged.

"Do you have a nervous habit?" I asked her.

"I think my nervous habit is noticing other people's nervous habits."

"I don't really think that counts as a nervous habit," Maddy said, "but it does make me curious what mine is."

"You scratch your head when you're talking to someone who's upset with you or when you're in trouble," she said without hesitating.

"For real?" Maddy said. "I had no idea. What's Elly's? He really wants to know."

Maddy definitely knew I didn't really want to know. I was positive that as soon as I knew what my nervous habit was, I'd start doing it more. Or I'd focus on it so much that it would become more awkward than it already was. I started to protest, but words were already coming out of Claudia's mouth.

"He doesn't make eye contact when he's talking about something where he has to remember facts," Claudia said. "It's sort of like he's looking into his own mind or something. I think it's cool, it makes it easier to concentrate on what he's saying."

"Doesn't everybody do that?" Maddy asked.

She paused and looked off, and I wondered if she was actually thinking or just doing an impersonation of me. "I'd say it's common, but not common enough to not count as a nervous habit."

"Fair enough," Maddy said. "So you must have an epic catalog of people's flaws, huh?"

"Well, I don't really view them as flaws. I actually like most people's nervous habits. They make people more real."

My brain busily tried to recall every time I'd talked about something that required me remembering facts. There were a lot. Which I didn't like thinking about, even though I did like thinking about being more real—whatever real was.

Life in the Mirror

Later that night I put one of my mom's bobby pins in my hair. I'd been thinking about it for a while. Not because I wanted decorative stuff in my hair, but because my hair drives me nuts and I just wanted to train it like a bonsai plant. I'd been thinking that if I could just do this then my hair might not be so bad. So I put one in to pin down an unruly strand in the front and there it was: doing what I wanted it to do for once. Un-unruly. With that success, I put another one in to train a strand in the middle of my head that sometimes sticks straight up. Then one for the cowlick piece, one on the left side, and stood back to see a normal-haired person who looked pretty okay.

But then the cowlick-y piece broke free, and I thought about what my mom said about genius hair and laughed to myself. I wondered if everyone's mom made their kid laugh like my mom made me laugh and I thought probably not. Like, everyone laughs *at* their mom, but not with their mom or because they think their mom is actually funny.

But my mom is funny. Earlier this year she told me a story about when her and my uncle were teenagers and they stole their dad's car in the middle of the night, and she made it into a big comedy of errors where they couldn't get the car started so they put it in neutral to try to push-start it and then got it stuck halfway out the driveway, blocking part of the road, and I was laughing so hard I could barely get breaths in between the laughs.

It didn't matter that their dad—my unknown grandpa—was mean, that he basically abandoned them a couple years later, or that they left their rural town and came to Portland together because most of their lives weren't funny stories. All that mattered was this moment where they were just regular country teens trying to steal a junker car and everything was going wrong.

When Rain and I were in elementary school and still best friends, she told me this sort of thing would mess me up. Like, someday I'd see my casual closeness to my mom as weird or inappropriate or something. She said a mom should be a mom and not a friend and sure, I can see that's a thin line and it could easily get awkward, but can't a mom be your mom and a friend at the same time? Rain's mom was a shrink, or something like a shrink (a therapist? A counselor? Are these things different?), and one of the worst things about being friends with her was that she was always diagnosing me with something.

Our breakup was foretold one late-summer day when I tried to borrow one of her shirts after we walked around in the super hot sun, and she said I had issues. I said maybe everyone else had issues, if a boy with a soaked-through sweaty shirt couldn't wear a girl's normal-ass shirt and vice versa. A few weeks later the Ramona Quimby incident occurred, we stopped being friends, and in time she's become my mortal enemy. And now I'm wearing bobby pins in my hair.

The Fourth-to-Last Day of Summer

Calling a season magical is dumb, but fall is magical. It's also much better than summer. These are just facts that can't be ignored.

I look forward to the end of summer all year. Since it rains in Portland for a good percentage of the year and we all complain about it, we're supposed to desire its opposite and take advantage of *every moment* summer offers. It's a lot of pressure.

But as soon as it ends, the pressure is off and we can go back to being regular humans who spend a decent part of the day inside and don't feel guilty about it. What I like best is this tiny sliver of the year where it's not hot but not exactly cold. When the leaves stay on the trees and get a chance to change colors before the rain knocks them off. Where the sun is out, but it's cold enough to wear a sweater. Since I look best in sweaters, this is my most stylish time of year. In summer, I just look ridiculous. I actually think most people look ridiculous in their shorts and tank tops, but some people pull it off better than I do.

In celebration of summer finally almost being over, and in preparation for a hopefully long tiny sliver, I dug my favorite auburn-colored sweater out from the back of the closet. I looked in the mirror, just soaking up how much more I identified with the person I was looking at than I had in months. It's funny to think that a seasonally appropriate piece of clothing could change self-perception and factor into a person's identity, but it's a very real thing. Without sweaters, and the weather to warrant their use, I would be a different person.

I slid the bobby pins back in my hair, pulling some other hair over them so they were little secrets and, for the first time in weeks, things felt okay. Good, even.

Then I was put into a small group with Rain.

It happened in drama class—a class I loved and, since it seemed to be Rain's least favorite class, a class I generally managed to forget she was in entirely. But I was put in a group with her and as we sat together, trying to come up with a short sketch with a couple other people, I tried to put our history behind us. She and I could momentarily pretend we didn't want to poke each other's eyes out, I figured.

While the rest of our group brainstormed ideas, she scrolled through her expensive-looking phone—the new kind, without a keyboard. Even though every news story over the past year seemed to talk about how fancy phones were talking over the world, I almost never saw one in real life. I didn't even really know what she could be looking at for so long. Texts? Infinite worlds I couldn't fathom? Regardless of what was behind her mysterious checked-out-ness, I took it to be a sort of agreement, a temporary peace treaty. She was making it known this wasn't a fight for territory; in this situation, she didn't care. At least that's how I interpreted it.

Because of this silent agreement and my general enthusiasm for the day, I was relaxing into the brainstorming. In a moment of inspiration and creative energy, I said, "Maybe we could make our skit an allusion to the play where the kid builds the horse religion in his head." The non-Rain others looked at me, nodding with interest. "But maybe instead of horses, we could have a character who was obsessed with some small and non-majestic animal. Possums, perhaps."

Then, out of nowhere, Rain broke out of her phone zone. "You're so oblivious," she said, locking eyes with me. "You don't even know what a loser you are."

In our locked gaze, I gave her a look that I hoped said, *hey, didn't we have an unspoken pact to be okay with each other for the half hour it takes to do this?* But she looked back at me as if my face was saying nothing at all.

"You think everybody gets what you're talking about," she said, "but we don't. Horse-religion play? No one has ever heard of that. What the hell does that even mean? You don't make sense to anyone at all and for some reason you don't seem to notice. You're a loser who's also a snob. Which is just insane."

I looked at the others, who were taking turns examining the ceiling and floor. I didn't know what to do, so the silence just took over as Rain stared me down, waiting for my response. I felt like running out crying—just flailing my arms, letting them flap against my body, howling like a child. But instead I said, "Well, I have to go to the bathroom. I hope you guys have some great ideas while I'm gone." I sounded like a robot. And I was fleeing. But at least I didn't allow her the pleasure of seeing me break.

I got a hall pass, walked slowly to the bathroom, and, when I got there, stared into the mirror. Just stared. This mirror experience wasn't like the mirror experience I'd had at home. I suddenly didn't look as good. My hair was jutting out at odd angles, clumsily adorned with randomly placed bobby pins that weren't secret and seemingly did nothing at all. It was as if I had bits of garbage in my hair. My little glasses seemed absurd, like a piece of a costume I left on after Halloween and had somehow still not taken off almost a full year later. My ears were potentially smaller than any other kid in high school and bits of gross facial hair poked through the skin on my upper lip. My sweater still looked good, though.

Eventually I closed my eyes, took deep breaths, and tried to empty my mind—which, for me, is nearly impossible. But I tried.

When I got back to class I put on my best performance of inner peace and confidence. I sat down, and my group looked at me nervously. Rain scowled, but that seemed to be a permanent state. I pretend-smiled and, in the silence that had formed around me, said, "So, what did you guys come up with?" And we continued on as if nothing had happened.

I went through the rest of the day going over Rain's words in my head again and again. Though I kind of wanted her to trip and fall in a public place, this was less about what she thought of me. What I couldn't let go of was the possibility that she was right. What if everybody—potentially even Maddy and Claudia—just wanted me to shut up? What if I was oblivious? That possibility was the hard part.

The Silent Bus

On the bus home, Maddy was caught up in the energy of fall—the way everything is dying in this nature-way that's beautiful but a touch unsettling and makes a person a little philosophical. "Have you ever thought about how you can go through years of life and never hear a phrase that everyone else knows?" she asked.

I looked out the window.

"Like, the other day, someone asked what my mom's maiden name was, and I had no idea what they were talking about. Maiden name. I figured it wasn't a common phrase, but then everyone was like, *how do you not know what that is?* How had I gone through life and somehow never heard this thing that everyone else apparently had known since birth? It's so bizarre."

I knew exactly what she meant. And it was something I'd thought about. A lot. But I couldn't bring myself to respond.

"So what's up?" she asked.

"Nothing," I said, barely letting the word out.

"Okay, sure. You're just really abnormally quiet for no reason. Makes sense."

"Yep," I said, both hoping and not hoping she would drop it.

Here's the thing: Rain is not the only person who has said something mean to me. If that were the case it would be incredible and I would like that, but unfortunately it's not the case. If someone else says something mean, it's usually a cheap shot about my name sounding like a girl's name or my glasses or clothes, and I can turn to my friends and be like, "Hey, you know what that jerk-face just said to me?"

The problem with Rain is that she got to know me and my secret insecurities so well over the course of our best-friend year that she manages—still, all these years later—to find the things I'm actually worried about. Like, that I'm an oblivious snob who everyone thinks is a loser, for example. So not talking with my friends about Rain's meanness isn't just a way to maintain their image of me as someone who can handle jerks, it's also to keep these ideas out of their heads completely.

Maddy, not knowing any of this, seemed sure she could break me. She tried the goofy technique. With her deep voice she can sing normal songs and make them sound really sneaky and eerie. She started with nursery rhymes before switching to songs that sounded like odd jingles. "Hey Sandy. Well, does your dog bite? Hey Sandy," she sang in a gruff hush, as if she was an old-time crooner and this was an intimate, meaningful song. I tried to keep a straight face.

She tried pieces of radio-pop songs, old crooner-type lounge songs, and indie songs that only she knew. Conversations around us were stopping mid-sentence, the eyes of the bus turning in our direction. She sang and sang and I wanted to resist, to continue with my wallowing, but eventually I couldn't take it any longer. She did it, she broke me. I let out all the laughs that had been building up inside since the first note left her body.

"That took longer than I thought," she said. "So, seriously, what's up?"

I stopped laughing as suddenly as I'd started and looked her in the eyes. "Maddy, do people think I'm a snob?" It was only part of what I wanted to ask, but it was something.

"Which people?" she asked.

"You know, like everyone."

"Well, I don't think you're a snob," she said, "and I'm somebody."

"Are you avoiding this question because everyone really does think I'm a snob or are you just being diplomatic? Because, seriously, I'm about to freak out right now."

"No dude, no one thinks you're a snob. I mean there are probably some people that think we're both snobs, but we probably think those people are dicks. And look at me; am I worried about that?"

"No?"

"Yeah, you're right. I'm not worried. So you should not be worried either. Because we're in this together."

"Like, in this school thing?"

"Like everything. We're in this everything together."

"Okay." I felt a gratitude I couldn't name and "okay" was a poor stand-in for that gratitude, but all words seemed wrong in that moment. "Thanks."

"Yeah, of course," she said.

"But will you tell me if everybody starts to hate me and I'm totally oblivious?"

"I'm sure that will never happen, but, yes, I will tell you if it does. I should probably say one thing, though, just to make sure we're on the same page."

"One thing?"

"I mean, I think you know this, but you're kind of like a grown-up. And it's not snobbish, but I think it's just unfamiliar to some people," she said. "It's who you are, though. So it's cool."

"Okay, I think I can handle that. But for the sake of clarity and my sanity, explain what you mean by grown-up."

"You know, like you're not caught up in the same dumb crap as everyone else. You're not acting like high school is going to be the best years of your life or the worst. I guess that's sort of like an adult-seeming perspective. And you read your uncle's books that don't really have plots and reference them in conversation a lot."

"Yeah, that stuff is weird, huh?"

"But cool."

"Are you sure?" I asked.

"Completely sure."

Unlike most times when she reassured me of my personal worth and goodness, I didn't actually feel reassured. I had these broad goals that seemed so simple in my head—help my mom, do more things, go more places—but they currently felt totally impossible. The fact that one person calling me a loser-snob brought me this low just didn't seem like a good sign of my ability to overcome obstacles. On the outside, though, I forced a smile and pretended I was done freaking out.

Telepathic Bad News

When I got home, my mom was there. Which has never happened in the entire history of me being a human being who goes to school. She's always at work when I get home. She never takes vacation days, and she goes to work when she's sick and pretends to not be sick. But there she was, sitting on Uncle's couch, his worn comforter folded next to her, staring out the window like she hadn't just heard me come in.

"Mom?" She didn't respond, and I wondered if she was actually there or was instead a figment of my imagination. I approached her cautiously, as I would imagine approaching a wild animal or a distracted ghost—not wanting to alarm her, but also wanting to get a closer look. I sat next to her slowly, trying to not make the couch squeak, observing the coarse texture of her arm hair, the small pores on her cheeks; anything to let me know she was, without a doubt, real and alive.

The moment before I formed an intelligible question, she said, "I got fired today." Her eyes fixed out the window, her head locked in place, it was as if she'd never said anything at all, as if she'd sent this message telepathically.

"Fired?" I asked. My mom worked harder than anyone I knew, so this seemed near impossible.

"I was being watched," she said. "For kind of a long time."

"Watched? By whom?" I asked. She sounded like a conspiracy theorist.

"My bosses. Secret shoppers."

"Why would they do that?"

"Customers had complained about me not giving correct change, ringing up items twice, entering the wrong codes for produce, forgetting to scan coupons, not providing receipts—a lot of stuff, actually. Also, the money had been off in my till. Quite a few times." She sounded hollow, emotionless.

"Whoa. But, I mean, you've worked there forever. They should have given you a warning or something first."

"They did. Many warnings. I knew about all this. And I was trying to fix it, but I guess I just couldn't."

I was trying to stay calm, but my insides were churning. I thought about how we were in a recession that some people said we were maybe never going to get out of. Up until now I'd only heard it as a buzzword or a headline, not something that actually mattered in my small world, but it felt like it suddenly mattered now. "What are you going to do?" It sounded more accusatory than I meant it, but she didn't seem to notice and continued looking out the window.

"Get another job. File for unemployment in the meantime, I guess."

I paused, not knowing how to say what I wanted to say, so I settled on, "Are we going to be okay?"

"Yeah, we'll be okay." She sounded both confident of it and far off, like she was in another land, a place where everything resolved easily.

"You're sure?"

She moved her head down and back up again, ever so slightly. "I have some money saved."

"Do you need anything? Like, right now?"

"No. I'm just going to sit here and think about things for a while."

It was then that I noticed how quiet the house was. "Where's Uncle?"

"I told him I needed some space."

"Oh. So, should I give you some space too?"

She slowly nodded again, so I went to my room and worried about her away from her. This is how we spent the rest of the evening. A couple of times I left my room to get some snacks from the kitchen and each time my mom was still right there, either curled up and napping or sitting up and staring, watching nothing. At one point I turned a lamp on for her, because she had a magazine open on her lap—just laying there, its words shadowed. She thanked me without looking up from the page. I'd never seen her like that. It made me feel wrong inside—her, like this.

My mom always did stuff; she never just sat. And while she wasn't the type of person who made a big show of her emotions, she also wasn't the type of person who completely shut them off. But that had to be what she was doing, because her responses were inhuman.

Before I turned my light off, I made a list of ways we could save money: types of food we didn't need to buy, using towels instead of paper towels, toilet paper instead of Kleenex, all the small luxuries we could do without. But that seemed to only address a small part of a problem that was only getting bigger.

What a Mystery Is

There's a woman, a poet, who wrote, "What's the appeal of a mystery? Someone is looking for something actively." It's so simple. And it reminds me that searching for something is that basic: we try to find something out and, in doing so, we get hooked and do it more.

I'm starting to feel like I'm solving a mystery that's only interesting to me. *What's happening to my mom? How do I help her remember more, remember better, stop forgetting?* There's no body, no murderer. The stakes are low to everyone who isn't me or her. But for me, the stakes feel so high, the possibilities so devastating. The chalk outline doesn't represent my mom's body, but her mind. Like, *This is the place where the thing that made my mom my mom once was.* That's my worry. That's what I think about more than once. A fate that's not death, but also not not death.

Not What You Think

That night I couldn't sleep. After flopping from one side to the other for hours, I sat up and got my clunky laptop out from under my bed. In the dark, staring at the glow, I searched memory loss. It brought up a broad and overwhelming assortment, and I couldn't believe I hadn't done it before this. Other than a brief dip into everything we don't know about Alzheimer's, I'd mostly searched for arguably related aspects of memory I thought were interesting—*is memory limitless, how to choose what you remember, how to remember important things*. But none of those, I could now see, were at the root of what was happening.

I tried *causes of memory failure*, which led me to *memory loss from stress, from medications, from depression, from head injury, from sleep deprivation, from blood-glucose levels, from stroke, from alcohol, from vitamin B-12 deficiency*, and I wondered if any of those could apply to mom.

Then I tried *memory loss help*, which told me about memory-improving herbs, super-foods, protein-rich smoothies, coconut oil, omega-3s, red wine, acupuncture, meditation, and these brought me, somehow, into the world of memory gurus.

Memory gurus, it seemed, led workshops to teach people the tricks of memory. Most were in India, but a handful were in seemingly random places like Juneau, Stockholm, Oklahoma City, and Halifax. Their websites and grainy videos didn't explain how they did what they did, which I suppose is how they got people to pay for their workshops. Some wore loud clothes and practically shouted with brightly colored banners draped behind them, while others dressed like preachers and spoke in calm, emotionless voices.

A part of me wanted to write memory gurus all off as ridiculous, but they also seemed like more of an answer than eating goji berries or taking some drops of an herbal tincture. Those things were saying "this could help" while the memory gurus were saying "this will work." They seemed so sure.

I typed in *memory guru Portland*, expecting nothing. And, at first, I got what I expected. But then a couple pages of search results in, I found Ada Dronning. She was from Northern California and lectured in a small suburb south of Portland called Vinton. I'd never been, but I vaguely knew it was near Beaverton, a dozen or so traffic-heavy miles away, down the twisty interstate and some other highway. She had a website that looked like it had been made when I was still in kindergarten. In a huge font over a light-gray background, it gave a very brief summary of her life. She was a child chess prodigy who became sort of chess-famous, it seemed. But then at some point, for some unexplained reason, she quit chess and moved to the outskirts of Portland to teach people the secrets of memory and perception.

Like all of the other gurus, her website was remarkably vague when it came to how she actually did this. It said stuff like, "I'll show you that memory isn't what you think it is" and "We must not focus on what we remember, but remember to learn when we don't."

I knew I could never convince my mom to go. She would never take it seriously. And I wasn't positive if I would either but, as I sat there, I knew I needed to go. Just to see. If for no other reason than to rule it out and move on. The site listed an event for Sunday, so I looked up the address. An hour bus ride. Though I'd never done something like it, I could. And I realized: This was it. The beginning of the new me who goes places. Does things. Leaves the apartment for more than school.

I closed the laptop and felt a determination I'd never experienced before. I was going to go, on my own, to see a memory guru, and I was going to keep it a secret from my mom. Maybe it wasn't a big deal, but in my uneventful life it felt like one. For some reason my mind went to how, in adventure stories, the characters always went on quests, and on these quests they ventured into the unknown. And my brain latched onto this. This, I decided, would be a quest to solve my mom's memory loss for her, and this memory guru would be my first unknown.

Welcome to the Working Weekend

Just when I'd given up on my fliers, I got a call. And, like that, I became part of the working world. While I was hoping they would lead to being offered a research position, a spot on an archaeological dig, or cataloging someone's personal library, they instead—more predictably—led to a job babysitting the kids in apartment six on the first floor of our building every Saturday. A three-year-old boy and a five-year-old girl who I'd seen playing in the apartment complex's grassy area. Based on this casual observation, they didn't seem like they'd be too hard to deal with, so I said I'd do it. Honestly I had no idea whether they'd be easy or difficult, since I'd never done this before. I didn't really even know if kids liked me, or if I liked kids.

What I did know when I got off the phone was I now couldn't travel on Saturdays. But at least I'd have money to travel on Sundays, a day of the week that suddenly mattered.

I went to knock on my mom's door to tell her but stopped in front of it, my fist in the air, paused mid-knock. Maybe it was rude to celebrate my job with her when she'd just lost hers. Or maybe the fact that this job was tied to a few barely thought-out lies meant I should plan my words more carefully. But those thoughts felt so icky, so calculated. This was big news; of course I would tell my mom. So I knocked. I heard a quiet murmur that I took to be something like "come in" and walked into darkness. "Are you asleep?" I asked. It was late afternoon.

"The lights just seemed a little bright," she said from the bed region, my eyes not adjusted enough to see her. "I'm awake, though. What's going on?"

"I just got a babysitting job in the building." My words came out jerky and awkward. "From the fliers. I just thought you should know."

"Elly, that's wonderful." Her voice was soft-excited, like the words were difficult to get out. "As you know, I had quite the informal babysitting career." I made a humming sound of agreement and then the room was silent. I wasn't sure if there was a facial cue I was missing, if it was strange to be standing on the edge of the room in the dark, if maybe she had somehow fallen asleep mid-response.

Right when I was about to throw some words into the air to break the silence, she started talking again. "One of my earliest memories is feeding your uncle oatmeal and the two of us making a huge mess, both thinking it was the most hilarious thing in the world," she said. "I was five, maybe six at that point. It was way too much responsibility for that age, but I suppose it worked out."

Like many of my mom's childhood stories, it was both sweet and mildly horrifying. But then something sunk in and I was briefly stunned—not by the story, but by the memory itself: how could she just bust out one of her first memories if she was truly in the midst of memory loss? I was so confused.

I told her I'd let her rest, she congratulated me again on the job, I shut the door in the slow quiet way I would for someone actually sleeping, and then I spent the rest of my waking hours debating inside my head: was that story a good sign or a bad sign? Was it a memory I should celebrate or be wary of? Could early memories be somehow easier to access than new memories? Even the details of life seemed unclear now—no story was just a story. Everything was heavy and tangled and hard to hold.

The Announcement

The next day was the first sincere rain of the season. A downpour to remind us where we lived, in case the unusually hot summer had made us forget.

I sat with Maddy and Claudia in the shop hallway closest to the Block, watching the muted chaos of the rain through the glass doors. I'd been containing my announcement all day, waiting for a time when I could tell Maddy and Claudia without any distractions. As Maddy looked at some notes from some class and Claudia picked at her sandwich insides, I knew the time had finally come. I decided to make my new choice sound as big as it felt inside and said, "Guys, I'm going on a quest."

I watched them exchange a look. "A quest?" Claudia asked.

"Yeah, I just decided last night. My mom's been forgetting things and it hasn't been getting better, so it's kind of a quest for knowledge. Like, trying to find the holy grail of how memory works." As soon as I stopped speaking, I realized how ridiculous this sounded.

They looked at each other again, and this time seemed to be stifling laughter. "That's really sweet of you, Atreyu," Maddy finally said.

"Not a funny joke. This isn't *The Neverending Story*, this is real life."

"Oh sorry, I mean your heart must be full of kindness, Frodo."

"Shut it," I said.

"Oh, pardon me, I meant to address you as Dorothy. Or is it Lancelot?"

I was on my feet. "That's it, I'm out of here. Maddy, you suck," I said, putting on my backpack. I couldn't believe that the first time in my life I had a real announcement Maddy would respond like this.

"Hey, hey, sorry," she said, getting onto her feet. "I just thought 'quest' sounded a little funny. But obviously you're being serious."

"I'm being very serious," I said, stopping but not taking off my backpack.

"Okay, I'm totally sorry. I screwed up. I thought it could be a joke, but I was wrong."

I continued to glare at her.

"It was a bad joke," she said.

"A very bad joke."

"I think it sounds cool, Elly," Claudia said from the ground.

"Thanks, Claudia."

"What are you going to do on your quest?" she asked.

"On Sunday I'm going to see a memory guru."

"A what?" Maddy asked.

"A memory guru. Which is a thing. I mean, I guess."

"Where are you going?" Claudia asked.

"I'm going to Vinton. That's where the memory guru is."

"Can we go?" Claudia asked.

I hadn't considered this possibility, so I felt thrown off by the seemingly simple question. "Maybe at some point," I said. "But I think I have to go alone at first. Oh, and I also have more big news: I got a job."

"Dude, that's cool," Maddy said. "What's your job?"

"I'm a nanny."

"Whoa, isn't that serious?" Maddy asked. "Like, are you going to be living with the family or something like that?"

"That's an au pair, I think. I mean, it's basically just babysitting. For some people in my apartment building every Saturday."

"Hold up, that's no good," Maddy said. "Saturdays are movie night."

"Not an issue; I'll get off work in time for movie night."

"As long as movie night is preserved, I have no complaints."

"Yeah, don't worry about it." As soon as it left my mouth, I wondered how early I would have to get up on Sunday morning, how late I could realistically stay up on Saturday night, and felt unsure of my words.

"I didn't realize your mom's memory was bad," Claudia said. "I mean, you know, bad enough to warrant a quest."

"Yeah," I said, pausing, unsure how much to tell them. "It's kinda bad. But mostly I just want to make sure it doesn't get worse."

There was an awkward moment. It seemed like neither of them knew what to say.

"But of course this might backfire, and I'll get forced into a memory cult," I said. I thought it would lighten the mood, but they responded with faces that seemed filled with actual concern. The awkward moment piled on top of the previous awkward moment.

"I really can't imagine you hanging out with kids," Maddy finally said.

"Don't dig your hole any deeper," I said.

"Noted. I'm sure you're great with kids."

"Thanks. I am," I said, knowing this was another statement that was only questionably true.

Interplanetary

The other day we were sitting on the Block when, out of nowhere, Claudia started talking about the human voice and all the different ways we can scream and sing and say things, and how these sounds can be so different and so strange depending on the person. How being human can sometimes seem sort of alien. And I thought of her words on my first day of babysitting, because it turns out kids not only make a lot of noise, but they also make a lot of really weird noise.

This is something you don't learn as an only child. From casual observation in public places, it seems like kids just talk too loud, use w's instead of r's and l's for some undetermined amount of time, and cry when they fall. But when you find yourself alone in an enclosed space with them, you discover this just scratches the surface. They emit vocal transmissions that don't fit easily into any category of human sounds I know of. Over the course of my six hours with the kids, I heard words I mistook for hiccups, song sentences, and unearthly howls of joy I mistook for expressions of horrendous pain.

I had been worried about entertaining them—I don't even have cousins, so my well of kid's games is pretty shallow—but it turns out they mostly just entertained me while I tried to keep up and stop them from hurting themselves and each other. What I should have been worried about is understanding them, because most of the time I had no idea what they were saying. It felt like I was on a loop of *whatwasthatwhatwasthatwhatwasthat*, over and over again.

They only cried once, when their heads bumped together and made a scary hollow clunking noise. But from that one time, I learned that crying isn't just a single sound, but a seemingly infinite collection of noises we group together. While I desperately tried to get them to stop, I also found myself listening in horrified fascination as the sounds shape-shifted and reached levels that seemed physically impossible for such small beings.

Though babysitting had its moments, as a whole the day was, more than anything else, pretty uncomfortable. I was definitely not a natural. When their dad came home from work, I think he noticed the shell-shocked look on my face. It was so shady on the first floor that I'd lost all sense of time. Their place smelled like dried oats and wet laundry. I rushed through the social niceties just to get out as quickly as possible. I took the short walk up the stairs to my apartment and considered the possibility that these kids might not only make inhuman noise but could be actual aliens.

Vengeful Ghost

Soon after I got home, Maddy came over for apparition-revenge movie night. Specifically *Ghost*, *The Invisible*, and *High Plains Drifter*. It was Maddy's theme and, though they all are to some degree since she always selects all of the movies, this one was even more hers. Because, while the theme's name felt great to say, I'd been skeptical that I'd actually enjoy the experience of watching and had largely not participated in the brainstorming because of my skepticism. I just hadn't been able to imagine myself getting behind ghosts killing the people who killed them. It was so base, so eye-for-an-eye.

But I would be a liar if I said I didn't get great enjoyment out of each and every one of those films. Though it did make me question the gender dynamics of the vengeful spirit world. Do women ghosts not seek revenge as often as men ghosts? Does earthly male socialization carry over to the spirit realm? It all seemed so unlikely.

Another unlikely element: apparition revenge takes a remarkably long time. You'd think it would just be like, *Oh, here's the person that killed me, they can't see me because I'm a ghost, I kill them, end of movie*. But no, all of these movies make it a lot more complicated than that. It was midnight by the time the second movie was over, and I thought about cutting it off so I could at least get some sleep before my early morning trip to Vinton. But I didn't want to let my quest get in the way of my friendships. So I got under the scratchy wool couch blanket and ate the tooth-chipping, half-popped popcorn at the bottom of the bowl, just to keep myself awake until the end. Finally, Maddy biked home and I set my alarm for three hours into the fast-approaching future.

The More You Know

Morning people talk about the early morning hours as if they're an essential part of being alive. Those hours are "magical" or "peaceful" and so "productive" while the mind is "fresh" or "clear." But I've been getting up early for school for a decade now and never once have I experienced any of those adjectives, nor have I been glad to be awake at six in the morning instead of asleep.

Since I wanted to sleep for as long as I possibly could, I slept in the outfit I picked out the night before. Which had seemed like a good idea at the time. But then it was three hours later. I looked generally wrinkled, everything fit funny, and it was immediately obvious why that was not a more common practice. I put on my bag, feeling a little like a pile of laundry with a backpack, and headed out the door to catch a bus to Vinton, the place where I would see Oregon's only memory guru.

I took the 9 bus to the 27—all the way trying to soak in the unfamiliar routes through my tiredness—then walked the ten-minute walk from the Vinton Transit Center to the event space and, for the first time in my life, I arrived early. But what I thought would be a conference hall with a big digital reader board out front was instead a nondescript storefront in a strip mall. I hoped the building just looked unimpressive from the outside but inside was even more disappointing. It was just a small room. Like one where a neighborhood association, or something equally boring, might have its meetings.

My triumph of being early was diminished by the fact that everybody was early. There were maybe 20 or 30 of us, not the hundreds I had expected, and I took one of the few remaining seats, feeling like I might have screwed up. We all sat on uncomfortable fold-out chairs, but everyone seemed oddly happy about it. Comfortable with the discomfort, even. They were all way older than me. Most of them were probably grandparents, if not great-grandparents. I must have been showing my discomfort, my out-of-place-ness, because a smiley grandma leaned in from the seat behind me.

"Is this your first time?" she asked.

"Um, yeah. You?"

"Oh no, I've been lots of times. Not as often as this guy, though." She motioned to the old guy next to me, and he let out a single, powerfully jolly laugh. "But I'm no stranger," she said. "You're in for a treat. It's so nice that you're starting so young. I wish I would have known these things when I was your age."

I didn't know what to say. How in the world did she expect me to know what "these things" were when I'd never been?

"In remembrance of things to come," she said, tapping her temple and giving me a look like *you know what I'm saying*, even though I obviously didn't and had, once again, no clue how to respond.

Luckily everybody started clapping, so I didn't need to say anything at all. I turned around and walking onto the small stage was a surprisingly tall woman with dyed blonde hair, pale white skin, and arched black eyebrows, wearing silky, flowy fancy-lady clothes in an assortment of pastels, some bits of tastefully gaudy vintage jewelry draped over the top of it all. She looked subtly buff, like an Olympic swimmer. The pictures on her website were poorly-lit living-room selfies, so I had no idea she would be a secretly strong giant. She was disarming, but it was something more than just her size. She moved as if she had been built rather than born—mechanical in a way that was somehow both soothing and enviable.

She approached the microphone with careful, precise movements and slowly said, "Hello. I'm so glad you could be here. You're all so." She held out the word while she moved her head mechanically left, then right, apparently taking everyone in. "Wonderful. And it's early, but— as usual—still you are here."

She spoke with the sort of smooth-and-even hushed voice you would want to hear if you were having trouble sleeping and put on a late-night smooth-jazz radio show to help. She paused, for what seemed like an unnecessarily long time, before finally asking, "When was the last time you ate chocolate?"

Everyone laughed like it was a clever inside joke. Which I suppose it probably was. *Is she on drugs?* I wondered. Is *everyone here on drugs?* I only knew what being on drugs looked like from movies, so I wasn't exactly sure what I was looking for. But being in that room felt the most like being in a movie of anything I'd ever done, so maybe everyone was on drugs. She took a deep breath into the microphone and the murmur of the room hushed.

"As you know," she said, "I'm more interested in forgetting than remembering. So today I'm going to take this a step further and say the most important thing I might ever say. So, please, try to remember." She flashed a sly smile while everyone chuckled. "Your style of forgetting *is* who you are."

Don't Try to Forget

The guru got into the audience with the mic, lightly touching people's hands as she went, like she was high-fiving but also not high-fiving. Everyone was smiling and looking at each other like this was special and for some reason it did feel special, even though I didn't know what it was normally like. I thought maybe it was a sign that I was here for my first time on such a unique day.

When she walked by the aisle closest to mine I surprised myself by leaning out, extending my hand, and she touched it while giving me a smile, holding my gaze as she continued talking, as if her eyes and mouth were operating fully independently of each other, somehow connected to two different brains.

"While we shouldn't try to forget, we should not berate or punish ourselves for forgetting," she said. "This really only makes the problem worse. We must notice what we forget and think about what that means for us as . . ." The room took a collective deep breath. "Real." People said it with her, some too quietly, some too loudly, all a little out of sync. "Living. Breathing. Human. Beings."

Hitting that last word in unison, everyone began applauding. Some made little hooting sounds. I clapped along, a little caught up in it.

She held up a hand, like she wanted to be called on. The applause died down, and she continued. "Mental athletes—those who participate in contests of memory—practice the Greek 'art of memory,' but also practice what they term 'the art of forgetting.' They can't risk having superfluous information pop into their minds during competition, so they go through a process of convincing themselves that certain pieces of information are meaningless."

Though the idea of mental athletes made me want to laugh—I

imagined bulging-muscled brains in tight workout clothing, bench-pressing weights and doing pull-ups—she had my attention.

The guru paused, making eye contact with, it seemed, each one of us individually. "This technique brings my mind to a short story by Jorge Luis Borges where a man couldn't forget, and he was unable to properly function because of it. He was constantly so overwhelmed with information that he couldn't lead a normal life. At the end of the story, Borges suggests that forgetting is what makes us human—that thinking inherently requires forgetting.

"We often don't think of the many unconscious ways we forget and how forgetting is actually helpful to us," the guru said. "We just notice when it is limiting and annoying. We see those moments as personal shortcomings. But if you think about the sheer amount of information we take in on a daily basis—especially in this new digital age—we begin to realize how it would be its own limitation were we to hold tightly to each fact or image or email.

"We as humans have what's called 'working memory,' which makes it so we forget information that isn't immediately useful. It's a very important filtering system and without it we'd be as overwhelmed as the man in the story. Our minds also have a 'curve of forgetting,' where our memory slowly loosens its grasp on a piece of information over time. This is a system of elimination—if we aren't using it, we lose it."

I wondered if this was my mom. Was she not using information and, consequently, losing it? Maybe her job had dulled her mind—she was so much smarter than she needed to be to cashier at a grocery store. But weren't most people smarter than their jobs allowed them to be?

"I think all this is important to talk about here, at our meetings on memory," the guru said, "because I believe understanding how we forget helps us remember. And if each of us begins to examine how and when we forget—which is your homework for the week to come—we can begin to see *why* we forget. When we compare notes, you will notice that there is an individuality, a complex personality, to how you forget. And maybe, just maybe, you might begin to see your forgetfulness not as a limitation, but as a gift."

She took two backwards steps away from the mic and the small room seemed to erupt. I didn't know old people could make so much noise or be so excited. Her talk was disorienting, but it also felt good—a little like waking up from a nap you didn't mean to take. I wanted to read the story she'd referenced, learn terms for the different kinds of memory, watch a competitive memory match—in a few short minutes she'd introduced me to so much. I felt the overwhelming sense that this is where I belonged, that this woman held the keys to my quest, and I couldn't wait to hear more.

The guru left the stage and people slowly started to gather their things. It took me a second to register what was going on. I'd thought this was just a pause to get the energy up, like I'd seen in the videos online, and that we were just getting started. I turned to the regular attendee next to me, who was standing up to put on his tan windbreaker and plain blue baseball cap. "So it's over?" I asked. "Already?"

He chuckled, again a little louder than I expected, then broke into a rapid fire string of words, the polar opposite of the memory guru. "Yeah, I don't want to speak for everybody, but most of us don't have the energy of our youth anymore, so she keeps them short for us. Plus we do this every week and, what with the way time goes at my age, the next one will be here before too long."

"Every *week*?" I asked.

"Every Sunday. You could say it's like our church. Oh, sometimes we get together other days just to meet up and talk—usually Tuesday and Wednesday afternoons, sometimes Friday evenings but not always. And a few times a year we have a big all-day retreat," he said. "But mostly just every Sunday."

I'd thought I was attending a lecture when I looked at it online, maybe something she did every couple months for her local fans, but really I was signing up for some old people's weekly meeting. I was even more out of place than I previously imagined.

"Don't look so sad," he said, "just come back next week. My name's Charles but everybody calls me Rigby. That's my middle name— Charles Rigby Johansen. Born and raised here in Vinton. You're eager for more, huh? Oh, I understand completely. I was after my first time too. That was almost three years ago, and I still haven't gotten enough. But let's see if there's something we can do about your enthusiasm at this very moment. Follow me."

I'm not exactly certain why I followed him without asking any questions, but I guess it seemed like a more interesting option than catching the bus home. We walked to the door where the memory guru was shaking hands and having conversation with people as they left. When our turn came she said, speaking just as slowly as she had on stage, "Rigby. So good to see your face. You are a ray of shining light. Always."

"Well, I appreciate that Ada and you might get to see more of this face today," he responded. "We have a newcomer and I thought maybe the three of us could get some coffee at the diner. He's looking for some additional bursts of brilliance."

"That sounds like a great plan." She turned toward me and, looking down from her towering height, asked, "And who are you?"

I hadn't introduced myself to anyone since getting there. "Oh, I'm Elly Fox."

"What a lovely name," she said. "I can't wait to get to know you. How did you find us?"

"Um, Google?" I said.

She laughed. "That's wonderful. I'm Ada Dronning."

"Good to meet you, Ms. Dronning."

"Call me Ada. I can speak for all who were here today when I say we're happy to have you. I imagine you're from the area?"

"Yeah, kind of. Portland."

"So you traveled. How special. We don't get a lot of Portlanders out here. Just let me close up shop, and we can go down the street and sit for a while."

Some people were slowly helping clean up, so we joined in by stacking chairs. It was impressive how fast Rigby worked. He was wrinkled and had to be in his late 60s, but he was lapping all of us. He was shapeless, almost stick-like, and just barely taller than me. His clothes seemed slightly too big, like a kid wearing his older brother's clothes, which made me wonder if he'd shrunk with age or if he was like me and it was just difficult for him to find clothes in his size. But his small frame was somehow strong enough to basically pack up the room by himself in no time at all, and the next thing I knew I was sitting with the memory guru and a very energetic old guy at a diner. For it being the first official day of my quest, I considered myself to be doing pretty well.

Brilliance, Redefined

The Three Rivers Diner felt like being inside another era. The booths were a once-bright blue, the walls a light pink, the floors check-ered. There was a jukebox in the corner. They had hand-painted signs for malts and rhubarb pie. None of it was fake-old like in Portland where everything was just made to look like it was from another era but was really brand new and silly—this was faded and chipped and dusty in all the right ways. I loved it instantly.

A middle-aged lady with an apron and a voice that was all gravel came by and said "coffees?" Ada and Rigby raised a finger, so I did too. They ordered pie, but I was unsure how long my babysitting money would last so I just stuck with the coffee, drinking it black like they did.

"So why did you make the trip to be with us, Elly?" Ada asked.

I hadn't planned what to say, since I didn't imagine needing to say anything at all. I imagined watching a lecture and getting some pieces of information I needed—my plans ended there. But I started talking about my mom, how I was trying to figure out what was happening because she wouldn't, her lost job, the quest that I had sworn I wouldn't attempt telling anyone else about, how I didn't have a dad but it didn't matter, and they both listened and nodded like I was making some sort of sense.

My coffee kept getting filled up and I kept drinking it, and the whole time Ada never broke eye contact. I felt like I could tell her any-thing and she wouldn't judge me. And since she didn't know me, I didn't need to protect some image she had of me, or need to make her think about me in a particular way—she was there to listen. I felt taken care of.

When I ran out of things to say, Ada said, "You've come to the right place."

"I have?"

"We're not offering a miracle cure, but we are offering a place to learn and grow. And you can commiserate with our members—many of whom have gone through this with their loved ones, or are going through it themselves."

While it was disappointing to hear there wasn't a miracle cure, I probably would have been skeptical if she told me there was.

"While we don't know the cause, what your mother is going through is a return to her birth position. The state of having known to again not-knowing. The diagnosis—and hence any potential cure—will be hard to determine, but the process is the same."

Even though it sounded bizarre, I felt as if I understood. "Are you saying that babies know stuff before they're born?" I asked, hoping it wasn't a dumb question.

She closed her eyes a little and smiled, looking a little like a cat basking in the sun. "Plato had this idea that we already know every-thing, or rather, we *knew* everything. That there's a universal source of knowledge we're connected to and each of us has the possibility to access, but cognitively we forget about it when we leave the womb. So life is a process not of learning, but of remembering.

"Whether we believe this or not, we can still look at memory loss as a return to the birth state. A return to innocence. I like thinking of it that way because it makes the loss less scary. And when the fear is gone, halting it and regaining losses can begin."

I never thought I'd believe that babies in the womb knew every-thing from some great source of knowledge that just exists, but in that moment I did.

"That idea might sound strange to some," Ada admitted, "but think about how we all intuitively seem to know the truth when we hear it. How do we know something is true if we don't already know what the truth is? How do we find truth without knowing what we're look-ing for? You see, Elly, we're more than a memory group. Our teachings reach far and wide. We question and expand the ways humans typically interpret the world."

"It's really fascinating stuff!" Rigby exclaimed out of nowhere, maybe to me and maybe to Ada, I couldn't tell. "Always just blows my mind. But I need to get home and do my Sunday chores before it gets too late. I hope you'll join us next week?" he said, this time definitely looking at me.

"If I'm invited."

They laughed. "All are invited," Ada said. "But unfortunately only some are wise enough to come."

Rigby walked out with a purposeful stride, and Ada and I silently watched from the window as he got into his giant old-man car and drove away.

"Rigby is a brilliant person," Ada said.

I felt like I was supposed to nod, but I didn't know if I agreed with this. Charming? Yes. Kind? Surely. But brilliant? I guess I just wasn't totally certain yet. Ada seemed to notice my hesitation. "Elly, I was raised to believe that brilliance was defined by a limited set of mental abilities. I was a chess prodigy, did you know that?"

I nodded, feeling a little weird admitting to having online-stalked her.

"Knowledge in very particular areas of study were looked upon kindly and knowledge in other areas of study were looked at as common, quotidian, pedestrian. But over the years leading the Fellowship, I've started to ask myself: what if all knowledge is equally important? Wouldn't that change what we call brilliant?"

She paused and started in on the important-slow-talking thing that I earlier thought was odd, maybe unsettling, but had quickly grown to think was actually hypnotizing, almost comforting. "Now, I think Rigby is brilliant because he knows things about the world that I can't seem to wrap my mind around. He could take my car apart and put it back together and it would be a better car. Me, I can't even change my oil. He can hear a bird from a mile off and tell you what it is. All birds sound the same to me. So I'm the genius and he's the village idiot, huh? I don't buy it."

It was like she had put words to a life philosophy I didn't know I had. Even though I thought there was probably a large gap between brilliant and village idiot, everything she'd said felt like the best way to be in the world—to see different kinds of intelligence all around you. She paid our bill, to my relief, and walked me to the bus station.

On the ride home I thought about all the showboating popular boys at school I make fun of in my head for being stupid, and I felt a little guilty. Maybe this quest could not only help me save my mom from forgetting but also make me a better person.

Memory's Friend

Before I got on the bus, Ada had given me some pamphlets, which she called "literature," and on the ride home I read them all. The organization was called the Acquaintances of Memory Fellowship: A Perception and Elevation Group, or AMF for short. The main introductory pamphlet said that it had been around for five years and had hundreds of followers across the Pacific Northwest. The people who meet every week mostly lived in Vinton, but the others received weekly emails and some would come for a big conference, the one Rigby had mentioned to me, at the beginning of each year.

I can't say I learned a lot from the literature. It was basically like her website with little sayings and ideas about what memory is and how we're supposed to think about it. I didn't understand why someone would hide the fact they were really remarkable in person with mysterious catchphrases like, "Be your memory's friend and you will begin to see it as tender and without blame." I wondered if there was a reason she wanted to keep how much she knew and could offer under wraps at first. Like, maybe she didn't want to make people think the group was too advanced or intimidating.

The next day I got a text while I was in English class. I checked it under my desk. *What would you say to meeting up next Saturday?* It was Ada. We had exchanged numbers when we were walking to the bus, but I didn't think she'd actually contact me.

OK. But what for? I texted back.

To get you caught up, she responded. *I can speak for the group when I say we want you to be a part.*

I almost couldn't believe what I was reading. *I could take the bus after I get done babysitting at 4...I'd be there a little after 5*, I think.

I'll pick you up from the transit center, she said.

Even though that was all we said, I couldn't pay attention to anything for the rest of the day. At lunch, I was more quiet than normal because I knew I'd have to cancel on Maddy for our movie night. For this one, we were supposed to watch movies named after holidays that aren't Christmas. *Groundhog Day*, *Independence Day*, and *Halloween* were all we'd found so far, but those were plenty for one night. I felt like a jerk, but I couldn't pass up this opportunity. For whatever reason, a famous chess prodigy, Oregon's only memory guru, and likely the source of knowledge I needed for my quest, wanted to hang out with me, and I had to figure out how to be there.

The Memory of Driving

That night I ended up in an online forum for people with parents who have various forms of memory loss. And there was a whole thread about how scary it was when the parent kept driving. Some kept driving after they admitted that their memory was going, and some even after they were diagnosed with the beginning stages of dementia or Alzheimer's. I had thought driving was just knowing rules and paying attention, but people on the forum said driving was as much memory. It's why people get stressed driving in new cities—when you don't know the roads, you become an exponentially worse driver.

I wondered about all the almost-accidents that might have happened since our almost-accident—the ones I just wasn't present for, the ones she never mentioned, the ones she didn't even notice. All of a sudden I was worried about a whole other part of my mom's life that I had no control over. I considered talking to her about it, but it seemed pointless. The thought made me feel like the people on the forum: powerless to stop their parent from doing something their minds no longer allowed them to properly do.

As I was reading, it occurred to me that most people on the forum were probably older than my mom. Did I really belong here? Is this how I spend my nights now? I'm not supposed to have this much in common with middle-aged people. But I don't have much in common with people my own age, so maybe it made sense. Maybe this is where I belonged. Worrying alongside people with as little control as me.

Armistice Day

"So I found another one," Maddy said, as I sat down next to her, thudding into the hard plastic bus seat. *"Armistice Day."*

I stared at her blankly.

"For tomorrow night. I did a million searches for non-Christmas holiday-titled movies and found this silent film about World War I. We can stream it on a random historical archive website, it looks really cool. I'd never even heard of the holiday, but it's about the war ending or maybe wars in general ending. So I guess it's kind of like Peace Day or something—which is pretty awesome, right?"

It was awesome. I wanted to be excited. And in fact, a part of me was excited. But somehow it was Friday, and I still hadn't talked to Maddy about canceling our movie night. When Ada texted me on Monday, I thought I had plenty of time and it wouldn't be a big deal because I would be canceling so far ahead of time. But I hadn't been able to bring myself to do it.

I was not the kind of friend who did this—I always made it. To everything. One time, in first grade, I went to my friend's birthday party even though I clearly had a stomach bug. I was so dedicated to going to his party that I pretended I was better so my mom would take me. I ended up puking minutes after walking through the door, but I puked *there*. At the party. And now I was canceling when nothing was wrong with me.

I just felt so driven, so excited that this lady who could be the key to me figuring out memory and helping my mom wanted to teach me everything she knows. And, the way I figured it, the faster I learned things the sooner I could help my mom. If speed wasn't so important and there wasn't this risk of my mom forgetting more every day, I wouldn't cancel. And if I explained it that way, Maddy would understand. So as she waited for my response, I decided I just had to spit it out before I lost my nerve.

"So about tomorrow," I said. "I've gotta go to Vinton after babysitting. It's a really important part of my quest, and I just can't back out."

She looked at me like she wanted to ask about the new plan, or maybe she was trying to figure out why I hadn't already told her about it. Did I keep secrets from Maddy now? Or was this just one isolated thing I didn't feel like telling her about?

"That's cool," she said, "we'll just start a little later. When do you get back?"

I hadn't expected this response. I expected to say I was busy and then have her understand what that meant. "I don't know," I said, "maybe as late as ten."

"Whoa, okay. Well, we can save *Armistice Day* for next time," she said. "I'm down to stay up late, but that would make it an all-nighter. Still, though, you're going to pretty much be going on zero sleep, huh?"

This was all so much harder than I had imagined just a moment before. Maybe there was a reason I had put it off for so long. "No, I'm not going to go on zero sleep," I said. The words came out more cutting than I meant them.

Her face seemed to be compacting. "Am I doing the math wrong or something?"

"I need to cancel our movie night," I said. "I mean, you know, reschedule."

"Oh. Okay. It's been awhile since we missed a movie night, huh?" She was using her fake voice; I almost couldn't take it. "So, what—next Saturday for movie night?" she asked.

"Of course. Next Saturday."

"Yeah, that'll be cool." She tried to smile, but it only kind of worked.

Watching Maddy fake being okay with this felt like what I imagined my heart being used as a punching bag would feel like. I never let any of my friends down. Even friends I wasn't really friends with. I didn't even let my acquaintances down. But there I was, letting my best friend down.

Poetry About America

There's a guy who wrote a book of poems about America who said he was never more human than when he was riding the bus next to someone who made him shudder. I thought about that on my way to Vinton, sharing a seat with a guy who unnecessarily took up most of our two seats. For some reason he wore tiny cut-off jean shorts in the final days of September and his oily cascade of hair was dangerously close to touching my shoulder.

With one of my butt cheeks hanging into the aisle, trying to stay on the seat while also trying not to let this person's body touch mine, I attempted to embrace the moment—to see it as, in some way, special. I didn't know if I felt human, but maybe I felt like a poem.

I texted Claudia, which I almost never do. But I had been thinking about her on these couple trips to Vinton, how she does her thing out in the world, seemingly without much worry or concern of getting stuck in seats next to guys like this one, and here I was out in the world. *Maybe we should go to a show sometime*, I typed, and I sat back stiffly and waited, feeling more nervous than I felt I should feel.

Sometimes I think Maddy and I are her consolation-prize friends— that if she wasn't stuck at a high school with limited options, she would be hanging out with some other people who aren't us. But even if that is true, I'm pretty sure she doesn't look at it that way. I think she just feels like the show scene isn't our style. Which is true. But being on the bus made me wonder if that could be different and it could be occasionally our style.

For me it's just an issue of passion; I like music, but it isn't my thing. And maybe I worry I would have to fake that to go to the shows— like, I wouldn't be honest with the people I met at the shows and this would get our relationship off to a bad start. But mostly I think it's just an unknown experience I sort of fear. While Maddy does love a lot of the same off-kilter indie-pop and punk-but-not-quite-punk music that Claudia does and the show scene would almost definitely be her thing, her parents are pretty strict when it involves anything other than hanging out with me, so she can't really go to shows without lying about it and sneaking around, which she doesn't like to do.

After a few minutes, I got a buzz. *Heck yeah!* she replied. *I thought you'd never ask. Anytime, just let me know when and I'll find us something.*

I relaxed my body. The new me, I thought, and the words sounded as sweet as a poem.

The True Meaning of Chess

I got off the bus in Vinton and Ada was waiting at the station with two bicycles. She was wearing workout leggings and a shiny windbreaker, grinning, like she had been waiting for my arrival for a long time and was so excited I was finally here.

"Did you push these both all the way?" I asked, realizing as soon as I said it that I didn't actually know where she lived. Maybe she lived right next door to the station.

"Just from my car," she said, motioning vaguely to her left. "Do you want to go for a ride?"

"It's been a long time," I said. I'd had a bike for a couple years in fourth and fifth grade, but it got stolen at some point. Then I started taking buses by myself in middle school and stopped thinking about bikes entirely. Why would I commute using something so statistically dangerous when there were buses to take me everywhere?

Ada took my reply as a yes, though, so she tipped one of the bikes into my hands and started riding the other. I got on the slightly-too-big bike and, while everyone says any action that uses muscle memory is like riding a bike, it turned out riding a bike was not like riding a bike. At least not for me. I was very wobbly and almost fell off a time or two, but Ada didn't seem to notice and led us to a trail that she said used to be railroad tracks.

After a few minutes of going on the straight and level trail, I stopped feeling like I might seriously injure myself and started enjoying it. The tree branches seemed to make a light whipping sound as we passed by them, as if we were carrying a small tunnel of air along with us, and I let my helmetless hair become a messy vortex. It felt good enough that I didn't care how stupid it probably looked.

When we came to a small park, Ada pulled into the grass, hopping off the bike more gracefully than I could ever imagine myself doing. "We study a lot in AMF," she said, giving her kickstand a little nudge. "But some days you have to get out of your head and have some fun." As I slowly came to a complete stop and maneuvered my body off the bike, she said, "Race you to the swing set?" and took off running. I trailed behind, laughing, still stunned that Ada had this playful side I'd never previously imagined.

Before I was even caught up, she was talking. In quick succession, she told me about everything from the minds of jungle predators to the principles of quantum physics. She told me that, in addition to being a memory guru, she was a "perception guide" and this was what the "Perception and Elevation" part of AMF's name was about. Then she started telling me the history of chess.

"It is said that chess was created to explain the abstract, the unexplainable," she said. "To make simple truths visible within the chaos of the world."   The whole conversation was giving me a second revised perspective on who Ada was. I had read her as generally soft and gentle in her demeanor, but she was also direct in a way that was almost a little aggressive. To some degree, I appreciated it since so many people in Portland are so indirect; it was kind of refreshing.

"It's often hard for those who don't play the game seriously to understand, but chess is a way of life," she said, while swinging higher than I'd seen anyone swing. "Even though I don't play anymore, it's still the way I see the world. Though I of course try to look upon the world with kindness and forgiveness, I will also forever see the constant, daily war of life on earth. I see small battles of opposing forces whether I'm driving down the street, ordering a drink at a bar, or pushing a cart at the grocery store. I see people vying for power positions. I see winners and losers."

It made me realize that probably a lot of people viewed the world this way, and I'd been a little naive to not see it.

"See how high I'm going, Elly?" Ada said, sounding a little out of breath.

"Uh-huh."

"Does it make you a little jealous?" she asked.

Having never been asked such a bizarre question, I said, "I don't know. I guess it is pretty impressive."

At that, she jumped off, landing like a stunt person on the bark, then turned to face me. "Many people say they're not competitive and, while I can see the ways they're not and why they believe this about themselves, I also think they fail to see the unconscious ways they seek power. The ways we all seek power. Even when participating in activities that are thought of as fun and careless." She paused for a really long time. I didn't know what to do, so I just kept swinging. Which felt completely inappropriate for the moment, but it would have felt more awkward to stop. Finally she said, "Do you see what I'm saying?"

"I think so," I said, unsure of what was happening.

"Good. It's getting dark, let's get some coffee before you catch the bus."

We biked back and by the time we reached Three Rivers Diner, the temporary oddness of the swing set had dropped away. She ordered us coffee drinks with names I had heard but had never had and told me about Norse myths, and how different cultures are still influenced by stories that are sometimes thousands of years old. She called it a form of cultural memory, which was evidently also a part of AMF. She talked about the need for ritual and ceremony in the modern world, how she saw AMF filling this need for members, and by the time we left I was brimming with more information than I could hold.

She walked me to the transit center and when my bus pulled in she asked, "I'll see you tomorrow morning?"

I couldn't imagine missing it. "Yeah, I'll be there."

"There are so many ideas and philosophies associated with our group, and I can't wait to go over them all with you," she said. "It's so unfortunate that you have such limited availability. What would you say to Saturday evening being a regular event?"

I had a flash of worry about ditching out on Maddy for the rest of eternity but tried my best to ignore it. AMF felt good. Right, even. I had to follow this out to see where it went, what I could learn. "Yeah, I could do that," I said.

"I think your youthful energy will do wonders for the group. I'm really glad you're a part of us now," Ada said.

I thought about how I'd never been a part of something, how long I'd waited for anyone to say that. On the ride home, I watched people get on and off the bus, switch seats, navigate this shared space, and I tried to imagine them as knights and rooks, kings and queens.

Anything Can Be Inspiring

Even after canceling with Maddy, the next morning was just as bad as I imagined it would be, perhaps even worse. I counted the time in my head: four hours and ten minutes of sleep. I couldn't believe I'd agreed to do this every week for the indefinite future.

I'm pretty sure the process of getting out of the house, onto the first bus, then the other bus, and into the meeting was done by somebody else who temporarily inhabited my body, because I remember none of it. I shuffled in right as people were clapping and Ada was approaching the podium. I found Rigby, and sat next to him as the applause died down and the dramatic pause started up.

She let the hush hang around long enough for us to feel uncomfortable before saying, "Memory." Then paused again, as if that word was just such a natural way to start a sentence she was unsure what to say next. "Is dangerous territory," she finally said, and then let us sit in the mild confusion of that sentence for a while before explaining.

"What I mean by this is that it can keep us from living here in the present. There are many—from great artists to people like you and me—who have given their lives over to the past. Isn't this interesting to think about? That we can choose to give up having new experiences to bask in past ones. When we consider certain memories positive, they often become romanticized—over time becoming bigger and better than the original experience. And herein lies the danger: the possibility of getting trapped in the romanticized past. Which brings us to our mantra of the week: Remember to remember, but never forget to live. Let's say it together a few times, to really get it in our heads."

We all joined in, but it came out sounding like "ra-ra-ra-ra-ra, ra-ra-ra, ra-ra-ra." It was obvious that none of us had any sense of timing and what we were doing was more a garbled assortment of syllables than a chant. But it somehow still managed to be sort of powerful. Something about all the voices rumbling together in the room made it not matter whether it was in sync, or even intelligible.

Somewhere during the chant, my mind traveled. I'm not certain where, or what exactly I thought about during that time, or what I missed in the lecture. I liked the idea of being in the present moment, but the outside-of-time world of my brain often felt better than the inside-of-time outside world, so I was used to going there; it was comfortable.

I reemerged at the very end of the lecture. "To embrace life is always the most inspiring thing one can do," Ada said. "So live. And inspire."

We all clapped. Though I didn't know what the context of those words had been, I did like imagining that my random choices were somehow inspirational. I watched Rigby put on his little windbreaker with the Members Only label on the pocket and scan the room, surveying the conversations that awaited him.

"So, you ready to go do some inspiring stuff?" I asked.

He laughed. "Well, we'll see! No extra-ordinary plans, but I guess you don't know what someone else will think about the things you do. There might be somebody out there who'll get inspired by me going to the hardware store. You just never know, huh?"

"Yep, I guess you never know." I tried to think of something clever to say, but I couldn't come up with anything. I was too tired to make my brain do what I wanted it to do.

He seemed completely unconcerned about the conversation dying in its tracks, and just kept smiling in a happy-go-lucky way. Then out of the blue he said, "Oh, I should get your email address." He pulled out one of the little pocket notepads I'd seen in drugstores but assumed no one ever bought and said, "Here, you can write it down on this."

"My email?" I couldn't imagine what in the world he would need to send me.

"I send out a daily newsletter to everyone I know," he said, seemingly satisfied with this fairly bizarre answer. Like, *that explains it all: a daily newsletter.*

I tried to be polite about it. "Okay, well, what are the newsletters about?"

"Nothing terribly exciting, I'm afraid!" he said, chuckling loudly. "Just what I did during the day, what movie I watched, what came in the mail."

"What came in the mail?"

"Like I said: no thrillers here. It's just when you get to be my age, you start to know fewer and fewer people. Most the people you used to know are gone and it's just kind of nice to know that people are there, even if you don't see them every day. So whenever I meet somebody new, I get their address."

I didn't know what to say. How do you respond to something so touching and so weird? "Is everybody in this room on your nightly mailing list?"

"As far as I can remember. But, you know, my memory's not what it used to be." We exchanged a smile. Any memory joke was a winner around these parts. "I'll try to get you on the list before tonight's goes out. That way you can read about yourself."

"Alright. Thanks, I guess."

As we were walking out, Rigby got caught up in conversation with the lady who'd talked to me my first day, and as I walked by I thought about how long ago that already felt. When I got to the door Ada had a crowd around her. I'd planned on suggesting we all get coffee again, but I was too exhausted to wait all these conversations out. I got on the bus, then the other bus, walked home, promptly got in bed, and went to sleep.

It was dark by the time I woke up. I checked my phone. 10:45. Fifteen minutes before I usually tried to go to bed. There was a text from Maddy, seeing what I was up to six hours ago. I felt embarrassed telling her I'd just woken up from an epic nap, so decided to not respond right away.

There was also an email from Rigby, just like he promised. For a guy who talked like he had caps lock on, it was surprising how quiet and very lowercase his email was. It showed a huge list of recipients, and the subject just said "Sunday news."

Hi all,

Normal Sunday stuff: had a grapefruit, coffee, went to group. Ada had inspiring talk about life. Talked more with a high schooler *who has joined the group. Stopped by hardware store on my way home to get a new spark plug for the mower. Went home and had lunch (tomato soup and toast). Watched another old movie,* Sunset Boulevard. *Very different, but well done. Had leftovers for dinner, now going to turn in. No mail today (Sunday).*

Until tomorrow,
Rigby

Even though it was a pretty uninspiring piece of writing, it somehow opened up a whole new side of Rigby. In a strange way, the message reminded me of this book of old Zen Buddhist poems my uncle had me read last year—both were incredibly boring and oddly beautiful. But instead of it being about leaves on the water's surface, it was about spark plugs and tomato soup.

I considered this for a while, then read it again, seeing if it would cause any great Zen-like revelations. When none came, I went to the kitchen to find a snack. My mom was sitting at the kitchen counter. "Good morning," she said, not lifting her head up from the crossword puzzle she was working on. "What wore you out so much?"

"Um, you know, the volunteer thing," I said, scanning the cupboards.

"What's that all about again?" she said, looking up.

"The thing at the old folk's home I told you about. With Maddy."

"Huh. It's a school project or something?"

I was sleepy, had no interest in responding, and felt unable to decide whether her questioning was normal everyday forgetting or big-deal forgetting. "Yeah, it's like an early college-transcript thing."

"Okay, right. So, do they work you really hard or what?"

"I guess." I tried to remember what I'd told her. "Mostly I just watched too many movies with Maddy last night and didn't get enough sleep."

"Hmm, maybe you guys shouldn't be hanging out Saturday nights when you have to volunteer so early on Sundays."

"Mom, don't worry about it," I said, not awake enough to navigate the conversation.

"Are you still going to be able to get your homework done? I don't think colleges are going to care whether you did volunteer work if you don't get good grades."

"Mom, it is entirely okay. I'm going to be fine." This whole interaction was quickly turning me from sleepy to grumpy. Truth was, I hadn't finished my homework and probably wasn't going to get it all done before going back to sleep. And a part of me was a little worried about it. But my mom was driving me nuts enough to not want to do it at all.

I briefly wondered why I was on this quest for her when she was this annoying, but immediately felt bad for thinking it. I took my not-quite-put-together cheese-and-crackers plate to my room to avoid any further questions and the very real possibility of me saying something extremely rude in response to my mom's questions, or blowing up at her for not remembering a lie I'd told.

I lay down on my bed and began texting Maddy back, but it was hard since I knew I'd soon have to talk with her about canceling our Saturdays forever. I felt more sentimental than usual, since we were on the verge of this big change, but I wanted to be casual enough that she wouldn't wonder why I was being so sentimental. After trying a dozen things that weren't what I wanted, I finally settled on *Sunday news: slept all afternoon. Remembered how my best friend inspires me (just by being alive). Now back to bed. Until tomorrow, Elly.*

Everything We Can Remember

No one actually knows if there's a limit to human memory. Or at least that's how it seems from researching it. There are cases of people with freak brain injuries whose memories, after their accidents, become seemingly limitless. And some people practice memorizing really impractical things—usually random number sequences or playing cards—and are able to remember more and more with practice. But then everybody else keeps forgetting stuff and no one seems to know, for sure, why. Even the people with brain injuries and the people who practice memorizing forget some things sometimes.

It's like the human brain is the bottom of the ocean or outer space—scientists can see bits of it and make theories out of those bits, but those theories are really only guesses at this point. There's so much we don't know.

My Current Failure as a Friend

I kept waking up all night long, wondering where I was, what life I found myself in. It was my little bedroom and our little apartment, sure, but I think my unconscious mind knew that everything surrounding it was different. The place was the same, but it also wasn't. When I finally woke up for good just before my alarm, I decided that this time I wouldn't wait. I had to tell Maddy right away. No matter how bad it was going to be, no matter how much she'd hate me for being such a terrible friend.

But again, the days passed and it never seemed like the right moment. Monday I was a floaty unfocused space cadet from messing up my sleep schedule, Tuesday Claudia was in a fight with one of her show friends and we needed to help her process it, Wednesday the Block had been tagged with a giant penis and we debated whether it was worth getting in trouble for spray painting over it or if we needed to find a new piece of concrete to call our own, and Thursday it had been painted over with that dumb-looking gray paint government institutions use to block out graffiti that we usually hate but were in this case happy about, and we spent the day trying to come up with some ritual to reclaim our block back from the stupid penis.

Then it was Friday morning, Maddy and I were on the bus, it was raining, she was saying words I couldn't pay attention to. When she took a sip from her coffee thermos, I saw my chance. I swooped in and said, "So I've got something I feel super bad about but cannot be avoided."

She made her surprised look, where she angles her head slightly, as if a new visual perspective might help things make sense. "Okay," she said, hesitantly. "What's up?"

"It's about our Saturdays. I have to give them up for the quest. I hate to do it, but I've got this woman wanting to teach me all this stuff and help me save my mom, and I've got to take every opportunity I can."

"So, you're saying you need to go to Vinton on Saturday nights?"

"Yes. And I am so sorry. Ridiculously sorry. Upsettingly, accepting my current failure-as-a-friend, sorry."

Then, to my surprise, she made her what-are-you-talking-about confused face, which is the same as her surprised look, only with a more wrinkled brow. "Dude, it's fine."

"What?" I didn't believe I'd heard her right.

"It's fine. You gotta do what you gotta do. You're on a quest, I understand. And you and I can still kick it after school during the week. Not a big deal."

Even though this was the best reaction I could have possibly imagined, I felt the need to fight against it. "Yeah, but we won't be able to do our themes."

"It's cool, we'll do all our theme nights at some point. Winter break is only a couple months away. We'll do a few then."

"Winter break? You can seriously think that far into the future?"

She laughed. "I mean, yeah, I don't want to. But this is important."

"You sure?"

"Completely."

She was so good at saying that word. Somehow she made that one word sound like it was the fact to end all facts.

Remember the Moves

I wish I could imagine a future situation without having expectations. But the second I imagine what something might be like I create an expectation and then I'm glued to that expectation. It just happens instantly; I can't seem to stop it. And if I've done something before, it's like my imagination just dies and I expect that this thing I've done before will be exactly the same as the previous time.

I got done with babysitting on Saturday, told my mom I would be watching movies at Maddy's, and caught the bus to Vinton. And the whole time there was just no question in my mind that I would end up swinging at some park with Ada and then go to the diner. I wasn't trying to imagine that, it was just the image in my head each time I considered what I was about to do.

But on the way to Vinton it started raining. And by the time the bus got to the transit center, it was pouring. Ada was waiting for me with a huge umbrella—a clear indication that she wasn't from the Northwest. No one from here uses umbrellas. It's dumb but true.

I hadn't considered that the rain might mean a change in plans, which I guess was silly, and was disappointed when Ada led us into a poorly lit hole-in-the-wall coffee shop next to the transit center called Angela's. The place was so spotless and sparse, it was as if nothing happened there at all. For having such a homey, welcoming name, it seemed completely disinfected, almost clinical, like all the places Maddy and I hated in Portland but even worse, because instead of replacing its life with design, it was both lifeless and design-less.

We sat down, but my stupid expectations made me feel unprepared for this new situation, and I had trouble keeping up with the conversation. It took a full cup of some badly made espresso drink Ada had ordered for me to snap out of it.

"How did you decide to start AMF?" I asked, maybe the first real thing to leave my mouth since we'd arrived. It wasn't what I wanted to ask, but it was something. "I mean, 'memory guru' isn't really a common career."

She smiled. "I had a gift, and knowledge that other people didn't have, so I felt I had to pass it on."

"But why did you become so interested in memory?"

"I didn't become interested in memory by choice, I had to be interested in memory. Memory is an essential part of a chess student's training. Chess students study the great games and remember the moves, as a way of getting inside the minds of the masters. Neuroscientists have done studies, and true international masters can be shown the board of a chess game for as little as five seconds and be able to tell you the location of all thirty-two pieces. Chess players train their memories around the chessboard."

I thought about what I remember and what I don't: movie titles but not book titles, the content of books but not the authors, the lyrics to songs but not song titles or band names. It seemed so silly in comparison.

"There was still a lot I had to learn when I started AMF, though," Ada said. "Especially when it came to connecting those ideas to perception and the brain's less acknowledged abilities. But it's still true that many of the memory techniques I learned through chess are actively incorporated into AMF."

I wasn't positive how to say what I wanted to say, so I just tried saying something. "I know you have a bunch of ways to help people remember, but is there a way to make people stop forgetting?"

She looked at me for a long time before saying anything. "You know, oftentimes there is. But I can't meet with your mother until we've done some more work."

I hadn't expected her to see through me. I started to stutter something, but she put her hand up to stop me. "You didn't let me finish," she said. "If you want, we can expedite the process of that work."

"Sure," I said. "But how?"

"I can offer you a position through our internship program."

A dozen thoughts flashed through my head—images of resumés, letters of recommendation, applications, the title *Acquaintances of*

Memory Fellowship Intern. I don't know what I wanted these things for, exactly, but I knew I wanted them for something. I thought of everything I could learn, my quest for knowledge expedited. It felt like some sort of big celestial door opening. She moved her eyebrows in a way that felt like a question. I had no idea how long I'd been quiet for, or what my face was doing.

"When can I start?"

We walked to the bus station together, and I purposefully didn't stand underneath her umbrella—just so I could get rained on and feel triumphant. Even though I knew it would make the bus ride home miserable, it was worth it.

One Stupid Letter of the Alphabet

While walking into drama class after lunch, Rain leaned toward me and, hovering around my shoulder, said, "How's it going getting your 'friend' to fall in love with you?"

I felt my nostrils flare, felt the way her presence made my whole body tense. "For the last time: Maddy is not my girlfriend, I do not have a crush on her. I've never thought of her that way. Ever. So lay off."

She seemed to consider this. "Okay, I'll lay off. But only if you tell me who you *do* have a crush on."

"No one."

"Now this I don't believe."

"Believe it," I said.

"You're into boys then? I guess I thought you just looked like a queer and that your whole get-up was just to lure some weird girls into your bed, but okay, I can see how you're actually a little dick-lover."

"I'm not into anyone, okay?"

"Oh, so you're asexual," she asked, her eyes getting wide.

I froze. "Yeah, sure, I'm asexual," I said, trying to coat the words with sarcasm. "Now stop talking to me."

Surprisingly she did. We each took our seats and the hour passed. But when we were leaving class, she said in a mock-friendly voice, "See you later, Little A!" She was smiling so big that I knew whatever had just come out of her mouth must have been mean—hurting people seemed to be her only joy.

"What did you call me?" I asked, though I knew I didn't want to know.

"I just want to be supportive of your non-sexual preferences. So I was just calling you by your new nickname: A. Or maybe Little A. I haven't decided yet. But you know, A for asexual. And also maybe Alien-

Boy—again, I haven't decided. I love that you're pushing boundaries and it's not just about being straight or gay. That's really impressive, A." Then she walked away.

It was so dumb—just one letter. She could have called me a whore-bucket or a dickface, something innovative. But I knew instantly that I'd have to endure her calling me "A" every single day for the rest of the school year, and it was somehow worse than other, more creative insult possibilities. The letter would make other people confused, which would mean they would pay more attention—they would get involved in the ridicule in a way that familiar insults simply wouldn't cause. Rain's powers over my self-esteem were great.

The Talk

Maddy and I had never talked about dating and sex stuff because neither of us had dated anyone. She had kissed two boys at middle-school parties, and she had a friend who was a girl and, though they had never kissed, their eyes somehow got shinier whenever they were together. I considered them in-love-but-untitled, since it was a crush that neither of them seemed to have any idea what to do with. But she'd never had a boyfriend or girlfriend or partner and never even mentioned liking anyone. Crushes, dating, and relationships seemed to occupy so little of her brain space that I almost couldn't imagine talking to her about that stuff, even though she was my best friend.

But Rain had once again hit on something I actually worried about. Though I didn't really understand what it meant to be asexual, I had heard the term and thought it might apply to me. Up until now I'd been too embarrassed to talk to anyone about it, but my mind was so weighed down with insecurities that, during the course of fifth and sixth period, I'd decided I was going to bring it up to Maddy on the bus home. It had to happen. I'd put it off for too long; even though it seemed profoundly awkward, I would start a conversation about relationships and sexual preferences with my best friend.

But as I turned my phone on as I walked out of sixth period, I saw a text from her saying she was staying late to work on a horticulture project—the annual plant sale was this weekend, and she'd warned me she might have to miss our bus ride home at some point this week. Just then, Claudia walked up. I looked at her and, even before saying anything, she said, "You okay, Elly?"

"Is my not-okay that apparent?"

"Yeah, you look sort of constipated. But I'm guessing that's not the problem."

"No, it's not," I said, sounding disappointed, as if I wished for that to be the problem. "Can I ask you a question?"

"Of course. I like to consider myself full of answers."

"Is it weird that I've never dated anyone? Ever?"

"Well, not really. I mean, I haven't dated that many people, either."

"Yeah, but I've never even been interested in dating anybody. Isn't that part kind of weird?"

She let her eyes go a little soft. "I guess," she said, "but you're probably overthinking it."

"I think I figured it was just something we would all do in the future. But now it feels as if the future is here and everyone's interested in this except me."

"Elly, that's an exaggeration. Not everyone is dating. When you want to date, you'll date."

"But that's the thing: I don't know that I will. I can't really even figure out who I'm attracted to. I know that sounds like another exaggeration, but it's true. Whenever somebody says some other person is hot, I end up staring at the supposedly hot person every chance I get to try to figure out what makes them hot and if I too find them hot. I mean, every now and then someone I don't know will walk by and I'll be like, 'Whoa!' But I don't know if it's because I think the person is hot or because some people are just magical creatures."

Claudia laughed, which made me feel slightly better. I paused before I asked the question I wanted to ask. "Do you think I'm asexual?"

"I really can't answer that one for you. I mean, I think I've only heard that word applied to invertebrates, so I'm probably not the most knowledgeable person here. But if you are, so what?"

"Well, it doesn't seem to be normal."

"When have you ever cared about that? Maybe it's a sexuality that just doesn't involve other people. Do you masturbate?"

It was definitely a question no one had ever asked me before. "I mean, I have. But not, you know, regularly."

"So maybe you're mostly asexual, or your sexuality will just happen later. Or maybe those times were experiments and you figured out you're ultimately not interested in sexual stuff. It's probably just confusing that it isn't immediately obvious where you fit. But you know, from my perspective, you're obviously doing alright. Really you're probably just smarter than everybody else. Do you notice how nuts everyone gets when they're in a relationship? You can at least be glad that you're way less stressed out than all the people who are dating."

I wanted to believe she was right and that I was just avoiding a headache, but I still felt off. I think I'd felt off about it, on some level, for a long time. But now that it had been identified by my mortal enemy, I suddenly had to think about it more and it seemed not just unusual but inhuman—from my uncle's books I'd learned about all sorts of sexual desires and how we're all sexual beings and how important-yet-repressed our desires are, but no one ever once said, in any of these books, "I'm not sexual" or "some people aren't sexual beings and that's okay."

While I sat there with Claudia, I even considered the possibility of trying to date someone just to put an end to this inhuman feeling and Rain's nickname. Or maybe just to find out what the big deal was. Even though I didn't really want to date anyone and had no idea who I would or could date if I tried.

I thanked her because she truly was the best person I could have talked to about this, even though I somehow felt maybe more lost than before. Now that I'd put words to these things, they were real and I had to deal with them, when before they were below the surface and I just had to stuff them down and ignore them—which was relatively easy, I think, because they were just about the absence of desire rather than a desire itself.

These thoughts now felt like a distraction from my quest, my internship that was supposed to start any day now, my mom, and all I wanted to do was travel back in time ten minutes so that I could just keep my stupid mouth shut.

The Intern

I spent most of the next morning and all of lunch spacing off, lost in some thought-loop about how robots in robot stories always learned to have human emotions by being around humans but humans never seemed to learn anything from the robots, when I got a text from Ada: *Can you begin your internship today?*

I was on my way from lunch to fourth period, and reading it was like waking up a second time—as if part of my brain was just lingering in standby mode until that message powered it on. I told myself to wait until after school to respond, so I could think about it and come to a decision that felt true and right. But instead I replied, *Of course*, and turned my phone back off as I walked in the door to U.S. history, for once unconcerned—despite yesterday's talk with Claudia, despite Rain calling me "A" again when leaving drama class today—about being called Elias and not Elly. Now I had a purpose.

For the next few hours I got texts from Ada that were just unattributed inspirational quotes without any context or commentary. Some had the feel of a real quote that a maybe-famous person once said ("The greatest work is the work you put toward a cause you believe in"), while others seemed too clunky to be widely quoted ("You can only work well and benefit others if you put care—and careful attention—into quality"). I wondered if Ada had just made them up, or if she was quoting herself from AMF literature, or what. But the odd thing was: they worked. It didn't matter what I thought of each individual quote, what mattered was that they were all inspirational and there were a lot of them. Each time I turned my phone on between those final classes there were a couple new ones waiting for me, and—after initially worrying how much all these texts were costing our family phone plan—I let the general sentiment of their accumulation seep into my bones.

On the bus my body seemed to be vibrating in the seat, the 9 to the 27, both surprisingly empty, the rain rolling down the windows in the steady river way that only allows peeks of the outside world. Then onto the flooded sidewalks of Vinton, wearing my extra-large thrift-store boy's section bright-blue raincoat, saying hi to everyone I walked past like I was the joy-inducing heroine of an old-timey movie when really I was just an awkward boy in a raincoat.

As I approached the meeting space, I could see Ada waiting at the table by the door. I'd never seen her at the table by herself—I was so used to her holding court there that she looked so lonely. Her hands were neatly folded and she seemed to be deep in thought. I got to the door and waved.

She let me in and locked the door behind us. "Let's head to the office," she said, walking me to the door at the side of the stage, the one she came out of before her talks. I'd always thought of it as an elusive backstage area I'd never see, but here I was, the door opening for me.

What was behind it was just a mostly open room, though, with a big desk placed sort of haphazardly into a corner, some supplies piled along the floor, and one wall filled with floating-style bookshelves littered with messy piles of books. It felt different than I imagined Ada—I assumed she didn't allow anything in her life to become as out of sorts as this.

"As you can see," she said, "the library hasn't been a priority. I loan books to members often, but I don't let others come back and search. I'd like to change that. And I'd like you to help." She walked us over to the shelves. "I'd like you to go through and clean this up. Put them into loose sections. Perhaps make some labels, even. I'll be leaving for the next couple hours, though, so do you think you can handle this on your own?"

I nodded. My own library to be in charge of; it was exciting.

"There's a stepladder in the main room that I'll grab now, and then I'll look forward to seeing what you did when I return."

After Ada left I didn't know where to start, so I just picked up the closest pile of books. They were different from my uncle's books and generally unfamiliar. Their covers weren't identical, but they had a similar aesthetic. While my uncle's books often had paintings and photos on them, these were all very computer-y and had images of far-off planets, the human brain, and water ripples.

I picked up another pile and they were similar, with a few motivational self-help and health books thrown in. I'd thought it would be easy to put them into sections, but I kept having to read and reread the back-cover descriptions. Even then, I wasn't a hundred percent sure; they almost all talked about quantum physics, the law of attraction, and neuroscience, often in the same sentence. It was hard to tell if most of them fit any single section.

I made stacks, even though I didn't have names for the stacks. I was mostly combining books that had a key title word in common: *secret, reality, power, spirituality*. The only book I'd read any of was the one about how the world was going to end in 2012 that my uncle had checked out a few weeks ago. There were more 2012 books too, which again made me nervous I'd never make it out of high school.

Oddly, there were almost no books on memory. There were books about the brain generally, but even that was a small pile. I wondered if it was because Ada already knew memory stuff so well that she didn't need books about it anymore. Maybe those were the ones out on loan? Or maybe they were in her home library? I kept getting waves of desire to read all of these, but I wondered if any of them would actually help my mom.

I continued organizing, having no idea if my system was a system at all, if this was what Ada wanted, and I imagined her coming back and instantly realizing I wasn't as smart as she thought I was. I braced for her disappointment as the day turned into the early evening.

When she finally came in, she looked at the wall and simply said, "So clean. Well done, Elly," and went to her desk.

I was both relieved and disappointed, but I tried not to show either.

"Do you want to come tomorrow?" she asked, as she dug through a pile of papers, her back to me.

I couldn't think of any reason to say no. "If you need it," I said.

"I can use as much help as you have time to give," she said, turning to me. "We'll do something different tomorrow. Something together."

In Remembrance

When I arrived the next afternoon, Ada was waiting outside the front door of the office. "I've got the car loaded up," she said. I didn't know what we were taking or where we were going, but I followed. We walked towards a white car the size of a small whale. Since I didn't know what else to call it, I assumed it was an SUV, but it was puffed up, almost swollen. The locks chunked, the car chirped, and I climbed in with a fair amount of difficulty.

"Big car," I said, because I didn't know what else to say. My mom had said many times that only jerks have cars this size, so I was trying to revise what I'd previously thought of as fact.

She was putting on leather driving gloves and adjusting her mirrors. "You have to be a presence in this world, or else you'll get trampled." She looked at me with her focused eyes. Since meeting Ada, I noticed that most people speak pretty casually and often don't hold eye contact with you, or they talk while they're doing something else. But Ada rarely did that. Most often, if she has something to say to you, she puts all her attention on you—like you're the only thing in the world. "A large vehicle ensures you at least won't get trampled while on the road. So yes, it is big. Very intentionally so."

I nodded. It made sense; I couldn't deny it. It was just different.

We stopped by a nursing home first. It was a wide building that took up most of a city block. "Grab the box," she said as we got out of the car. I looked behind me and on the backseat was a banker's box full of brown-paper lunch bags that each seemed to have a few small things in them, their tops folded over and taped shut. I grabbed the box, which was lighter than I expected, and followed her inside.

After we checked in at the front desk, Ada power-walked us around the complex as I tried to keep up. Each time we stopped at a room, she went in, closing the door behind her, while I waited. I could only hear bits of conversation—everyone mentioned the care package or the contribution, though I was unsure what our little paper bags would be contributing to. Or how much care could be contained in something so light. But the thought seemed sweet.

After a dozen rooms, Ada said it was time to go. I eyed the lonely last paper bag in the box and she said, "Don't worry, we've got another stop on the way back."

As soon as the car doors shut, she said, "Thank you for not asking too many questions in there. I like getting out in the community and visiting the members who are no longer physically able to join us. But some members of this particular care facility's staff don't like their residents being part of a 'non-Christian organization.' So I try to be discreet when I'm there. Having you along was helpful—a younger person with gifts is often treated as less suspect."

I hadn't imagined anyone considering AMF a harmful organization; the idea seemed so silly.

On the way back, we stopped by a small-but-wide house off the main road. Vinton was basically one long main street with businesses all along it, so I didn't know the rest of the city looked like a rural town. It was like the city was a collection of movie set props and the real Vinton was back where we were, in the tall grass and evergreen trees and rusted mailboxes.

We parked and I hesitated, unsure if I was staying or going.

We watched the door open slowly as we made our walk down the decorative cement-block path. A walker came out first, followed by a magnetically wide-eyed woman with hair dyed the color of pomegranate juice.

"Eleanor!" Ada shouted, more celebratory than I'd ever heard her.

"Who have you brought?" Eleanor said, her voice joyous but strained.

"This is Elly."

Eleanor looked at me, her eye contact as purposeful as Ada's, maybe even more so. "We're name twins," she said with a little smirk. "That's nice; I like that. Well then, come inside, come inside."

In the living room, she got us seated on the couch and backed herself up to a recliner. Once she was settled, she turned to me and said, "Young man—it is 'man,' correct?"

I'd never been asked so casually. "Yeah, that's fine," I said, waving my hand as if I was bestowing a gift, trying to match her casualness.

"Young man," she continued, "what are you learning?" She spoke so slowly that each word was almost its own lovely, raspy sentence.

"Well yeah, I've been taking in a lot since I joined the group."

"Of course—any intelligent person would," she said. "There's so much to know. Do you ever have these moments where you think there might be a limit to how much you can know? You say to yourself, 'well, I'm probably pretty close to having figured it all out,' but then you realize the universe of knowledge is infinite and you're a damn fool?"

I wanted to say how I felt like a damn fool every day now—how people always assumed I was smart and just a month ago I even took a stupid online IQ test because I thought I was smart too, but I'd come to realize everyone was probably wrong and now I didn't know what I was—but instead I said, "I think I know exactly what you're talking about."

"A kindred soul," she said, somehow putting the weight of the entire world into her words. "I know you're both on the clock, so I won't keep you long, but I just wanted to sit down together for a brief moment. Because it feels good to sit with kindred souls, doesn't it?"

"It does," I said, more sincere than I'd possibly ever been. Ada remained unusually quiet, smiling, seemingly content.

"Do you want to know the secret, Elly?" Eleanor asked.

"That might be nice to have," I replied.

"There is no secret. That doesn't mean there's just nothing, mind you. It just means the things we call secrets aren't secret."

"I don't know if I know what you mean."

"The keys to life on earth," she said. "They're just there. Out in the open. We just have to pay attention enough to see them."

"Thanks for the secret," I said. I tried to soak up this moment—*be in it*, my brain kept saying—because this was something special. This was so different from my life with Mom and Uncle, or even Maddy or Claudia. I wanted to say it was better, that I felt more alive, but that felt mean. So I tried to just tell myself it was a different kind of good and to enjoy it while it lasted.

Eleanor looked at me knowingly. Ada leaned over the TV trays and said, "Before I forget," and handed over the paper bag.

"Appreciated. And I have this for you," Eleanor said, gracefully slipping Ada a small envelope. She then brought the pointer and middle fingers of her left hand to her temple, tapping it twice delicately, and said, "In remembrance of things to come." To which Ada responded by putting her own fingers to her temple and mouthing what seemed to be the same phrase.

On the way out the door, I searched my brain for where I'd heard this before, coming up empty, until there it was: the first day at AMF. The woman who talked to me as I sat down nervously, wondering what I'd gotten myself into, feeling out of place. She'd said it.

We got in the car and I asked before I could second-guess whether it was an okay question to ask. "What did she mean when we were leaving?"

"'In remembrance of things to come'? That's a phrase I came up with in the early days of AMF. It's an important phrase to me, because I actively advocate against nostalgia."

I wondered what was wrong with nostalgia, but I felt like asking might make me sound stupid.

"Have you heard of Marcel Proust?" she asked.

"I mean, I know the name. He's like a French writer or philosopher or something?"

She laughed. "He's surely not a philosopher, but people study him as if he is. I honestly wish you didn't recognize his name; I despise Proust."

I felt mildly accused, like maybe I'd been paying attention to the wrong names. Maybe she would be less disappointed if I knew the names of the authors in the AMF library.

"It's not actually him I despise," she said, "just the ridiculous legacy people have made for him in our modern world. And largely all from one small scene where the protagonist of his impossibly long novel takes a bite of a cookie and is immediately thrown into the past—a single example of involuntary memory that has become a symbol for the poetic beauty of nostalgia. It's absurd.

"I view his enduring legacy as nothing more than the seduction of nostalgia. The antithesis of a life well lived. He gave up the present for the past—writing a pointless seven-part novel while he wasted away in bed. Some would argue that it was worth it, sacrificing life for art, but I believe that to embrace life, regardless of your ability or state of health, is always more important."

"So is that where the phrase comes from?"

"Oh yes, 'in remembrance of things to come' is a play on the two English translations of Proust's novel—*Remembrance of Things Past* and *In Search of Lost Time*—and it's become a cornerstone of AMF. It's a reminder to live in the present, that the world keeps moving forward. The touching of the temple combined with the phrase alerts AMF members to other members—it's a bond between us."

"Am I allowed to use it?"

She laughed. "Of course—you're a member, aren't you?"

"I guess I wasn't positive I was fully there yet."

"You're there. And I have a feeling you might help carry AMF into the coming generations."

I didn't know what to say to that and she seemed done talking about Proust, so we sat in silence as she drove. Did she expect me to be a leader in some way? I thought the internship was temporary—a way to get to a place where she could meet with my mom—but maybe it was bigger than that.

I also thought about how often I looked back on me and Maddy's years as friends, my childhood with my mom and Uncle, as times that were so precious and good, and I wondered if that was wrong to do. My mom liked to tell me that when I turned five I was already nostalgic for four. Was I living in the past instead of the present? Had I always?

Other than AMF, the present seemed pretty awful and I worried I wouldn't be able to find any happiness if I couldn't, at least on occasion, look back on good times. I saw Ada's point—there was a limit to how much lingering on old memories was healthy, sure—but wasn't her position a little extreme? And how were you supposed to remember the past if you just never thought about it at all?

My mind drifted to my mom and how she had been out of work for over three weeks, but I somehow saw less of her than I did when she worked full time. After that first sad day on the couch, she'd mostly been in her room, usually with the door shut. Outside of her room I only saw her deeply involved in some cleaning project, so focused I usually chose to not bother her. I figured she was coping in her own way, that maybe it was a process and I shouldn't get in the way of it.

I was a jumble of feelings—excitement for what this internship might lead to, worry that I wasn't paying enough attention to what my mom was going through, fear that I might have to give up a way of thinking that felt really good—and they all mixed together in my body, becoming some combo-feeling I'd never experienced before, as I watched tiny strip mall after tiny strip mall out the window.

What We're Not

On Friday we had a half day. I had no idea it was even happening until I got on the bus in the morning—school mostly seemed like a distraction now, a bunch of wasted hours I could be using to learn things I cared about more, that might actually benefit my life right away, not just in some vague future. But Maddy asked me what I was doing before going to Vinton, so I pretended like I knew what she meant and said "hanging out with you," because I knew it was what I was supposed to say. And I did miss her. But mostly, at that moment, I just felt obligated.

Hanging out with Maddy is a little dream-like; other than our movie nights, we never go in with a plan. We just follow it out and see what happens. Oftentimes, we just end up lying on her bed and staring at the collage we made on her ceiling. It was two years ago, when we were still in middle school, so some of it seems a little silly—pointless secret messages and inside jokes buried among a pile of pictures we cut out from a box of old magazines we picked up at a neighborhood yard sale—but there was still just so much to look at. I felt like we always somehow found something new, something we'd never seen before, even though we were the ones who cut the images out and taped them up there.

The song she had on kept repeating: *There are a lot of ideas I got from my friends.* Maddy loved songs like these—ones that were all artsy and didn't sound good in the way normal songs sound good, but sounded ecstatic in the way not-normal songs can.

I had no idea who the band was, but as we lay on her bed, staring at her ceiling, listening, I didn't care. I just cared about that idea, the one they brought up over and over again. Finally I asked, "We have friends, right?"

She laughed. "Yeah, I'm pretty sure we have friends. What sort of question is that?"

"Well, I was just thinking about this song. That idea, you know? How ideas get passed around. And I was thinking about how many ideas I get from you and Claudia and Ada, but then I wondered who else I get ideas from and if anybody gets ideas from me, and I just don't know. It kind of seems like I have three good friends, and then I just know a lot of other people. But those are acquaintance-friends and not friend-friends, you know?"

Maddy paused. "You call Ada a friend now?"

"Yeah, what else would I call her?"

"I don't know, like, 'mentor,' or 'teacher,' or something. Doesn't she call herself a guru? Call her your guru."

"No, that would be weird. I mean, at least it would be weird since we started this internship. It's different now. I mean, sure, she's my teacher and my boss too, but we're friends now."

"Okay, I get that, and I don't want to be uptight about this, but I thought this internship and giving up our Saturdays were supposed to be part of your quest."

"They are," I said, still not understanding what she was getting at. "Why wouldn't they be?"

"Well, it just doesn't sound like they really are—or maybe it sounds like they only partly are," she said, her voice getting thin, like she was struggling to get it out, which made my heart race in a way I couldn't seem to control. "It sounds like you're telling me Saturdays, and now a bunch of other days I guess, are in part just a day you hang out with your new friend instead of hanging out with me."

I didn't know how to respond. "It's not like that. Really."

Her face advertised how little she believed this. "I was trying to be understanding," she said, "and trying not to feel ditched because I want to believe in your quest—even though you haven't told me anything but the most basic details about what's going on with your mom, or where this is all leading—but this makes me think it's something else now. Like, not really quest-related at all."

"Seriously, Saturday's are part of my quest, the internship is part of it, I just—"

"Whatever, I get it. I'm being nuts again, I guess. It doesn't matter."

"Maddy, listen."

"Just never mind. It's fine. Really, forget I said anything." She stopped talking, her body tense, and her sudden silence made it clear there was nothing more to say, even though there were obviously a thousand things we could and maybe should have said. It's what I imagined the vacuum chambers that astronauts trained in were like: the sound of the absence of sound.

We lay there not saying anything for what seemed like eternity, letting the song play on repeat. Maddy often accidentally hit the repeat button instead of the shuffle button, so I was used to randomly hearing a song again and again. It was usually on in the background, though, something we talked over. But here I focused in, listening to every little move the song made, because I needed something to pay attention to that wasn't the sound of my best friend silently hating me.

Eventually I caught a lyric I hadn't noticed before. *We're not defined by what we're not*, it said. In my head, I tried to cut the tension swirling around us by thinking of things that are defined by what they're not: nonfiction, antimatter, unknown, asexual. I thought about how it was a sad thing to just be the opposite of something else. Then I realized that, in that moment, I was a sad opposite half, and also the kind of person I'd always believed I wasn't: inconsiderate, tactless, disloyal.

Nowhere to Hide

While babysitting, I got choked up in the middle of reading the kids a picture book about hippos. It wasn't even sad. The hippos were best friends who had to talk things out because every day they had misunderstandings, and I just got caught up in how real it was, how you can't prepare for misunderstandings, how hard it is to be a good friend, and my eyes started leaking.

I used to think hiding your true feelings from children was probably easy—you just put on a happy face and they go along blissfully unaware. But I found out that it's actually kind of difficult. Especially if you're the only adult-like person in the room. I don't know if it was my voice that changed or what, but they started staring at me and asking what was wrong. They were truly sweet, and this made me even more sad.

To somehow explain my sadness, I went into lecture mode. I told them about the value of friendship and what it took to be a good friend. To which they squirmed on the couch, and tried to hand me other books. "This one," they said. "Read this one instead."

Keep it Casual

I'd been waiting for the right moment to talk to my mom. All week I could feel my time with Ada getting closer to some next phase, and out of that feeling I'd become preoccupied with telling my mom about AMF—just to let her know there was this option out there, something I wanted her to be a part of. I didn't want to scare her off, though. There was a lot to explain, a lie or two that had to be accounted for, and I needed it to not sound like a big deal.

She was cleaning the kitchen when I came home from babysitting to grab my things, and I somehow sensed this was the moment. She was a little distracted, so it wouldn't be like a serious talk; it would hopefully seem completely casual. I approached her cautiously, to feel her out.

"Hey you," she said, continuing to the strip of counter behind the sink. "How you doing?"

"Good. Got done with the kids a little early, so I thought I'd get a snack before heading to Maddy's."

"What's the theme tonight?"

I hadn't planned a fake movie-night theme, so I said the first thing that came to mind. "Movies where people recite poetry at some point."

"That's the theme?"

I nodded.

"They're usually just so much punchier than that. Maybe you could call it . . ." She looked to the ceiling, and opened her hand like she was letting the words free: "Poetry movies." She seemed satisfied. "You see what I mean? It rolls off the tongue a little better."

"I definitely see it, Mom. I'll pitch it to Maddy; I think she'll like it." It felt like I'd lost control of the conversation, so I tried to reign it in.

"So Mom, I have this friend."

"I'm so glad to hear you're making friends, honey," she said, smirking slightly as she scrubbed.

"No, what I mean is that I have a friend who I think can help you," I said, as confidently as I could.

She stopped scrubbing and looked up at me. It was awkward. And definitely not casual. "Help me with what?" she asked.

Even though I think she knew the answer, I said, "With your forgetting problem, Mom."

"Uh-huh." She paused again. It was even more awkward. "Well, I know you have some really smart friends, but I don't think any of them can help me with that."

"Well, she's kind of a professional."

She squinted her eyes. "Like in the way that you're a professional?"

It seemed like ages had passed since I'd made my professional-for-hire sign. "No, she's a real professional."

She took her rubber gloves off and turned to me. "How old is this friend?"

"I don't know. Your age, maybe."

"You have a friend who's my age?"

"Yeah, her name is Ada. She knows a lot about memory. And forgetting. Maybe especially forgetting."

Her body seemed to tighten. "And how is she your friend?"

"I went to her lecture."

"About memory?" she asked.

"Yeah, about memory."

"Because of me."

"Because of you."

"Huh."

I don't know why, but I thought I might still have a chance to save it. "I think you should come with me on Sunday," I said. "And at some point, she can do a free private meeting with you and maybe figure out what's wrong and—"

She cut me off. "I think we probably need to talk about this later. I don't know how much later. Maybe much later." Then she walked to her room, shut the door behind her, and I was left standing alone, wondering how exactly that had gone so bad, so fast.

Edit the Sad Parts

Since I didn't know what else to do, I left my mom a note that said I was going to Maddy's for movie night and went to Vinton instead. Ada and I sat in the clinical coffee shop, and I let her words wash over me. She said something about the hippocampus and angels, the medulla and past lives; I don't know if I absorbed any of it. I felt dumb, like I was wasting the trip, her time, a lie.

When I came home, I put the tea kettle on the stove, and my mom's door creaked open.

"How were the poetry movies?" she asked, appearing in the kitchen.

I was unprepared. "Yeah, fine. A lot of inspired recitations. Who doesn't love a poem on screen?"

I felt the pressure in the air change and knew the water was about to boil.

"You want a cup of tea?" I asked.

"That might be good."

As I pulled down the mugs and loose-leaf tea, I felt my mom wanting to say something. Another thing just below the surface, waiting to come out. I basically knew what it was before she said it, but I also needed to wait for her to say it.

"Do you want to sit down and have a talk?" she asked.

"Yeah, okay," I said, thinking how this was both exactly what I'd been hoping would happen all night, and exactly what I'd been hoping wouldn't happen.

We arranged ourselves on Uncle's couch in a way that felt too formal. I crossed my legs and then uncrossed them. "Sorry about my temper earlier, Elly. That was...well, not how I would have wanted to react. I was just startled." She fidgeted with the string on her tea bag.

It was clear this wasn't a prepared speech, just a collection of thoughts that had accumulated over the course of the evening and were just now coming together.

"I have at least a dozen questions about who your friend is," she said, "and how you've been meeting with her, but maybe those questions don't matter. Or at least they're not what matters most." She cleared her throat. "I think something in me is changing. And I might not be the same self you've known your whole life."

My face became instantly, almost unexplainably, a mess of salt water.

My mom looked as surprised as I was. "Maybe that sounded a little more intense than I'd intended," she said. "I'm just not the do-it-all, organized mom I've always thought myself to be. Not anymore, at least."

"I'm trying to help you," I said. "And I found someone who can really help you."

"That's not the kind of help I need. This is a natural process, there's nothing your friend can do for me. And obviously, as we've seen, it means I won't always be as on top of things as I'd like to be. I don't know how to give up control over my life, but I think I'm going to have to learn to give up some. I might need you to be around more—do more of the household chores, maybe make dinner once in a while. Just so I can juggle things easier when I get a new job. So, however you've been meeting with your friend, I need you to stop doing it."

"Are you serious?"

"Elly, most parents would not be so calm about this situation. You tell me she's a professional and you trust her, then fine. I believe you've been taking care of yourself and staying safe. But I don't feel comfortable with it continuing."

"So you're giving up and asking me to give up with you." It wasn't a question.

"No, I'm just accepting that my memory's not what it used to be, and I'm asking you to help me with simple, daily responsibilities. To make our lives easier. That's all."

She was fooling herself. Telling herself a story that made this normal. And I was the only one in the apartment who seemed to be admitting that. But there wasn't anything to say that would change it for her.

So I said goodnight, got into bed with all my clothes on, and lay there staring at my decidedly un-collaged ceiling.

Normally I believe I can edit the sad parts out of life. That I can deal with something sad just by thinking about it differently. And so far it's worked. But I couldn't find a way to edit the sad out of that conversation. It was like my mom just told me she was turning into a zombie. That she would basically be dead, but her body would still be wandering around, and I'd just be helping her with chores and finding brains to eat. And I didn't know what to do with that.

As much as I wanted to believe I could be responsible and keep my emotions together in the name of helping my mom, I just didn't know if it was true. I would much rather find the secret miracle-cure that would make everything better, which I think was my unofficial hope for the quest. But not even Ada was offering me that. As much as I hated to admit it, there didn't seem to be an easy way out.

The Poets Speak of Memory

There's a poet who asks, "If our memories were scraped away, or just lifted from us, what world would we want?" Which makes me wonder about starting fresh, the potential beauty in that, how I'm maybe fighting against something not worth fighting against.

"But what is memory if not the language of feeling," says another poet, "a dictionary of faces and days and smells which repeat themselves like the verbs and adjectives in a speech." Which makes me wonder about the emotional world that would be lost—without memory, can we really feel in a human way? Can we love?

"Define loneliness?" writes another. "It's what we can't do for each other." Which I use as proof. For what, again, I do not know.

Apologist

When Maddy got on the bus Monday morning, I expected her to walk past me, to pretend I didn't exist, but she sat down beside me, and quietly said hi, not looking at me directly but not avoiding my eyes either. I took this unexpected opportunity and let my words loose—the day-long backlog of feelings, regrets, and fears. I told her about not being able to go to Vinton anymore but still going, about the sad parts, and she just listened. The words blurred together. I begged her to be my friend again, and she looked at me like I was nuts.

"Elly, I never stopped being your friend. I was just mad. That's it. We're good."

She didn't look like she was good—her face without a smile, her gaze not fully holding mine —but I reminded myself that things like this take time. We'd never had a real fight. So I took this acceptance of my apology and we acted out the goodness we supposedly were, playing the part of a pair of best friends.

Drifter

My mom got a swing-shift job stocking shelves at "one of the boxes," her name for any non-local grocery store. When I asked which one, she said "What does it matter? They're all the same," and I laughed but she didn't.

She got interviewed, hired, and started all in the same day, so it felt sudden, especially after our talk the other day. I'd imagined her being out of work for a while and us having to experience this recession in a real way I hadn't previously considered and still couldn't really imagine. I was of course glad she'd gotten the job and we didn't have to go through that, but the fact that I was still processing her words from the other day, still processing whatever was happening with me and Maddy, made it seem more strange or chaotic than it was.

Since she was at work from the late afternoons to the late evenings, I spent the next couple days bussing to Vinton for my internship as if I'd never been told not to go. I expected to feel elated—I could do the thing I wanted without my mom knowing and she wasn't sad on the couch, worrying about money. But nothing felt right; I'd somehow lost the point of things.

I wanted Ada to teach me something, or take me into the community again, maybe get Eleanor to break through my wall of pessimism. But Ada was in and out each day, briefly apologizing every time, telling me something new had just come up, occasionally bringing me little snacks to eat and knick-knacks to bring home. I wasn't mad, but it just wasn't what I'd thought the internship would be. Was I learning anything? I wasn't sure.

For the next couple days there were laundry lists of new monotonous tasks to slog through—dragging computer folders onto external hard drives, organizing loose paper clips and rubber bands, shredding old papers. Instead of being a distraction, the simple, repetitive actions just gave me more time to dwell on my failures, the people I was letting down. I felt like I was wandering through life when I was supposed to be embracing it, ignoring the moment when I was supposed to be paying attention to it. But my brain felt stuck, unable to do anything different than what it was doing.

The Importance of Forgetting

The next time I was in the AMF office, Ada was still in and out, but she was at least around more, and I could feel how my whole attitude was different in her presence; it felt like I was actually a better person—someone more positive, okay to be with, not boring. I was going through the office closet, repacking everything into bankers boxes, while Ada loaded them into her blimp-like car to take them to a storage unit down the street.

I loved how, in Vinton, everything was actually down the street, given how all the businesses were all on one long main road that ran from one end of town to the other before turning back into highway. In Portland people will say down the street and mean "it's in a totally different neighborhood three miles away."

When Ada was packing up she told me about stuff—not really teachings, but not not-teachings either—and I did my best to follow the things she was saying. She wasn't making eye contact like she normally did, but I actually found that more comfortable. She seemed to be in a flow, monologuing her thoughts and philosophies, but I didn't mind that the conversation was one-sided. I thought about how nice it was that she never asked me about what I liked or did. The truth was I didn't really "do" anything, and nothing I liked defined me in the way that other people's likes defined them. I guess I just took things day to day, liked some things when I liked them, and when I tried things I usually wasn't good or bad at them, but maybe slightly quicker than some people at being okay.

Since I turned 15 in July, every adult has wanted to know what I do. I used to be able to get away with saying things like *I like to read*, but now people seem to expect me to have figured something out that's more than reading and I just haven't.

During a brief lull, I asked, "Do you ever miss chess?" I didn't really know where it came from.

"I loved chess, I loved the competition," she said, "but I hated that my parents were involved. My mother was a mean-spirited person, my father a rule-obsessed disciplinarian, and they treated my success as their game. They pressured me while training, shamed me when I lost."

I realized how privileged I was to have a parent I liked and who liked me and didn't force me to do anything. "So you quit because of them?"

"In part. I also quit because of love, of all things. I met him right after I graduated high school, when he was traveling through a nearby town. We met at a party thrown by a girl who had recently quit the chess circuit, thereby planting the idea in my mind. I wanted something different and he was different. So I followed him back to his hometown, here in Vinton. It stopped being fun when we settled here—it was suddenly too different. But I'd followed him a long way, given up a lot, and we both knew that, so we tried to make it work for longer than we should have. It was only after we finally ended it that we became friends. And we remain friends to this day. He was the one who led me to the texts that gave me the groundwork for AMF." She motioned to the wall. "Many of the books you cataloged the other day, in fact, were his recommendations."

"Does he come to the meetings?"

"No, he left Vinton long ago."

"Did you ever think about leaving?"

"Of course. But it's become my home over time. And AMF's success here lets me know that the universe believes I'm in the correct place."

She packed up the last of another carload, left, and I opened a box filled with a hundred-some copies of a pamphlet called *The Importance of Forgetting*. It was bigger than the folded single sheets of "literature"Ada had given to me after my first meeting, something more like a small stapled book.

I opened it to an introduction from Ada, complete with a small slightly younger-version picture of her at the bottom and her signature. Her hair was bigger, her eyebrows thinner. I looked for a date and found it in the corner of the page: "copyright 2004," the year AMF started.

I wondered if this was the first piece of literature. Five years ago didn't sound that long, but this looked like an ancient text from a wholly different organization.

I put a copy in my backpack and repacked the rest into a bigger box. On the bus ride home, I read it. It had a little bit of everything: the Old High German origins for the English word "forget," oral societies keeping "equilibrium" by choosing to leave behind memories that were no longer relevant, why children under three in large part don't form long-term memories, and so much else I'd never heard come up with Ada or at the meetings.

I was fascinated, and I thought of my mom's question, the ones she asked at the end of every Uncle-book I read: *where is it taking your mind?* And suddenly I didn't know what to do with all the things I'd just read. None of it seemed to apply to my mom's situation, and there weren't any big conclusions at the end to help me make the connections. I could see this being intentional—like Ada wanted people reading the pamphlet to make their own connections—but I also thought that maybe this is what had changed most over the years. Like, maybe Ada has made more of those connections over time and this publication was the first step of figuring that out. Maybe that's why these were in a box at the back of the office closet.

I wondered about the title and if, after reading this, I believed forgetting was important or just interesting. But I felt this is what studying with Ada was like—you learn by making connections, each piece adding onto the other pieces. I'd come looking for some secret, but I'd ended up being a student. I thought about how I'd been a student for most of my life, and I hadn't felt like one at all until now.

There are Worse Things

I unlocked the door of our apartment and opened it to a sound I'd never heard before. My feet instantly became stuck in the doorway, my body frozen from that feeling of something being familiar but not familiar at the same time. In my apartment there was a woman yelling. She was definitely mad and, from what I could tell, mad at my uncle.

I got past the doorway and followed the sound down the hall. Even though it's not a big apartment, getting across seemed to take forever. It was like I was holding my breath while trying to walk on the bottom of the pool; I was using all my strength, and it seemed like I should be going faster, but I just couldn't.

I got to my mom's open door and there I saw it: my mom, the most stable-seeming person I've ever met, screaming at Uncle, throwing whatever she could get her hands on at him. Pillows, pens, crumpled pieces of paper. I couldn't even make out her words, they seemed to just be part of some larger unintelligible blame—an endless string of *you, you, you, you, you.*

Uncle saw me first. We made eye contact for an impossibly long time before my mom followed the path of his gaze. Her confusing words trailed off. She very suddenly seemed to lose the steam behind her anger, and she stared at me like a person who was coming to after being hypnotized. We stood in a silent triangle before I finally asked the only question I could think to ask.

"What's going on?"

Neither of them seemed to have any idea how to answer me, so we all just continued staring at each other. I know there are things in the world that are much worse than seeing your otherwise-solid mom lose it, but at that moment it didn't seem like it. It was as if I'd just seen my mom turn into that lady in *The Exorcist* whose head spun around

360 degrees.

Even though fake parental-like comfort would normally be annoying to me and I wouldn't want that at all, I couldn't believe they weren't trying to tell me it was okay or trying to soothe me in any way. For the first time ever, I wanted them to lie to me. Instead, we just stood there and stood there, until I finally couldn't take it anymore.

"Well, as fun as this is," I said, "I'm going to my room."

I shut my door and immediately wished I was like Maddy or Claudia and knew exactly the right song for every occasion. I wanted to blast some painful, overly-dramatic song until the neighbors banged on their ceiling/my floor. I didn't know why I wanted this so bad, why I was trying to perform this moment instead of just feel it.

But I didn't even know how to do this. I just had an iPod that Maddy and Claudia had curated for me with an assortment of songs. Ones I put on shuffle nearly every day. Songs attached to band names I never paid any attention to. I knew what I needed was right in front of me, but I didn't know how to find it. I tried to think what this was like—a labyrinth? a great paradox?—but maybe this was just not being able to find a song on a machine full of songs and it didn't equate to anything bigger or more mysterious.

I plugged the iPod into my speakers, hit play, and it picked up where I had left off. It was a hand-clappy, group sing-along kind of song. It was like some people trying to pretend that singing camp songs had become cool and it was completely wrong for this moment.

I collapsed on my bed and was staring at the wall when there was a knock. My uncle asked if he could come in. I turned down the music and told him he could.

He sat down on the edge of my bed, crossed his legs, and took a deep breath. It seemed so much like the end of a movie we would watch in health class—ones about getting your period or getting peer-pressured into using drugs. I'd wanted this comfort just moments before, but I couldn't take being the kid in the PSA. Plus, I'd never seen the "What to do When Your Mom Flips Out" one, so I had no idea what my lines were or what lessons I was supposed to take away from this moment.

"I'm sorry you had to see that," he said, trying to force eye contact.

"What exactly was 'that'?" I asked, focusing on the sheets of my bed.

"I honestly have no idea. It came out of nowhere. I walked into her room to tell her about some better job openings I'd heard about at the new New Seasons, and all of a sudden, I was under attack for something."

"But for what?"

"I couldn't exactly tell. I always worry she'll get sick of me being around, so at first I thought it was about that and maybe I'd have to move out. But it was about stuff from when we were kids, fights we had twenty years ago. Now she's telling me she's not mad at me at all and doesn't seem to remember what she just said. So I'm not exactly clear how to feel. She's lying down now and taking some time to get grounded." He paused. "I think I can talk her into seeing a doctor."

I nodded. What was there to say? I wanted her to go to a doctor. It would stupid not to. But I also wanted to just figure it out myself so she didn't need to. And, as much as I tried to ignore it, there was a part of me that didn't want to know what was wrong.

We sat.

"Is there anything you need?" he asked, clearly attempting to wrap it up in some way.

I shook my head from side to side. It felt loose, exaggerated. What could he give me that I didn't already have? I wanted to ask if he needed anything—I mean, he had been the one getting yelled at—but I couldn't make myself form the words.

"Okay, well, just let me know if anything comes up," he said. "Alright?"

I nodded up and down, cartoonish.

He left and out of habit I pulled my laptop from under the bed. There were no messages or wall posts on MySpace, no likes to the things I'd reposted on Tumblr. The only thing truly waiting for me was Rigby's nightly email. The fact of it felt pathetic, even though I was sort of honored to know Rigby and to probably be the youngest person on his list.

I'd gotten into the habit of scanning his emails before going to bed. Most of the elements remained the same, so it was kind of like those games where you look at two pictures that seem identical and find the tiny details that are different. But I needed a distraction bad enough to actually read-read it.

Hi all,

Normal Thursday stuff: eggs for breakfast, went to post office and mailed bills, coffee at Angela's. Then lunch (hamburger and salad) and pinochle at the senior center. I didn't win any of the games, but that was fine. Good conversations. Watched an old movie, Harvey. I'd seen it many years before, but forgot it was about an imaginary rabbit. Very strange idea, but you can't beat Jimmy Stewart. Had chicken and cubed potatoes for dinner. Turning in soon. Mail was Car and Driver and donation requests from organizations I'm not familiar with (already giving to my favorite organization anyway, not much else to go around).

Until tomorrow,

Rigby

On the surface, it wasn't life changing, but somehow it made the ground a little more solid. It made me think about how there could be an almost endless number of days that might await me, most of which would probably be pretty plain. Days where nothing unexplainable and disturbing happened. I'd never thought to reply to Rigby's emails, but I felt like I needed to communicate with someone who would listen but who wasn't attached to some idea of who I am. And I couldn't think of anyone except Rigby. So I gave it a try.

Dear Rigby,

Hopefully this isn't too out of the blue. I'm just having a hard time and thought you'd be open to listening. I usually like to think I have all the answers. And since I have the answers, whatever I'm doing is the right thing. But sometimes I'm pretty sure that all my "answers" are just the things I want to happen and not really the answers at all. The past two days have been full of not-real answers. I had this belief that I was helping my mom by going to our group and hanging out with Ada, but my mom doesn't think I'm helping at all, and now my mom is not only forgetting things but also being unlike herself in a somewhat scary way. I don't know where my plan went wrong exactly, but if you have any advice on how I could undo this it would be really appreciated.

Yours,

Elly Fox
P.S. - I get your nightly emails and enjoy them. Thank you.

It was strange how easy writing to Rigby was. I felt like I could say anything and embrace feeling like a total mess. To him, I was just the one young person who came to his memory group.

Within a half hour, there was an email back:

Elly,

What a nice surprise to hear from you. It's rare anyone responds to my emails. Sorry to hear the circumstances aren't more fortunate, though. I won't claim to be the best at giving advice and, as it is past my bedtime, my brain isn't running on all cylinders. But I do seem to remember that Martin Luther King, Jr. once said something about how the biggest question in life is "What are you doing for others?" Sounds like your intentions were following this idea, so I think you're ultimately on the right track. From experience, I can say that most things take a while to work out, and most things don't always work out like we plan but usually work out in some way. So I suppose I'm just saying don't give up quite yet? Working with limited information, but that's my knee-jerk response.

Your friend,
Rigby

I read it a few times and wondered why his nightly emails weren't like this. It was like his emails were both a way of reaching out and hiding his true self. While I couldn't imagine things eventually working out, and I didn't know if intentions were enough, I decided to believe he was right on one count. Maybe things take time. I'm generally impatient, all my plans had changed, and maybe I didn't know where this all was headed, but I was still on a thing I was calling a quest. And I had to keep going.

Something You Can't See

I had planned on telling Maddy all about my mom's trance-like anger state, but here's the thing: my imagined conversations live in a world where the reality of the other person doesn't exist. It's consistently a problem. In my head, it goes like this: I tell my story, the other person reacts, we talk about it. But in the moment it's never that simple, because the other person also has stories to tell, their own imagined conversations to make real.

When Maddy sat down next to me on the bus, she was bursting at the seams with a bike adventure she had gone on the night before. She and her neighbor had gone out riding together, took some unknown routes, got lost in an industrial neighborhood, and ended up at the Denny's on MLK where they met a guy with one arm who told them about a thing called phantom-limb syndrome. It happens when a person loses an arm or a leg and the nerves keep trying to use it like it's still there. I was trying to roll with this story, but all I wanted was to tell my story. Maybe even get a hug. This was made even more difficult by the fact that this syndrome was—despite being a real thing I should know about—impressively disturbing.

She was describing the constant clenching that happens at the spot where the limb was cut off when I got a text. I pulled out my phone. It was Ada.

For tomorrow night: Bring a deck of cards (preferably one you've had for a while), a blanket, a handkerchief or piece of fabric, a book of matches, and a small pocket knife.

I had no idea why I would need any of that stuff, since up until that moment I hadn't needed to bring anything except myself. I read it a few times, thinking it might start to make more sense. It didn't.

"Who's the text from?" Maddy asked. I'd stopped paying attention. I wondered what she'd said before this, what I'd missed.

"Oh, Ada. It's just stuff to bring for tomorrow," I said.

"I thought you couldn't see her anymore."

"Yeah, I'm not supposed to." But after yesterday, I wanted to go. Needed to go, even.

"Well, if you end up sticking around and you're not really grounded, me and Claudia and some of her friends are all going to the dance. You should come."

"The dance? As in, the school dance?" I was both upset that they were considering going and upset they hadn't invited me sooner.

"Yeah, the homecoming one."

"Are you for real?"

"Come on, it'll be funny. And we're going as a crew, so we won't be stuck with a bunch of couples. We'll kinda be messing with the whole concept of a school dance, really."

"It still sounds horrible," I said. "I would spend the whole dance in an existential crisis not being able to talk to anyone. Not even you guys."

"I really can't imagine you not talking."

"Well you've never seen me at a dance," I said, smiling, feeling the moment become lighter. "Besides, I should find a way to meet with Ada. I think it's just too late to cancel now."

Maddy turned her head toward the window and said, "Huh." She said it in that way where "huh" is no longer a question but a statement.

"What?"

"You know this is the same situation that happened a month ago, but in reverse."

I had no idea what she was talking about. "No it didn't," I said, trying to make the words sound playful while fearing the possibility they were somehow not true.

"It did. When you canceled movie night a few weeks ago. You canceled on me the day before so you could hang out with Ada. I mean, it's not a big deal, but it's just sort of offensive that it was okay to cancel last minute then but not okay now."

"Well, Ada's like a mentor or something. You know, it's different." Somehow it sounded less convincing aloud.

"Right, I've heard how it's different."

"What does that mean?"

"Remember just a week ago when you told me it would be weird to call her a mentor because she's your friend now?"

I had forgotten, but suddenly I remembered.

"It's just frustrating that you don't see what's going on."

"What don't I see, Maddy?" I was getting worked up, trying to defend myself with sarcasm and volume. "Show me the world through your sage-like eyes."

"All this double standards crap. Like, even if you're not intentionally ditching me, it totally feels like it. And if there will always be all this stuff that's okay to do to me but not to Ada, I'm going to continually be offended."

I tried to stutter out some response, but I could tell it wasn't helping. She'd stopped listening, her arms crossed tight, her gaze directed out the window. We rode the rest of the way without saying anything.

The first half of the school day I tried to fool myself into thinking that what had happened wasn't that big of a deal, that Maddy probably wasn't as mad as she'd seemed. But at lunch I showed up at the Block and it was just Claudia. I could tell from her face—her lips tight as she forced a smile—that she'd talked to Maddy about the bus ride. I couldn't tell if she was mad or trying to act clueless and doing a bad job.

I wanted to talk to Claudia about how when things go wrong it just happens so fast, and you end up feeling like you missed something—even when you were sitting right there and you couldn't have missed anything. But there's some inner thing, something you can't see, that you definitely missed.

I didn't know how to say all that in the moment, so we just ate while making small talk about our classes, the new piece of Block graffiti that said *Lickz*, and afterwards I spent the rest of the day trying to figure out that mysterious missed thing: how Maddy had gotten so mad at me, where I'd gone wrong.

When I got to the bus stop at the end of the day Maddy was there, but she didn't acknowledge I was there, even though I knew she knew I was there. As we waited, I thought about how horrible it would be if I sat down next to her and she got up and moved to another seat. I considered just walking home so as not to risk that possibility, even though it was a long walk—one I could do, though I didn't especially want to—but the bus came before I made up my mind. So I just got on and sat next to Maddy like I always did.

Luckily, she didn't move. But she also didn't say anything. She didn't say anything for long enough that I began to think this was just the way it was going to be from here on out. Silent Maddy and me, hanging out silently, forever and ever.

Then out of the blue Maddy blurted out, "You remember when you told Claudia and me about the quest?"

"Of course, you made fun of me. How could I forget?"

"True, then I apologized and soon became very supportive and understanding. But do you remember that after you told us, you joked about potentially getting forced into a memory cult?"

"I don't know, I guess. It does sound like a joke I'd make."

"I held onto those words this whole time. There was something about them I just couldn't shake," she said. "And, well, it happened."

"What happened?"

"Ada, her whole forgetting fellowship, all those old people you hang out with—Elly, it's not a joke. It's a frigging cult."

I felt all my muscles clench. "No. No way. I realize I haven't brought you with me, so you don't know what it's like, but I can assure you it's not a cult."

"Yes it is. She's just got you brainwashed so you don't see it, but it's happening—it happened. I've wondered if it was an actual cult since day one, but after this morning I'm positive. Her brainwashing has turned you into a total jerk."

"Okay, what? First you tell me my new friends are a cult, then you tell me I'm brainwashed, *then* you tell me I'm a jerk? I was so ready to apologize for this morning, to say I screwed up and say I was totally in the wrong, but now I'm not going to do it. Because I am not a jerk."

"That doesn't make sense."

"Yes it does," I said through my teeth. "Think about it. As of this moment, I'm the one who's not going to talk to you."

And we went back to riding the bus in silence.

People, Being People

When I got off the bus, I was fuming. My jaw was still tight, my eyes were narrowed, and if anybody tried to mess with me on my way across the pedestrian bridge or in the two blocks it took to walk from the end of said bridge to my apartment, I was going to let them have it. Whatever that meant.

But it's amazing what a small bridge and two blocks can do. In that walk I'm pretty sure I felt the entire range of available human emotions, and by the time I walked through my apartment door, I was somehow once again ready to apologize. I went to my room, lay down on my bed, and texted Maddy immediately, even though I had a feeling she wouldn't respond. *Hey, sorry about freaking out on the bus. And especially sorry about this morning. Let's talk sometime.*

Combined with Ada's strange text, the Mom-losing-it incident, and the Mom-forbidding-me-to-go element, I felt pretty certain I should not bus to Vinton this weekend. Maybe I would even suck it up and go to the ridiculous school dance. I decided that even though canceling at the last minute made me feel like a bad person, in this situation I had to do it. And I needed to tell Ada about it right away, before I changed my mind. I pulled out my laptop.

Ada,

Our meetings and AMF have been so helpful to me, and I've just wanted more of it since I started. And I still do. I want to learn so much more. But I feel like maybe I've been relying on you too much. I think I've been thinking of you like you're this problem solver for me and my confused life. And that's not fair to you. I should figure out how to learn a little from everyone, like you taught me. I'm beginning to believe that no one holds all the answers, and that's one of life's great challenges—

it's like a puzzle of truth that we have to put together piece by piece.

Maybe we each just have an internal balance of knowledge? Like, if one person is really good at one thing, they're probably terrible at another. And the person who doesn't seem super remarkable is possibly kind of good at everything, while the remarkable-seeming person is only good at one thing. Do you think this is true?

What I'm trying to say is that I should maybe stick around Portland this weekend. My mom is being weird, and other things are going on. Sorry for the last-minute notice,

Elly

It felt like I'd barely hit send when my phone started buzzing. It was Ada.

"Hello Elly." Her voice sounded deeper than normal.

"Hey Ada," I said, for some reason feeling nervous.

"I got your email." She sounded neutral about this. Factual.

I didn't know how this was humanly or digitally possible but resisted questioning it. "That was quick," I said.

"I don't think it's a good time to skip a weekend. We've got to get you caught up with some of the basic techniques of the group before the big conference in January."

"Oh, okay," I said, seemingly unable to defend myself. "Let me see what I can do about the thing with my mom."

"Would you like me to talk with her?"

This seemed like a terrible idea. "No, I think I can figure it out."

"Good. I'll see you tonight then."

I couldn't imagine going anywhere—it felt like my emotions were fist-fighting each other to figure out which one would reign. "Okay," I said. "Tonight."

I knew my mom had worked a bunch of days in a row and was bound to have a day off sometime soon, so it was a risk to go to Vinton any of these next few days, but I decided it wasn't worth talking to her or trying to convince her of anything. I was just going to go. People on quests do the thing that gets them in trouble because it's ultimately better for everyone in the end—it's what you're doing for others.

Though I was having a hard time dealing with the total and utter strangeness of my phone conversation with Ada, I just kept reminding myself that she was probably right. It probably was as important as she said, and who knows what I would miss out on learning if I skipped this weekend. I didn't like missing anything. Even a school dance that sounded horrible. But I especially didn't like missing a potentially life-changing/mom-helping session with Ada. I left a note that said I'd be at Maddy's late, and crossed my fingers she didn't check to see if this was true.

New Plans

I got off the bus, exhausted, and there Ada was, waiting.

I approached her slowly, more nervous than I can remember being around her. "Change of plans," she said, her words coming out in a rush, as if they were making up for my slowness. "We'll do the thing I mentioned tomorrow night."

"Oh, so I'm coming back tomorrow night too?"

"Of course; it's Saturday night, isn't it?"

I wasn't sure if she was asking a real question or not—it seemed as if the email I wrote had never happened.

"I keep wondering about your innate abilities," she said. "Your powers."

She'd never mentioned powers—mine or anything else's. "My powers?"

The question seemed to fluster her and she waved her hands in front of her like she was sweeping the question away. "We will cross that bridge soon enough," she said. "Just bring the cards, blanket, handkerchief again tomorrow night. Matches and knife, just in case."

I'd forgotten all of these things tonight. "What exactly is all that for?"

"Soon enough, soon enough." She blew out air like my simple, timid questions were pushy and unreasonable. "Let tomorrow arise naturally."

This time I decided to say nothing.

When we sat down at Angela's, the bad-lighting coffee shop hole, I noticed for the first time how overdressed she was. She always had something flow-y, a piece of old jewelry or two, but tonight she had a blazer on and all sorts of accessories I'd only seen under the display cases at antique stores—a couple brooches, a pendant necklace, several bracelets, pearl earrings. It felt like too much.

She said, "You seem to be dealing with something."

For the first time ever, I didn't want to tell her what was going on with me. "I mean, like I mentioned in the email, some things are just not going especially well," I said, hoping to some degree I could just leave it at that.

"It's your mother?"

"And Maddy. But yeah, mostly my mom."

"She refuses your help?"

"Yeah, she does." I paused, wondering if I should even say more, and then just said it. "I'm actually not supposed to be here."

She narrowed her eyes, as if she was trying to figure out what I meant by my words. Once she decided she understood, she leaned back. "The fools always try to impede the wise."

I felt my face twitch or flinch. I wasn't positive, but it sounded like she'd just called my mom a fool. "What do you mean?"

"Those who are on the righteous path are always thwarted by those off the path."

I sat there waiting for more. When it didn't come, I tried to change the subject, but she stopped me.

"Memories are how we make meaning of life; forgetting is how we sculpt it," she said. It was something I'd heard her say in meetings, a mantra maybe. One sleepy morning I think I'd chanted it along with everyone. But now she was here, directing the mantra at me.

"Here is the secret," she said, pausing long enough that I wondered if I'd missed something. "Forget your mother."

"Forget my mom?"

"It sounds radical, sure, but don't you see? She's the source of the pain. You keep trying and she keeps making your life worse. Forget the sorrows you feel!"

She was getting so worked up. It wasn't that I'd never seen her excited, but she usually seemed more collected, like some embodiment of what being enlightened looked like, even though enlightenment is an internal thing and probably doesn't look like anything.

"This is the sculpting of reality to which I refer," she said, slightly elongating each word. "This is freedom."

I didn't know what to say and I think my face told her that I didn't know what to say, so she kept talking, filling the space.

"You care about your mother because she gave birth to you," she said. "Fine, okay, that makes sense. It's animal attachment—a basic biological response for species survival. But you didn't get to choose this relationship. It was forced upon you. Have we not evolved past this? Think: would you be friends with your mother if she wasn't your mother?"

I didn't want to tell her that I thought I would. I worried it would make me sound stupid or un-evolved, like an animal, even though I sometimes think animals are maybe smarter than humans. So instead I said, "I guess I don't know."

"Of course you don't know!" Her voice squeaked in a way that pierced my eardrum a little. "Because not only have you not been given a choice in whether your mother is someone you want in your life, but you've never been given that choice in this society. It's an unspoken assumption that we'll all trudge through our family-of-origin relationships, but we don't have to. And you don't have to make a chosen family out of the limited options of a public high school. Elly, you have a chosen family in AMF—let's wean you off these dysfunctional families. Your life can be healthier."

I was too stunned to say anything real and useful, so I went for the practical holes. "But how would that even work? I've got years until I can legally move out on my own."

"It's a process—I'm not talking about doing this tomorrow! Like I said, you can wean. I have connections—people, AMF members, who can get you on track for real jobs, who can connect you with scholarships, paid internships. Don't let the ambition-less environment you were born into hold you back; work on forgetting the imprinting of your birth family, move toward the future you want."

I could see in her eyes that she was expecting so much from me—a celebration, a mind-blown new self emerging from a cocoon—but I was too shocked to even fake it. The thing was: those were powerful revelations for someone else. There was someone who needed to hear that. It was probably what my mom needed to hear at my age. And, judging by her excitement and what I knew about her history, it was probably what Ada needed too. But it wasn't what I needed.

"Okay, I see," I finally said. "Yeah, those are some ideas. They're interesting."

"Interesting? These are life-changing." She was clearly frustrated. "Maybe you're not ready for them," she said with a toss of her hand. "Maybe you need to go through more sorrow, more trials by fire. Fine, be miserable a little while longer." She leaned across the table. "Just think about what I said." I could feel the warm breath from her nostrils. She tapped my temple, a little harder than felt right. "In remembrance of things to come, Elly. In remembrance of things to come."

I nodded. "In remembrance of things to come."

"Let's reconvene tomorrow night," she said. "I should take care of some things."

Though we had only been there ten minutes at the most—which in the past wouldn't have seemed worth the hour in each direction on the bus—I was internally relieved. She walked out the door without saying goodbye.

Babysitting for Satan

The next morning, I learned that kids can sense when you're under-slept and they maliciously use it to their advantage. I'd woken up so tired I'd felt like crying, then walked past the bathroom, heard my mom crying in the shower, and wondered if crying in the morning ran in the family. I wondered why she was up so early when she didn't have to be, but I couldn't think much further than the dull pounding in my head, the pressure behind my eyes that seemed to be saying *close us, close us, close us.*

Somehow I slept-walked myself ready and floated down the stairs to the first floor. I made eye contact with the kids, saw their eyes register my state, and somehow witnessed the moment where they collectively decided to make my morning worse. My previous belief that the kids are aliens or fully realized empathetic beings has been revised, and I now believe them to be hellions. And not in a fun, *oh, those little hellions* loving-grandma sort of way. But in an actual-devil-children, sent-by-Satan sort of way. If I hadn't been frantically trying to stop them from breaking things and beating each other up all day, I would have looked up how to perform an exorcism.

I left the apartment and got on the bus without considering not getting on, the whole time wondering if I was forgetting my mom. How could I be forgetting my mom when my mom was all I could think about?

The sky seemed darker than it had the day before, and I wondered how mid-October could make me so aware of the coming winter solstice. Was fall over already? I felt removed from everything, like I hadn't been paying enough attention. Or I'd been paying too much attention to the wrong things. One of the two.

In a Field

The 9 seemed to drag through the darkening winter-fall sky, stopping too long at bus stops with no one, the driver calling out riders for rules that didn't matter when no driver ever called out the sketchballs that did matter, and I missed my connection to the 27, stood at an uncovered bus stop in the middle of nowhere for a half hour, texted Ada to let her know I was running late, didn't hear back.

I got to Vinton and Ada was waiting at the station with a big woven bag. Over the past 24 hours I'd been trying to figure out what happened at the coffee shop. Whether I should come again. But I'd convinced myself it was just her issue—her past and her mom, not my present mom—that she was pushing onto me. She didn't really know the situation, but I couldn't blame her for trying to look out for me.

Before I could even say hello, or further explain the late bus, she asked, "Did you bring the items on the list?"

"Yeah, of course," I said, a little offended she would even question me. I felt like she should know my reliability at this point. Like how I was there in Vinton against all odds, for example.

"Good," she said. "Follow me."

She led me through streets I'd never been on, a couple times cutting down dark residential alleys with plant canopies, walking so fast I could barely keep up, all the while saying nothing. Eventually I couldn't take it anymore and asked, "Where are we going?"

She didn't answer.

"You know how memories are stories?" I asked. I didn't really know what I was saying—it was some half-formed thought from the past month—but I just wanted the moment to slow down, to be comfortable and calm. "I mean, I guess that's a dumb question, but I've been thinking that life isn't usually a very good story."

Ada was far enough ahead of me that I had to speak at a volume that wasn't quite shouting but wasn't not-shouting. "Like, our memories of a typical day—or even just a part of a day—aren't very interesting unless we take details out and sort of weave it into something that can be told to other people." I knew I wasn't being articulate; maybe I wasn't even making sense.

"I guess I'm just saying that our idea of a traditional story feels off to me because it doesn't seem to be how things really happen. Or how our memory works. I think of memory like a collection of interconnected moments, you know? Which isn't really like a traditional story at all."

Ada stopped and turned to me. "You have a lot to learn," she said. It was as if she was telling me I had something in my teeth: *here's an unglamorous fact about you, now do something about it.* She turned back around and kept walking while my body recovered from the small punch in the gut I'd just received.

We emerged into a field. Or a park with nothing in it, I couldn't really tell. A thin layer of fog hovered in the air, and it felt colder than it had all fall. Ada got a blanket out of her bag and laid it out on the damp ground. I sat down and the dampness immediately seeped through my clothes. "Turn off your phone," she said.

"My phone?" I asked.

"Yes, we can't have anything that will distract you."

I turned it off and started putting it back in my pocket.

"No, not there," Ada said, as if I was making some totally obvious mistake.

"Huh?"

"You can't have it in your pocket."

"But it's turned off."

"The phone has you trained. Even when it's off you feel it in your pocket, and the feeling reminds you of what could be awaiting you once it's turned on. Your phone is full of rewards and you are Pavlov's dog, salivating."

I knew what she was saying; it made sense and was surely true. But it felt so bad to not be trusted. "So I should put it in my backpack then?"

She watched me put the phone into the front pocket of my backpack like she thought I might, last minute, pull a fast one on her. Once she was sure the phone was safely out of my reach, she said, "Now get out the deck of cards."

I pulled the deck out of my bag—some old casino cards I'd found in a drawer, probably left over from my uncle's gambling days—and she snatched it out of my hand, popped the cards out, fanning them in front of me. "With intention, pick your card." I didn't know what type of intention I was supposed to have, but I was a little afraid to ask, so I just tried to look really focused and hoped she wouldn't call me out for having no clue what I was doing. I picked a card.

"Now stare at it," Ada said. "Soak it in. That is your card. It belongs to you and also represents you." It was the four of clubs. Which seemed like an insignificant, or at least unimpressive, card to represent me. It felt like reading a horoscope that said you were going to have a boring life. But I stared at it. And I don't know if I soaked it in, but I tried.

"Do you have it as a part of you now?" Ada asked. "Do you know it?"

I tried to ignore the fact that those questions sounded kind of nuts to me. "Yeah, I think so."

"Good, now give it to me."

I gave it to her and she said, "You see that fence out there?"

I looked out into the field and could sort of make out a chain-link fence through the fog. I nodded.

"Wonderful. Let's put that blindfold on."

I didn't know the thick handkerchief on the list was supposed to be a blindfold, but I got it out and handed it to her. She got behind me and tied it so tight that I worried about circulation to my brain.

"Now wait here," Ada said.

So I sat by myself on a blanket in a damp, foggy field with a blindfold on, using my brain to worry about my brain.

The Waiting Game

Ada was gone for what seemed like a very long time. I'd never thought about how slow time goes when you don't have anything to look at. Usually I'd be unconsciously amusing myself by looking at stuff, but since I couldn't, all I had were my thoughts to keep me busy. I thought about how my brain might explode, how wet my butt was getting—how I could actually feel the wetness getting wetter—how I was going to volunteer to work with the blind as soon as I cured my mom's memory loss and this was all over.

Then I wondered if this would ever be over. Or if my future was a perpetual quest that would never lead to anything.

I also tried to avoid thinking about the possibility that something had happened to Ada—a head injury, perhaps? Or maybe she had a silent, hard-to-diagnose illness that sometimes affects the brain, like Lyme disease. She had always been strange, but I thought that just came with the territory of being really smart. But now I was unsure. I had no idea why she had brought me here. I was blindfolded, cold, and waiting for someone who thought I had a lot to learn and wanted me to disown my mom.

I was just about to take off my blindfold, walk away from this field, and take the next bus back to Portland when Ada's voice came out of nowhere. "It's time to rise," she said.

I didn't know how she'd walked quietly enough for me not to hear her coming, but from the sound of her voice she was standing right next to me. It seemed that as Ada became weirder, she was also becoming more superhuman.

"Do you remember your card?" Ada asked.

"Yes," I said, though I'd actually forgotten all about my card and didn't remember what it was until after I'd said yes. But I didn't want to let on that I hadn't been thinking about what she told me to think about. I also had a probably irrational fear that Ada could read my mind, and she knew I hadn't been focusing on my card and that I'd instead been thinking about her mental health.

"Focus on your card," she said. "Really focus. Don't let any of your mental or physical energy be distracted. Just think of the card."

I tried, but in the last couple of days I'd learned that getting distracted was my specialty. I used to tell myself I was very focused, but I now knew that I had been completely lying to myself. Ask me to focus on one thing, and I will immediately think about something else.

"Do you have it?" she asked.

"Yes," I said, knowing I didn't have anything at all.

"Good. Now find it."

"Find what?

"Find the card."

"Where?"

"In the fence."

"The fence?"

"Walk to the other side of the field and find it in the fence."

"With the blindfold on?"

"With the blindfold on."

"I don't think I can do that."

"You can. And you will," she said.

I wanted her words to sound supportive or inspirational, but really they felt like a command. Or maybe a threat.

The whole thing felt like I was being forced into something I had never wanted to do. My idea of this quest had mostly consisted of me traveling, listening, talking, and reading, but never included me being physically uncomfortable. The fact that I hadn't been able to sleep in on Sunday mornings was already pushing it. My idea of excitement was taking the bus to places I'd never been before. Finding a playing card in a fence while blindfolded? That wasn't exciting, that was just dumb. But I saw no other choice, unless I wanted to face some unknown wrath from this new, possibly unstable Ada.

I put my arms out in front of me and started walking. Doing this felt somewhere between a Frankenstein impersonation and a trust fall. I'd never been to a summer camp, but I'd seen a lot of movies about going to summer camp and they always did trust falls—those things where you fall backwards into someone else's arms. After watching a few summer camp movies when I was younger, I'd tried this out with my mom in our living room and I screamed. Like, shrieked. When I recovered, I looked up at my mom—my body tilted, hovering, her hands in my armpits—and we laughed so hard she dropped me. Which only made us laugh harder.

I walked slowly and jerkily across the field and wished I could just get this over with like a trust fall. But I couldn't see a way to end this quickly, to rip the Band-Aid off. Nor could I imagine a moment that followed this where Ada and I would laugh joyfully. I plodded along, thinking about how all I had to do was just make it to the fence and then feel around for a while. I knew that probably wasn't the point, I was probably supposed to magically just go straight to it. But finding the card was obviously better than not finding the card, so I wasn't going to take any stupid wild guesses—I was just going to do what I knew would work, even if it meant feeling the entire fence, link by link.

The fence hadn't seemed terribly far away before I put the blindfold on, but it was taking forever to get there. I was at the point of believing I had somehow walked at an angle and missed the fence entirely when the weight of my torso hit against it. It turned out the fence was pretty short, so my Frankenstein arms went right over it. Even though I was going incredibly slow, I still crumpled a little, the wind ever-so-slightly knocked out of me.

Hunched over, cradling my gut, everything seemed to suddenly get a touch brighter. I felt around my face to confirm my blindfold wasn't leaking light. Then I realized: the brightness was my card, alerting me that it was close. For the first time since starting this exercise, I was filled with hope. Maybe all this had not been in vain, and maybe Ada's oddness was just a way of helping me tune in to this extrasensory thing that I had in me this whole time but would have never otherwise known about. Maybe she could see it in me all along—my powers—and this was what I needed to hone them.

I began feeling along the chain-link, sure my hand was at any moment going to brush along the four of clubs, my four of clubs—glossy, shimmering—when my blindfold came off. I turned my head and Ada was standing silently behind me with my blindfold in her hand, her eyes fixed, lips tight.

"Your card's down there," she said, pointing into the distance. I was at one end of the fence, and my card—which I couldn't see because it was so far away—was evidently at the other.

"You failed," she said, then turned away from me, walked across the field, and put her useless wet towel into her woven bag. She walked into the street, turned a corner, and disappeared. I thought about chasing after her and having her explain what it all meant, or at least helping me get back to the transit center, but I just let her walk away. I let her leave because she was, in a way, right. I had failed. But not at this game, because failing implies that you tried to do something you actually wanted to do. I'd let Ada take over my life and, by doing that, had completely and totally failed at my quest, failed at being a son, failed at being a friend.

Still a Professional

Elly Fox, Professional Idiot. Professional Fool.

Entering Absence

I wandered back through random alleys and side streets, not paying attention but just hoping one of them would spit me out at the transit center and I could go home. I felt like I should have been worried about walking in the dark, alone, down alleys in a place I barely knew, but I just wasn't. No one else was even in the alleys. I thought about how maybe alleys were like the woods. Like how fairy tales and movies have made the woods at night seem so creepy that maybe everyone's scared of the woods now, even creeps.

It was depressing to think about how my quest had turned into all Ada and nothing else. I could see how I'd gotten caught up in her small-town-famous status, her big-to-me organization, the fact that all these people looked up to her but she for some reason wanted to spend all this time with me. I thought she had some things figured out and wanted to help me figure things out, but I hadn't truly thought about how this would all practically help my mom for what seemed like a long while now—I'd let her importance become the reason for spending all this time with her.

But now that she was apparently gone from my life, what did I have?

I seemed to remember a list or two I'd made a month ago, before her, but I couldn't remember what had been on those lists. I knew my quest and my ideas of adventure had at one time been more than Ada, more than the Acquaintances of Memory Fellowship, more than just taking the bus to the same crappy suburb over and over. But somehow I'd lost all those ideas, all that inspiration.

Eventually I came out to a main road I recognized, found my way to the transit center, and miraculously got on a number 27 right before it left the station. I initially wanted to believe this good series of events meant that things were looking up. But I felt my mom was probably waiting for me at home, ready to express her justified disappointment and anger. I couldn't pull off the lie about going to the dance. Because I now wanted nothing more than to be at the dance with my friends, on the sidelines, shaking our heads at how foolish everyone was. I wanted it too much to be able to lie about it. So I spent the trip formulating not-so-brilliant excuses and self-deprecating apologies, unsure of which tactic to take in my new world of lies, my life as a liar.

When the bus dropped me off at my stop, I dragged out the two-block walk to my house as long as I could, hoping against all reason that my mom and my uncle would go to bed in that extra minute or two. I got to the apartment and slowly unlocked the door, expecting the worst—expecting to have them sitting there, facing me, tapping their fingers with stern looks on their faces—but no one was there. The lights were on, it was sort of messy, but was quiet in the way that only places without people in them are. Somehow sleeping people, even ones who don't snore, make a type of noise. Or not really a noise, but they give off a presence, a feeling of life. I walked through each room to make sure I was right, thinking about how people make noise without making noise and wondering if the whole card thing—despite my anger toward it—had heightened my senses. It was then I remembered my phone. It had been in my pocket, pretty much continuously, since I got it last year, and I had just assumed it was there, not buzzing. But it wasn't.

I got it out of my backpack and turned it on, feeling an odd sense that it held the key to something important and that there was a very good reason I never took it out of my pocket, never turned it off. The screen loaded, displaying 15 missed calls, 10 voicemails, and 21 text messages, all from my uncle.

Not Unicorns

I opened a text, some words without context, starting mid-sentence, and I knew there were twenty more 150-character fragments of the whole story, probably received out of order, that I didn't have time to go through and make sense of. So I skipped reading, skipped the voicemails, and just called.

Uncle asked if I was okay but didn't ask where I'd been. He sounded calm but a little shaky as he explained the situation. While I'd been in Vinton searching for a playing card in a fence with my phone off, my mom had a seizure. Collapsed, out of nowhere, while making dinner in the kitchen, and hit her head on the floor. The seizure seemed to end when she hit the ground, but her head was bleeding and she couldn't remember any of it, so my uncle drove her to the emergency room and she'd been there since.

I got off the phone and took the 27 to the 19, going on stretches of each route I'd never been on before and, in another situation, I would have viewed it as a fun expansion of my bus knowledge, but my mind was in a universe where this viewpoint wasn't possible. I'd messed up.

In my head, it seemed certain that my mom's stress and worry over not knowing where I was had somehow caused her to have a seizure that placed her in the emergency room. Which, if this were true, would be further proof that I had totally and utterly failed. And the quest, or whatever it was that I had been doing, clearly hadn't been for my mom at all. It was some selfish thing where I wanted to feel like I was a good person and ignore the fact that, at my core, I was rotten.

A month ago, I imagined that I just needed to travel to be a better person. I imagined a self-proclaimed guru could teach me everything I needed to know. I imagined I could fix my mom's memory loss. But I might as well have been imagining unicorns and mermaids. Or Lisa

Frank art where kittens have wings and puppies sleep on rainbow-colored clouds. Because I had basically been living in a fantasy land.

When the bus let me off at the hospital, I ran inside, my backpack flopping from side to side. I got to the front desk, expecting words to exit my mouth and then be immediately rushed up to some room. But instead there was a woman on the phone, lazily speaking with half-mast eyes, who gave me the one-finger wait signal before I could even say anything.

The phone call did not take one second or one minute or one of anything, but took what seemed to be many ages. Lifetimes. I couldn't believe this place had the nerve to call itself an emergency room when it prioritized somebody on the phone over somebody frantically running up to its front desk. When she finally hung up, I let out a string of words that became more like one word. "WhatroomforSusanaFoxpleaseshe'smymom."

The woman looked at me for a moment, in that slow way that seemed to be her specialty and most certainly didn't belong in this wing of the hospital. "Susana Fox, you said?"

I nodded and she looked at the computer for an amount of time that seemed unnecessary for such a simple request.

"Looks like we saw her briefly before she was admitted to the hospital and then transferred to diagnostic imaging. So you can go up to the desk on the third floor."

"Is she okay?" I asked.

"The computer just tells me where she is."

I wanted to freak out, tell her I had no time for bureaucracy and red tape, but instead I turned around and ran to the elevator.

When I got to the third floor, I talked to another receptionist and he made a call. A nurse eventually came out, told me my mom was getting an MRI so they could figure out what was going on, and then quickly walked away. I had no idea what an MRI was. Obviously it was a type of test, but what kind? Were there needles and blood, or sensors and heart monitors, or what?

I usually hated being treated like a know-nothing child, but I actually wanted these people to see me as clueless just this one time. Because at this moment I *was* clueless. And nervous. Scared, even. I tried calling my uncle, but his phone must have died—straight to voicemail, again and again.

Over the next hour or so, I learned this important fact: despite what TV medical dramas may suggest, hospitals are not fast-paced worlds full of handsome people. They are the most slow-moving, awful places in the world. I was in that waiting room for over an hour, while my mom got one test. I couldn't believe that a single test could take an hour, but evidently it was possible. So I waited.

Scanned

At some point, a nurse brought me into my mom's room. She was hooked up to beeping machines and an IV pole, and I couldn't tell if she was asleep or awake. My uncle sat in a chair next to her, looking pale enough to be hooked up to some machines himself.

I didn't know what to do with myself. Was I supposed to sit or stand? Cry or smile? Talk or be quiet? I wanted an etiquette guide for this moment, but I was pretty sure that such a thing didn't exist.

I was about to sit and not cry when my uncle stood up, walked over to me, and gave me a hug. Which made me start crying. I was buried in his hoodie, thinking about how unlike me this was. Or how maybe this was exactly like a new me. A me who cries all the time. When it got to the point where I was just sniffling and no longer bawling, I whispered, "Is she awake?"

"She's pretty out of it, but she's awake."

"Should I talk to her, or just leave her alone?"

"Why don't you let her know you're here?" he said. "That would make her happy. She was worried about you."

I knew they were probably both pissed at me. And with good reason. I was pissed at me. I tried to ignore this as best I could as I slowly walked up to her bed. She didn't seem to notice me, so I said, "Hey Mom."

She turned her head toward me and sort of smiled. "Hi Elly."

"How're you feeling?"

She scrunched up her face and looked at the various things connected to her body. "Well, I've been better," she said with a half-smile.

I allowed myself to smile a little too, and we just looked at each other for a long time. Eventually she broke the silence and said, "How about you? How are you feeling?"

"I've been better, too."

She didn't say anything in response and the moment felt awkward, but an awkward that also felt good. Needed, even. Life is awkward, so maybe embracing awkwardness is the ultimate experience of life.

This distilled human experience was broken when a woman walked in and announced she was the doctor. We all politely said hello and she shook hands with each of us.

"As you probably know, we might not have fully confirmed MRI results for a couple days," she said.

I definitely did not know this.

"It could be quicker, but once I've gone over the images I'll want to run them by my colleagues, and during that time I think it's best for her to stay in the hospital for observation," she said, talking about my mom as if she wasn't there. "She has a mild concussion from the fall, and since we don't know why the fall happened—combined with what you told us, Mr. Fox, about the patient's recent memory issues—it's best that we keep a watch on her and that she not exert herself in any way."

We were all silent, letting this sink in. My mom's eyes were barely open, but I saw her look at my uncle in a way that I interpreted to be some type of *how could you* thing for outing her memory loss to the doctor. Which I don't think would have been a betrayal in any other family, just a fact.

The doctor waited for someone to say something. Her eyes seemed to search around the room, trying to figure out what she was missing, who she should be waiting on. "So, I can't provide many answers, but do you have any questions?"

My uncle and I looked toward my mom cautiously. The doctor didn't seem to consider the possibility that my mom might just refuse to stay in the hospital. It was probably rare that she had her recommendations challenged. But my mom was stubborn enough to say that "observation" was not enough to keep her in a hospital bed. My uncle and I knew we couldn't speak for her. She didn't look at either of us, or at the doctor, but looked to the side of the doctor, where she didn't have to make eye contact with anyone.

"I don't like it," she said to the wall. "I don't want to stay here." For a minute that seemed like all she was going to say, but just as the doctor's mouth was opening to likely voice appropriate concern, my mom said, "But if it's what you think is best, I'll do it."

No one made a sound, but I could feel a collective internal sigh of relief.

Night Drive

My uncle and I drove home in his tiny car with the radio on. It was the soundtrack to my uncle and my mom's life, the local NPR station, which they both play constantly in their little machines. I wondered if this was my future, my inheritance: notably small vehicles and boring radio.

I read the Post-Its on the dashboard ("Buy notecards," "Revisit dream journal," "'There is a silence that paces us all.' - Mia Zapata") while the radio played the morning news from the BBC. It seemed surreal that a new day could be starting somewhere else when it felt so deep into the night here. Every bar we drove past seemed to be overflowing with people. The night had gotten colder during the hours I'd been in the hospital—it was probably the coldest it had been since February or March—and everyone seemed underdressed and clumped together in great masses. The radio went on and on about countries I wouldn't be able to find on a map and leaders I'd never heard of. I felt the weight of my insignificance.

"So where were you earlier?" my uncle asked. I was so lost in my pity party it was like he was speaking to me from another universe. I turned to him and he was looking straight ahead, out the windshield, as if he had just asked the most casual question in the world.

"Do you want the truth, or the lie I came up with?" I asked.

"How about we start with the lie?" he said, not breaking a smile.

"I was at the homecoming dance with Maddy and Claudia."

"So you risked getting in even more trouble with your mom to go to a dance? That doesn't seem like you. What's the deal, do you have a crush on somebody?"

Even though I knew he was just playing along with this temporary game of the lie, the crush question was still uncomfortable coming from my uncle. It felt as unsettling as if he'd out of nowhere started telling me about safe sex. I tried to pretend like I'd only heard the first part.

"I suffer from FOMO." I felt silly saying it, but it was the first thing that came into my head.

"FOMO?"

"Fear of missing out." I said it confidently, not mentioning that I'd only found out what it meant a month ago when Claudia told me. "It's a problem. In this case, it makes me need to go to anything my friends are going to. Even horrible things like school dances."

"I see. That's somewhat believable. What does the truth sound like?"

"I went to Vinton to meet with the memory guru. I imagine Mom told you about her."

"Your mom told me the little she knows."

"Well, she left me in a field. It was a bad idea to go. But again, FOMO."

"A field, huh? And you made it home by yourself?"

"I'm pretty street smart, I'll have you know. I did grow up in Brooklyn."

"The sleepy Brooklyn neighborhood of Portland, Oregon, you mean? I think I'm familiar. Those are some pretty mean streets, if I recall correctly."

"Okay so maybe it's not street smarts exactly, but I guess I'm just wise enough to not get into any sketchy situations."

"You're fifteen. And you got left in a field."

"You're thirty-six. And you live on a couch. And since when did fields become considered sketchy?"

"I'm just saying I don't think you've lived long enough to be wise yet. Smart, sure. But wise?"

"Fine, then I'm smart enough to not get into any sketchy situations. Is that better?"

He took a very purposeful-sounding deep breath, which I think meant he was both amused and frustrated by my response. "So you went to Vinton because of your fear of missing out?"

"Yeah, mostly because of that. And because I wanted to help Mom." I thought about my mom alone in her hospital bed. How strange it was to leave her there, how wrong it seemed. "But I figured out tonight that helping Mom was just my excuse," I said. "Really I'm so self-obsessed that I just wanted to be celebrated for helping Mom and it was barely about her at all. It was selfish, but I was pretending it wasn't. I also went because I didn't want to give up. I didn't want to fail."

We pulled into our apartment building's parking lot. He turned off the car and said, "What you did was really irresponsible. But I don't believe you were being selfish." Then he got out of the car. I followed him inside. I went for the couch, moving aside a stack of books so I could lie down, and he went for the kitchen.

"Want a piece of toast?" he asked.

"Sure," I said. Then I closed my eyes and, without meaning to, fell asleep on his bed.

I woke with a start, shoved out of some dream about dead-end streets and brick walls, and found myself covered in sweat. I still had my glasses on, all my clothes, and a big down comforter had been laid onto me. There was a cold piece of toast in front of me on the coffee table, butter solidified into its pores. The apartment was still dark, so I knew I couldn't have slept more than a handful of hours. But I was wide awake. I got my phone out of my pocket. 6 am. The time I got up to go to Vinton every Sunday morning for the past month. I never wake up early without an alarm and, even though it was probably just because I was slimy and miserable, in the moment I felt it was a sign. My mind was made up before I could wake enough to think rationally. I was going to the Sunday meeting.

I left my uncle a note: *Will be back to be with Mom. Had to go to Vinton. FOMO strikes again!* I tried to be funny with it, but I honestly didn't know if it was the right thing to do or if I would regret it later, and I didn't know if my uncle would be as understanding. But I couldn't concern myself with those things. I had a bus to catch.

Regarding the Pain of Us

Walking into the meeting room felt like breaking a rule no one else in AMF knew existed. Like I was secretly throwing some sort of something in the face of Ada's power. I had no idea what to expect— her ignoring me seemed equally as likely as her making a scene and kicking me out—but I felt ready for anything.

I waved to people I barely knew, said hi to others I'd never said hi to before. Internally I felt sour, like everything wrong was rotting in my belly, but it expressed itself on the outside as strangely giddy. I didn't see Rigby, so I didn't have a friend there, but that meant I could sit wherever. So I went right up front with the people who had wheelchairs and canes. I asked if I was stealing anyone's seat and they welcomed me as if I was an old friend, a couple of them patting the open seat like I was a cat they were trying to coax up.

Ada always started right on time. She knew her crowd—mainly old people who didn't like to wait—so she gave them what they wanted. 8am sharp, every time. So when it was 8:05 and she wasn't on stage, it was definitely odd. Five minutes late is nothing as far as I'm concerned—to me, that's basically on time—but it wasn't like Ada. I looked behind me at the sparse room. A couple people were checking their watches and everyone looked a little confused. I thought about my mom and wondered where the rest of the group was, where Rigby was, where Ada was.

A few more minutes passed before a ruffled version of Ada appeared from the back room. Her hair was matted like she'd been wearing a beanie for days, and her puffy eyes suggested she had gotten even less sleep than me. She stepped to the mic, made a move like she was going to speak, took a breath, and then paused.

I tried to make eye contact. I was in the front row, no more than six feet from her. Her eyes were looking in my direction, but she seemed to be looking past me or into me. Definitely not at me.

"I don't want to sound cruel," she finally said, clearing her throat, her voice desert dry. "But I want you all to experience pain."

Collectively, we shifted in our seats.

"There's a saying that's quite silly, but is perhaps surprisingly true," she continued. "'No pain, no gain.' It feels ridiculous to say, doesn't it? I imagine people getting doused in energy drinks when I say it."

We all laughed, which felt good after a whole room of followers had been told their leader wanted them to feel pain. Even though I didn't feel like one of the followers anymore, I still felt the relief the laughter brought. But I also worried that I'd ditched my hospitalized mom for a cheesy basketball-coach speech.

"But 'no pain, no gain' is accurate in that we all must go through a period of hurt and stress to change and grow. Chaos teaches us so much more than a neutral state of calm and contentment can."

I felt like she was speaking directly to me. Like she knew my mom was in the hospital, like she knew that I felt like a failure. And maybe she was telling me that everything she had put me through last night was just a strange lesson. It didn't make it right. But maybe it gave it a reason.

"I'm not suggesting any of us seek out chaos, or try to get hurt," she said. "That's simply self-destructive. I just want us all to be prepared. Because, for better or worse, it will come on its own. And we must remember that our times of pain can be occasions for great learning. Because when we come out of it we will be wiser, more fully realized, human beings."

We all clapped—the sound notably skimpy—thinking that Ada was just getting started, but she walked off the stage. The minutes passed, and it became clear she wasn't coming back. People murmured a little, and eventually we, a couple people at a time, got up to leave.

I slowly put my peacoat and backpack on, feeling torn between telling Ada off for abandoning me last night, and telling her that her lecture was exactly what I needed. There was something that now felt a little less difficult because of it, but it also made me angrier at her for toying with my emotions. I had so much on the tip of my tongue. But when I turned to leave, she wasn't at the door.

On the Outside

Leaving an AMF meeting was usually part of the meeting; it typically took as long as the lecture itself. Because on the way out, one-by-one, each person would have what amounted to a philosophical talk with Ada. Her not being at the door was like a play ending at intermission. It was basically a wholly different event.

And people wanted that second act. They waited all week for it. So they weren't giving up easily.

A line formed at the door, and I stood with them for a minute. But there was no Rigby to talk to, and I wasn't about to let Ada abandon me again, so I squeezed through the line, saying an indiscriminate string of *excuse me, pardon me, sorry*, until I was outside and running to the bus station.

I got there right as the 27 was pulling out. Out of breath and watching the bus drive away, I looked at my phone, knowing what to expect. There was once again an overwhelming amount of messages, missed calls, and voicemails. All, of course, from my uncle.

While I was scrolling through it, my phone rang.

"Elly, what the hell?" Uncle spoke like he somehow knew I was going to answer this time after not answering all the times before. "Why did you do this?" He didn't wait for my response. "Did you think about how I would have to show up at the hospital and tell your mom I straight up lost her kid while I was asleep?"

I definitely hadn't thought about that.

"And then instead of just answering your phone to let us know you're alive, you just shut it off for a while? That just made things so unnecessarily scary."

It hurt. My uncle had never been truly mad at me.

"I just had to see," I told him.

"You just had to see." He said it like he was trying to crack a code, like my words were a series of anagrams he needed to rearrange to get to the real meaning. "And what was the thing you had to see?"

"You know, I had to see what would happen. I had to follow this out."

"Follow what out?"

"What I started, Uncle. This woman I decided to follow. I don't get why so many people think they can just stop something they started. Because I can't. I need to see things through to the end. And there was something I needed to understand." Even as I spoke, I thought about how some answers just didn't sound good when said aloud.

"Well, I hope you found it."

"I don't think I did."

He let me sit with those words for a long time. "Then that's not much of a reason."

"I know," I said. I wanted to retract what I'd said, tell him something he could understand, something that might even make him proud of me. But to do so would have taken more strength than I had.

"I'm coming back," I said. "I'm just waiting for the bus."

We spent the rest of the day apart together in a hospital room, my mom in an ongoing state of headache agony, my uncle not talking to me. I didn't know why we had to do this—it surely wasn't what my mom wanted—but Uncle seemed to think it was something I needed to endure. Finally, as it got dark, we left.

The whole ride home, I wished I knew how to make the tension better, knew the right action to take, the right words to say, but I didn't. And I added these to the long list of things I didn't know.

Fever Dream

The next morning, I sat down next to Maddy and, before I even had my backpack situated by my feet, she said, "You missed a really fun dance."

I couldn't believe this was the way Monday was starting. After everything. The field. The seizure. The meeting. The hospital room. The serious lack of sleep. The bus should have been the one place where things would be okay. Where I could talk with Maddy about anything and everything. Or where I could at least tell her about my weekend, in all its awful glory. But the first thing out of her mouth was this. A dance.

"I seriously doubt it," I responded.

"No, really, it was cool. I mean, at first it sucked. Something was up with one of Claudia's friends, so Claudia only stayed for fifteen minutes, tops."

"This is why I'm friends with her," I said. "She's very wise."

Maddy ignored this. "So I was stuck by myself, right? Of course I knew some people, but I didn't want to just drop into a group and be like *hang out with me!* you know? So I was on the sidelines, drinking punch, trying to look like I wasn't stranded at sea, and then Rain came by."

The second her name left Maddy's mouth, all the other sounds of the bus fell away. It was like when a fever kicks in and the world feels like it's shrinking, like the world around you is suddenly being sucked into a cave.

"We started talking and just didn't stop. For maybe hours. It was really awesome. I'd actually always thought she was prissy or something, but she's not at all. She just kinda tells it how it is, you know? And she swears up a storm while she does it—it's really hilarious."

Rain had once again found a way to hurt me. She was going to fool Maddy into thinking she was a good person, take her away from me, and then destroy everything kind and beautiful about her.

"Do you like her?" I said, my voice sounding as close to a growl as I had ever heard it get.

"Like, like-like her? I have no idea. I mean, sure, she's cute. But we just hung out once." Maddy gave me an uncertain look. "What's going on with you? Whatever you're doing is very freaky, and I think you should stop."

"Maddy, listen to me: Rain Mallory is a horrid human being. Do not go near her."

"Whoa, what are you talking about?" Maddy said, her eyes huge. "I hung out with her all Saturday night. She's definitely not horrid."

"It's a trick. You're under her spell. You just can't see it."

"Seriously, what's your problem?"

"My problem is Rain. She's the problem."

"So you're just telling me who to hang out with now?"

"No, I'm telling you who *not* to hang out with, and that person is Rain Mallory. That's it. You can hang out with anybody else in the entire world. Just not her."

"This is so unfair. You think you can stop hanging out with me and then tell me not to hang out with someone else? Elly, that's messed up."

My brain felt like all its synapses were firing at once. I said, "This is a nightmare brought to life on earth, and only you can make it end."

"You sound insane, Elly. I'm not going to stop hanging out with Rain, I'm going to hang out with whoever I want to hang out with. And I am going to stop talking to you. Starting now."

"I am so sane, Maddy. I can see so clearly what she's doing. I—" The bus wasn't even all the way to the bus stop by the school, but Maddy squeezed past my legs and headed to the front. I heard myself yell *wait*, as if from somewhere outside myself, but she didn't wait. She didn't even turn around. And as soon as the doors opened, she was gone.

Skip

At lunch, Maddy ate with Rain. I walked past them while getting a burrito. They both ignored me. Claudia met me at the Block, like usual, and I kept a fairly stoic face at first. But as soon as she asked me where Maddy was, I started bawling. Which I've definitely never done in front of Claudia before. And certainly not at school. But I couldn't hold it in.

And then I proceeded to spill my guts about everything that had happened on the bus, over the weekend, and everything I had felt—even slightly—in the last 72 hours. I was a mess.

I was pretty sure the handful of people who were using the alley behind the shop buildings as a shortcut to somewhere else were staring, I could hear laughing, but I couldn't stop. Finally Claudia said, "Let's get out of here."

We walked to a bus stop and were on the 9 heading downtown before I even considered what was happening. "Where are we going?" I asked.

"I don't know. Somewhere other than school," Claudia said. "Maybe we just walk the Park Blocks?"

I told her I hadn't walked along them since a field trip to the art museum in elementary school, which I probably wouldn't have admitted had I not been such a wreck.

We got off and within a few minutes we were walking along a strip of land that was like a mega-median cutting through downtown. There were hundreds of crows in the giant, newly de-leafed fall trees, all talking at once. There were fancy people walking fancy dogs, people sleeping on benches, a handful of hippies selling things off patterned blankets on the ground. I thought about how the place I called Portland didn't look like this at all, and how maybe everyone meant something different when they said "Portland"—each based on their own neighborhood, all the different sights they'd seen, adventures they'd adventured.

Somehow we ended up close to Powell's, the bookstore that takes up an entire city block, the one Portland is famous for, and I had to admit to Claudia again how rarely I'd been. "Maddy and I mostly go to the smaller Powell's on Hawthorne," I said. She just nodded, but I could see she thought it was a little surprising.

Once we were in the aisles, briefly entering little worlds, one after another, the events of the last few days temporarily faded away. She took me to the weird-book wall and we laughed at all the baffling old titles and covers, taking turns reading excerpts, and I was immediately aware of how little I'd been laughing of late.

But I couldn't leave it be. For some unknown-even-to-me reason, I couldn't just let it feel good.

"I don't know what Maddy's problem is." I had meant to keep it in my head, but I said it out loud. "Rain Mallory? Really? She's gotta know, on some level, that I can't stand her."

She pursed her lips, slid them to the right. "She does? I didn't know until you told me at the Block just now."

"Okay, I mean, I know she doesn't know the details, but she knows Rain and I are former friends. Former." I paused, hoping this argument would ignite some small form of agreement in Claudia. It didn't. "She has to know there are reasons for that."

"I don't think that's an obvious conclusion. I mean, you two were friends in elementary school. That almost doesn't count as a friendship anymore. Everyone just makes friends indiscriminately at that age—someone can just say 'do you want to be friends?' and the other person can just say 'sure' and it's somehow automatically a friendship."

I knew, because of my own embarrassment, I hadn't told Claudia and Maddy the real situation, but—especially over the past month, with Rain going so hard on me, semi-publicly—I assumed they had sensed it in its most general form. Which, I could see now, was like expecting someone to read your mind. "But why her?"

Claudia paused and looked at me like she felt sorry for me, like I was an upset baby that needed a nap. "Maybe she just likes her," she said.

I couldn't imagine a worse answer. But then she gave me one.

"Plus, I think she just feels totally ditched."

"But now she's the one ditching me."

"Okay, that's true, but you guys used to hang out all the time. And for an entire month now you've spent every spare moment with this weird older lady who nobody else can meet. Did you expect her to just be sitting there waiting for you when you were ready to hang out again? I mean, it just doesn't work like that."

"But you're not mad at me, right?"

"No offense, Elly, but I just don't expect anything from you beyond lunch at the Block, so that's the only reason I'm not disappointed by your recent vanishing act. If we actually hung out outside of school, I'd probably be pissed at you too."

I was stunned. Claudia had never said anything like this to me. "I thought you were supposed to be cheering me up right now."

"True, but I also have to be real. I'm not mad at you, but I can see why Maddy is. And yeah, I left her at the dance by herself. But only because my friend was having a panic attack. It sucked ditching Maddy like that, but it was an emergency. I mean, it worked out for her, I guess, but ultimately you weren't there for her."

Her words were small daggers being shoved into my chest. She was right, and it was the most painful kind of right there was.

In the Paper

When I walked into the hospital room, my mom looked asleep. My uncle instantly rose to his feet and gave me a hug. "I'm so glad you're here," he said. It was only when he let me go that I got a good look at him: his hair stuck out at various angles, his clothes seemed more wrinkled than clothes could be wrinkled, his anger from the previous day gone.

"What happened to you?" I asked.

"It's been pretty rough. She's been having migraines all day." He paused. "She was in a lot of pain, Elly," he said, his eyes watery.

I tried to hold it together, to be a rock for my uncle in the moment, but I felt myself starting to tear up.

"And of course she blames the hospital itself," he said, trying to laugh. "She says it's a 'toxic environment' that makes people sicker. And that's why she's having migraines when she's never had them before. That I never should have brought her in."

I couldn't tell if he thought this was all ridiculous, or if he was starting to believe it. "It's good that you brought her in, Uncle," I said. "It's not the hospital. We know that."

He nodded.

"How long has she been asleep?" I asked.

"An hour or so. She'll most likely be asleep for the rest of the night. She has more painkillers in her system than she's probably had in the course of her entire life. I wasn't able to get the night off work, though, so could you stay here with her? Just in case."

"Of course." I tried looking him in the eyes. It didn't work, so I looked at the floor. "And hey, sorry about yesterday." It felt too casual, but I didn't know how else to say it.

"Yeah, I didn't handle that well at all. I have no idea how to do this." He ran his hand through his long hair part of the way, then just held it there, his head hanging.

"Do what?"

"Like, actually parent you. Or actually take care of my sister instead of her taking care of me. Having too much responsibility just really scares me. I've always avoided being in charge because of that. And now I suddenly have a lot of responsibility, and I don't really feel like myself. I know that's stupid, but the gravity of it all has just hit me really hard."

"I honestly didn't think about what you were going through at all." I paused. "I should have."

"Thanks. I'm not totally certain I've thought about anything from your perspective either, so maybe we're even. But just so you know: the fact that you've never done actual bad or dangerous things before and then did a whole bunch of bad and dangerous things in a row? That was a real curveball." He smiled.

"Yeah, I was trying something out. It didn't go especially well." I paused. "How much does Mom know?"

"Most of what I know. I've been keeping her updated. Ratting on you, one might say."

I let out a short laugh. "Yeah, I figured. I just wanted to know."

"I should head home and get cleaned up before work. But the MRI results will be confirmed tomorrow. Then we'll know for sure what we're up against." He put his arm around me in a way that I think was supposed to be casual but instead betrayed the level of desperation he felt.

Hours passed. My mom slept, nurses came in occasionally. I tried to read things, tried to draw, but mostly I stared at walls, at my mom, at the monitors.

Eventually I got out my laptop. I'd thrown it in my backpack that morning and had unexpectedly ended up lugging it around town with me when we skipped. My shoulders hurt. As I waited for the computer to connect to the hospital's Wi-Fi and wondered what might be waiting for me online, I felt only soreness and dread. I was so used to being excited about getting a message of any kind, but right now I couldn't think of anyone I was on good terms with. I felt like any message would either be somebody reminding me that I'm an awful person or yet another piece of bad news.

The laptop felt heavier than usual, like the unread messages inside it had their own mass.

When I finally got connected, I was both relieved and disappointed to see the only new thing was just Rigby's latest email. I hadn't been reading his nightly news all week and had felt vaguely guilty about it. I knew he didn't expect anything, but I couldn't help feeling like he was just another person I was letting down. He missed Sunday's meeting, so maybe he had a cold or his own emergency. If I was really his friend I would have checked in, or at least I would have taken thirty seconds to read his email yesterday.

I read the new one and it was barely distinguishable from every other one I'd ever read—different errands, different things in the mail, but mostly the same. It made me not feel so bad about missing a whole week of them. But just for good measure, I decided to read Sunday's, and was surprised when it was notably different.

Hi all,

New type of Sunday. Went to farmer's market for last time until April (it closes for the colder months). Bought discounted apples and a cup of drip coffee. Tried to run some errands, but many things were closed. Had more time than I was used to, since leaving AMF earlier this week because of fraud. So didn't go to meeting, or coffee after. Have to get used to my new schedule.

Until tomorrow,

Rigby

I read it again. It didn't make any more sense than it had the first time through. *Because of fraud?* I started writing back, but there were too many questions and I needed answers right away. I stepped into the hallway and called.

I remembered how, when he'd given me his number, he was so impressed as he watched me enter it—he said he'd never seen how a cell phone worked up close before.

"Hello?" I could hear his voice was full of a sweet, sincere curiosity that somehow made my heart feel good in the midst of my franticness.

"Rigby, it's Elly. I just read your email from last night."

"Oh, I'm glad to hear you keep up on—"

"Yeah, I've actually been doing a bad job at keeping up on them, and I'm sorry. But I need to know what the fraud is all about."

"You haven't heard about Ada?"

"No, what about her? I was at the meeting yesterday and she was there."

"You didn't see it in the paper?"

"The paper?"

"The newspaper," he said, matter-of-factly.

"Ada was in the newspaper?"

"Yep. Right on the cover of this morning's *Oregonian*. I mean, it was sort of toward the bottom of the page, and it was very short, so I could see how you might miss it."

"Rigby, I don't read the paper at all. I've never read the paper. Not even once."

"Oh, well that's different!" he said, chuckling. "Guess I just assumed everyone read the paper. Maybe it's a technology thing."

"Maybe it is." I was getting impatient but trying to keep it together so I didn't say anything rude. "I'm also fifteen. But since I didn't read it, can you tell me what it said?"

"Well, Ada was taken into custody yesterday after the meeting. I'm actually surprised anyone even came. Most of us here in Vinton found out on Friday or Saturday. Word about it spread through the group pretty fast, even before formal charges were made. But some people might have not believed it, especially the handful of people who have been with it since the beginning—they're pretty devoted. I know I didn't want to believe it. But the evidence is there."

"Rigby, what are you saying? She's in custody? Like, in jail?"

"I think it said she made bail. I can't remember for certain, though. But yes, she was in jail."

"Because of fraud?" I asked, realizing I didn't exactly know what that meant.

"Unfortunately, yes. Elder fraud, they're calling it."

"But, uh, how?" I said, unsure if that was the right question.

"Well, do you know Cynthia?"

"I don't think so."

"She's in what we call the 'remote group'—ones that are no longer able to make it to the weekly meetings, you see. Not one of the higher-functioning ones. She's been fading, mentally-speaking, for a while. I think she joined the group with the idea she'd get some of it back. And Ada paid her a lot of special attention. To the rest of us it seemed like a really kind thing she was doing for somebody who seemed like a pretty hopeless case."

I wondered if this was the way people would talk about my mom in the future: a hopeless case.

"Cynthia started declining this week, so some family flew in from out of state to be with her and talk to lawyers about her will and all that—her 'affairs,' as people say. She didn't have any kids, so these were cousins, I believe. Anyway, as it turned out, she largely didn't have any money left to will to anyone. They followed the paper trail. Ada had somehow managed to drain all Cynthia's money into AMF. And we're not talking pennies here. Cynthia might have been a little senile, but she also wore furs to our annual conferences. Her late husband was in some variety of finance, if I recall correctly."

My mind flashed back to the nursing home, and I flinched.

"We all know the truth now, though," Rigby said, in a way that seemed too casual for this situation. "Better now than later, you know? At least it was before January rolled around, so we didn't end up giving any more of our money to the group. Speaking for myself, it'll be nice to not be on such a tight budget."

Rigby seemed to be speaking another language, or talking about a group I had no connection or relationship to. "What money did you give to AMF?"

"Well, the annual dues."

"Annual dues?"

"Well, I paid them annually, but I think most people paid them monthly. You didn't have to pay them? She was probably trying to hook you before asking for money. Was worried about scaring you off, I bet. The dues scare a lot of people off. It's not the cheapest club you could join."

I'd always thought of AMF as notably cheap—the simple meeting room, the plates of cookies that made my teeth hurt, the burnt coffee smell, the way we would help fold chairs at the end. I never could have imagined that people gave large sums of money to it. I'd never heard mention of dues. Not at the meetings, not through Ada at our Saturday meet-ups, not at Three Rivers or Angela's, not in one of Rigby's emails.

"No, I didn't have to pay them."

And there wasn't much else to say.

Visiting Hours

We got off the phone, and I walked back into the room, my mind full of things I didn't want to think about. My mom in migraine pain I couldn't imagine. The coming test results that held answers I was in fear of. And now there was Ada. In jail.

I was trying to wrap my mind around it, but I was also lost in the details of the situation. It felt like I couldn't understand it without first knowing a hundred other things. I turned over all the things I thought I knew but didn't know. Like what, exactly, it meant to drain someone's bank account. Or what all of the membership dues were even used for. Or where the very concept of money itself came from or meant.

I felt like I needed a crash course in economics to fully know what had happened. I was sure this probably wasn't the point, and I should just judge it for what it seemed like: AMF was a way for Ada to steal money from old people. But I couldn't do that. At least not yet.

I ran to the floor's check-in desk and asked where I could find a paper. They said there were boxes on the sidewalk out front, so I sped-walked out through cars stopping and starting along the various entrances and drop-off spots and bought a copy of *The Oregonian* with the quarters I luckily had in my pocket. I let the bottom half of the cover flop down and there it was, a tiny blip on the sidebar: "Former Child Chess Prodigy Arrested in Vinton."

A Vinton resident is facing both federal and state charges for elder fraud and financial exploitation after an investigation into billing practices at her memory-services educational facility revealed multiple inconsistencies, according to local authorities.

Former chess prodigy Ada Dronning, 39, was arrested at the offices of MemoryCorp, LLC yesterday following an investigation spurred on by allegations made by the family members of one of her clients, Cynthia Jenkins.

"Our family is shocked by the level of exploitation," said Theodore Price, Jenkins's nephew. "My aunt has suffered from age-related dementia for many years, and Ms. Dronning took advantage of this. She coerced her out of money, as well as family heirlooms and jewelry."

Investigators confirm they are also looking into past allegations of Dronning exercising undue influence in the affairs of the senior citizens with whom she worked as a memory coach.

Born in Northern California, Dronning became a nationally known competitive chess player at the age of 10. She moved to Vinton in 1999 and has run MemoryCorp since 2004. She was released on bail from Multnomah County Jail and will be facing her second arraignment on November 10th.

I read it again, read it a third time, pulled out my phone, texted Ada: *I want to talk.*

I stood on the sidewalk, staring at my phone in one hand, gripping the newspaper so tightly in the other I could feel the little crinkle lines forming under my fingertips. After some amount of time I couldn't be sure of, she wrote back: *Anytime. Meet at Angela's?*

I hated how casual she was. I hated how available she was. I hated that she wanted to go to Angela's. I hated Angela's. I wished I could throw my phone against the sidewalk and she would receive a message that said *Elly has smashed phone in frustration with you.* But instead I wrote: *Sure. Tomorrow morning?* I couldn't even imagine going to school right now, so I just wouldn't go. I decided it without even having to decide it—it felt like it was already true by the time I had the thought. I had some things to find out.

Random

Angela's was empty except for Ada, her back turned away from me at a small table by the counter. Even empty, the place—a narrow, shotgun-style, strip-mall space squeezed between two other bigger strip-mall spaces—felt claustrophobic, as if it were a funhouse illusion, some trick of mirrors and lights.

"I thought you would come," she said as I approached. Even though she'd just been in jail, she somehow looked more put together than the last time I'd seen her. Her confidence was impossible to miss; it was overwhelming.

"You did?" I said, sitting down, feeling timid, again reminded that the difference between talking to a person in your head and talking to a person in real life was great. I didn't know whether I was there to tell her off or give her a last chance to explain herself. I was just there, as she evidently knew I would be.

She nodded. "I also assumed, correctly, that you would be the only one to reach out."

"No one else has?" It was hard for me to imagine.

"No one from the new group—the ones who have been with me for fewer than three years. The original group, while small in comparison, still stands with me. Though I've been legally advised to not be involved with AMF at this time, the original group is currently in the midst of planning our next regional conference—it won't be in January, but I trust it will happen in time. The new group unfortunately believes the surface of this situation is its reality, even though a core group teaching they ostensibly believed a week ago is to not mistake the surface for truth." She looked away from me, toward the wall, and smiled about something. "People like to use the phrase 'innocent until proven guilty, but it's hard to find anyone who will stand behind it when the time comes. Humans love to believe in justice, but we find it so difficult to practice."

I somehow knew our time together was limited, that she might leave at any moment, and I wasn't about to let it slip away into a monologue. "Why didn't I have to pay membership dues?" I asked. It wasn't the question I cared about most, but it seemed most relevant.

"You had next to no income or savings of your own. It wouldn't have been right to charge you." She paused. "I also thought you had a better chance of putting the lessons to work in your life. You were so much younger than the rest."

"So you didn't charge me because you thought I'd benefit more?" I could see now how everything she said had small holes.

"People get charged by what they can afford and their stage of life."

"How do you know what people can afford?"

"Everyone had an intake survey when they joined. I don't ask questions about money directly, but I ask a series of questions that unveils a person's relationship with money."

"But I didn't have to take one."

"You told me everything I needed to know the first time we got coffee."

I thought back with embarrassment to the amount of trust I'd placed in Ada when all I knew of her was a ten-minute talk on a small stage in a strip-mall complex. The thought of it made my body tense up.

"I believe in distributing resources," she said. "I don't believe in wealth."

"If that's true, where did the money go?" I felt like a courtroom lawyer, trying to catch her in a lie.

She remained unfazed, almost emotionless. "I have a decent house. I have quality possessions. But I share the majority of my money with the world. I'm a philanthropist."

"Does that mean you donate money?"

"To those who need it, yes."

"But why even have all that money in the first place?" I asked, my voice getting louder. I didn't want to seem like I wasn't in control of myself—a few people had wandered in and were waiting on to-go drinks—so I tried to speak normally. But what came out was an almost-whisper. "It doesn't make sense to me. I mean, shouldn't everyone get to choose for themselves which charities their money goes to? Or if their money goes to charity at all? Wouldn't you have been even more of a philanthropist if you didn't charge anyone? AMF couldn't have cost that much to run, you could have easily got by on donations."

"It's a sad fact," she said, shaking her head, "but due to the system we live in, people tend to invest more energy into something they see as having monetary worth." She looked at me like I was supposed to figure out the rest. I stared back blankly.

"If I charged people only what it cost to operate," she said slowly, "they would have been less invested—they would have seen it as cheap, not worth their time. This is no different than what schools of higher education do. You think a university is just covering their overhead when a single graduate student pays $30,000 dollars for a year of school? The university is using this same philosophy. And making much more than AMF ever did, I might add."

I didn't want it to, but it made some sense. Maybe all those people wouldn't have cared so much if their money hadn't been on the line. I felt sideswiped by how broken everything was. I hated that this was reality, and I hated Ada for being able to see it and for having an excuse, a way out.

"But Rigby was living on a budget to be in AMF!" I yelled. I could see myself from the outside, losing my cool in a coffee shop, looking like some stereotypical image of a teen fighting with their cool, collected, seemingly reasonable mom. I wanted to tell everyone that she wasn't reasonable, wasn't innocent, wasn't my mom.

"Rigby is a perfect example of this idea," she responded. "He was born at the beginning of a world war, in the wake of the Great Depression. Even when people of his generation get to a point of financial comfort, they're still careful where their money goes. Anything they do put their money into, they make certain they get its full worth. So, because he pays for it, Rigby is one of our most dedicated members." She talked as if he was still a member, as if AMF as we knew it wasn't over. As if her trial was going to wrap up tomorrow afternoon and everyone was going to forgive and forget and her flock would be reunited. "He gets charged what he can afford. He's certainly charged less than Cynthia. He has humble means, he hopefully has many more years to live, he has a niece he's close to who could inherit what he has left when he passes. Cynthia is the exact opposite—she has nothing left but money."

She got as close to my face as she could without it seeming abnormal to anyone in the counter line that had built up alongside us. "Everything I did," she said, enunciating each word, "I did with her permission. There were some legal hoops I didn't jump through, but I didn't steal from her."

"But Cynthia wasn't really with it. How can you get permission from a person who's not doing okay?"

Her nostrils widened. "Did you know Cynthia?"

Suddenly it felt like I was the one on trial, the one with questions to answer.

"Well, no."

"I *know* Cynthia," she said, her voice unlike I'd ever heard it. "And when we made these deals, she was with it enough to know what she wanted."

There was nothing I could say to that. I felt like a small dog being intimidated by a big dog. Any idea I had of interrogating her, of catching her in a lie, seemed over. She saw it all as a competition—just like she saw everything else—and I was losing.

I wanted to ask her a hundred other questions: Why did AMF still call itself a memory organization if she wanted it to be something else? Why did she introduce me to Eleanor? Was that truly a special connection she orchestrated, or a way to manipulate how I saw her relationship to the seniors who followed her? Did she even like me, or was I just a little chess pawn she batted around her life-board for a month?

"How did we end up here—you and me?" I asked. "Why me?"

"It was random." She said it quickly, as if it was a clear, sensical question she'd been waiting for me to ask.

"Random?" I thought about all the kids at school that used this word for everything, even things that weren't random at all.

She leaned forward again, holding my eyeballs with hers. "Some things have deeper meaning and symbolic importance. Some things are orchestrated. Some things are random. This is one of those times when it's mostly random."

"So, what? This whole thing has been meaningless?"

"As humans, we make meaning everywhere we go. Our brains

make sure that nothing we do is ever meaningless. Do I think there's a reason our paths crossed? Of course. But the occurrences that followed that meeting happened because you and I were both making random decisions or assumptions, and outside forces interrupted our acquaintance just as it was beginning. Do I think there's a reason these events occurred simultaneously? I do not."

I felt my heart go fragile, but I tried not to let on. "But why did you give me all of this attention?"

"I saw that you didn't have many opportunities, and I knew I could offer them to you. I thought you getting invested in the organization would be good for your future. And I thought you could be an assistant—a protégé, perhaps. You needed someone to foster your development and sense of ambition because your parental figures weren't doing so."

I felt defensive—how could she say that when I'm here, already fostered, existing as a pretty okay person, at least most of the time? I stuffed the feeling down. "But why would giving me these opportunities also mean I needed to give up everything else?"

"Again, none of this was planned, Elly. It just happened. I didn't know Cynthia's family would falsely accuse me, I didn't know it would end up spiraling out like this. I got stressed and said some things I didn't intend to say. You didn't need to give up everything else, true." She paused, and when her voice came back it was more proper and filled with something sappy and weighted. "I simply don't believe it's noble to raise a child without access to opportunities."

I could finally see how fake she was now. I was done with it. "I mean, why not? Like, every movie and TV show is about well-off families and how messed up they make their kids—even though those kids have every opportunity—so is that more noble? You were raised with opportunities and you hate your parents."

She looked at me like I was a child. Which maybe I still was.

"And what do all the opportunities even do?" I said, my words coming out faster. "Do they make you a better person? Do they make you kinder, gentler, more caring? Don't they really just get traded in for some fun experiences most of the time—at best the beginning of skills for some future career, probably one working for some immoral corporation? Am I a worse person because I didn't go to horse camp, or take sailing lessons? I've been feeling like I've missed out and, sure, I have. But I also got to experience what it feels like to just hang out and be close with my family members and my best friend, and that wouldn't have happened if I was always going from opportunity to opportunity. Why should I be finding an internship, or working on my transcript? I'm 15. Just because you didn't have a childhood doesn't mean that's a generally good life path."

I could feel our time running out, could feel her getting ready to leave, could feel the eyes of everyone in this hallway of a coffee shop on me following my outburst.

Maybe I couldn't win our dog fight, but I could at least find out one more thing, something that had been nagging at me.

"You remember that first meeting I came to?" I asked.

"Of course," she answered, her tone lighter, softer, as if I hadn't just yelled at her, as if she hadn't just backed me into a corner a few minutes before. "How could I forget such a memorable occasion?"

"What was the chocolate thing about?" I asked.

She looked at me, blank.

"You know, that thing you asked everybody," I said. "About the last time they had chocolate. I thought it was going to be part of the philosophy or something, but I never heard anything about it again. I guess I've just always wondered what the deal was." I left out the fact that I'd bought dark chocolate for my mom in hopes of it helping.

She thought about it for a moment longer. "Oh. Yes, I think I remember now. Funny you held onto that. The chocolate statement was based on an idea from several shamanic societies."

This was definitely not what I was expecting her to say.

"Loosely-based, I should say. When the sick come to the healers, the healers ask three questions: *When was the last time you danced? When was the last time you sang? When was the last time you told your story?* These actions are powerful medicine that have been written off as frivolous by our culture, since they don't directly lead to the production of anything."

She let the words hang there for a while. I could feel their weight.

"The week before you came," she continued, "I told the group about this. I jokingly said that I was going to propose adding a fourth very important question to the list: 'When was the last time you ate chocolate?' Then I passed out dark chocolate squares."

"Wait, that's it?"

"That's it," she said. "It was just a joke."

"Just a joke?" I said, barely getting the words out.

"Yes, like many things in life."

I felt certain I was being made fun of by the universe. I'd been gullible enough to take a questionably culturally offensive joke seriously, but it wasn't about the chocolate thing—that was just the trigger for this bigger feeling. It was like some grand, cosmic joke. One that was definitely, in some way, on me.

"Why did you leave me in a field?" I said, now wanting to stand up for myself, show her I was done being ridiculed.

"Again, I was under a lot of pressure." She seemed to be stifling a yawn. "I was being investigated."

"That's no excuse. I trusted you. And what did you do with that? You blindfolded me, told me I was a failure, and left me."

"Look, now that I'm fully in this legal situation and not worried about its looming possibility, I'm no longer living in fear. Humans do things they wouldn't normally do when acting out of fear. And, if I'm to be completely honest with you, I had yet to test anyone's deeper sensory perception skills in this way. When you were unable to find the card, I saw your failure as my own—a failure of myself as a teacher. As a leader."

I stared at her.

"Clearly I rushed the process, and I didn't respond well when the outcome wasn't positive. I wasn't operating with a clear mind. But you came out of the experience with greater resolve; I can see it. I wish I could apologize, but why would I apologize for making you stronger?."

I couldn't believe I ever put any faith in this person. "Why didn't you help me cure my mom?" I said. "Like, at all."

"Elly," she said in a voice usually reserved for toddlers. "If you've learned anything from your time in AMF, I hope you've learned that cures aren't the goal."

"Bullshit," I said, surprising both of us. "A cure was *my* goal. It was my quest, actually. Now my mom's in the hospital. I wanted to make sure it never got to this point. And I really thought you could help me figure out something that would prevent this from ever happening.

But instead I'm here, still listening to you tell me what's *not* important. Or about the importance of forgetting. Which is crap. You know that, right? It's nice to know our brains filter some things out intentionally, but no one who comes to you benefits from that piece of information. It's not what they're looking for and not what you're claiming to be. Those who stay just get caught up in all the fun facts and the feeling of being part of a group."

"My messages are real: enjoy life, pay attention, don't get hung up on the past," she said, somehow sidestepping everything I'd just said. "I believe in these principles."

"Those aren't principles. They're just a list of good things."

Her face showed no emotion. "I'm sorry to hear that your mother's in the hospital. I hoped it wouldn't get to that point either. But there are things we can't control. There are bigger forces at play."

I imagined Greek gods and goddesses, hanging out on clouds, watching my life like it was a TV sitcom. That's when I knew I had to leave.

"Good luck in jail," I said, as I stood up and walked away.

The people in line watched me. A door opened. I walked through it. Then I got to the sidewalk and stopped.

I had come out of a dark room into an unlikely late-fall sun. The sun can be shocking in the Northwest. Sometimes a whole week can pass without it peeking out from behind the clouds, so when it finally makes an appearance it can seem confusing and new. I stood there and thought about how when you stare at the sun—the source of all life on earth—you temporarily go blind to everything else. Maybe there was an analogy there and maybe there wasn't.

I was going to face some future I didn't want to imagine. I crossed the parking lot to the bus stop, feeling like I was going to puke, and caught the 27 back to where I should have been all along.

Defining Okay

I don't mind the stuff that makes riding the bus seem so horrible to other people. I don't mind the guys who get in pointless arguments with drivers and other riders, the amount of sticky liquids that cover the floors, or standing for extended periods of time when it's crowded. I don't even mind the smell of pee with no identifiable source that makes you repeatedly wonder if you're sitting in it. Those are all part of the experience.

It's the times I'm not on the bus that I mind. At a bus stop, outside in the cold, not going anywhere. That's the worst.

And that's what I was doing. Not going anywhere. I'd walked past the transit center, trying to get as far away from Ada and Angela's as I could, and I hadn't stopped until I reached the final bus stop before leaving Vinton: an uncovered bench on the far end of downtown, before the town became a highway again.

I waited there, in my thin red cardigan, as the brief moment of sun turned into a light rain. But the kind of light rain that covertly soaks, leaving you feeling like a towel that has just dried someone off after a swim. By the time the bus came fifteen minutes later, I had advanced from towel to sponge and was cold enough for my brain to have shut off. It wasn't much warmer on the bus, so I sat in my seat with my body clenched, trying to gather heat. I stayed like that for the whole ride and the transfer back to the hospital.

I came into the room. There were no doctors, just my mom and my uncle. My mom looked more awake than I'd seen her all week, my uncle was sitting on the edge of the bed holding her hand. Neither were crying, but both were puffy-eyed. And I knew they knew. They'd received the diagnosis and it was bad. I could tell. It was all too much.

So I just let go of my body. I couldn't hold it up anymore.

I collapsed.

I hit my shoulder pretty hard on the floor. I heard my mom make a yelping sound and heard the words "faint" and "seizure," as I stared at the ceiling in a strange, sort-of-painful trance that wasn't either of those things. It was like it had been unintentional and intentional at the same time. I knew what was happening as it happened, I maybe could have even controlled myself enough not to fall, but now that I had fallen I couldn't respond or get up.

My uncle was in my ceiling view. "He's got his eyes open," he reported to my mom. "Can you hear me, Elly?" He sounded like someone speaking to a person with a hearing problem, or like how some people speak to people whose first language isn't English.

I gave something that approximated a nod.

"What happened?" he asked, quieter this time, almost whispering.

"I don't want to lose Mom," I said, actually whispering, still staring at the ceiling.

"I don't want to lose your mom, either," he said, even quieter. "I don't think we will."

"Is she dying?" I asked, unsure if the words had left my mouth or if I'd just made the lip motions without making any sound.

"No, not dying. She just needs help. Are you able to get off the floor?"

"I don't know."

"Can I help you?"

He gently grabbed my hands and pulled me to my feet. My mom had her brow compressed, her chin wrinkled. "Are you okay?" she asked.

"Yeah," I said. "My shoulder kinda hurts." I stood there, feeling my body. "Are you okay?"

"Depends how you define okay." Her voice was scratchy and low. She hadn't been talking much of late and it seemed difficult for her. "But I'm better than I thought I might be. If that makes sense."

"It doesn't."

She smiled. We still had the same sense of humor. "This is going to sound worse than it is, okay?"

"Okay."

"I have a brain tumor."

I almost semi-fainted again, but I curled my toes into the soles of my shoes, grasping the floor with all the toe strength I could muster.

"It's most likely benign, though," she said quickly. "So, not cancerous. But it's pushing on my brain tissue and crowding things in. And that crowding has been making a lot of things happen. It's why I've had outbursts of anger, why I had the seizure, why I'm sleeping so much, why I'm having headaches, why—"

"You've been forgetting?" I finished.

"It's likely why I've been forgetting."

"You're not going back to your birth position?"

"I don't know what that means, but I don't think I'm doing that."

A brain tumor was a real answer. And in some way it felt like such a relief to have a real answer. But it didn't seem like a good answer at all. "How..." I started to ask, but I couldn't think of a question that sounded intelligent. "How do we make it go away?"

Her face compressed and wrinkled again, but in a different way. "I get brain surgery," she said.

"Seriously?" I hadn't thought about how that was the obvious conclusion. "Mom, that's fucked up."

She gave me a brief Mom-glance. "It hopefully won't be," she said. "I'll just need to go through it and then have a long recovery time."

"So it *hopefully* won't be, but does that mean it might be?" I asked.

"Well." She looked to my uncle. His head was bobbing back and forth.

"There's a very low-percentage chance that things could go wrong," he said.

A few minutes ago it felt like I couldn't handle any information and now I wanted it all. I didn't want to be shielded from the truth. "Like what?"

"Why don't we not think about those parts?" he said. "With this type of tumor it's all about placement, and this one is in as good of a place as it can be. Maybe we should just focus on that for now?"

While that was nice to hear, it wasn't enough. "No. I want to know."

My uncle clearly couldn't do it, so my mom took back over. "So good tissue could get removed in the process. Evidently it's not always clear where the borders of the tumor begin and end. So I could have permanent problems with headaches. And memory. The tumor, or a new one, could also come back after this one's removed. So we'll just have to keep a very close watch on it."

"When's the surgery?" I asked.

"Tomorrow."

"Tomorrow?" After all the waiting—waiting for the problem to get better or worse, waiting for her to go to the doctor, waiting for the test results—this felt very sudden.

She could see the shock on my face. "I know," she said. "I feel the same way." She yawned a giant, long yawn and when she came out of it she looked exhausted. It was like all the talking had sapped her.

My uncle noticed it, looked at me, and started to get out of his chair. "We should probably head home and let your mom rest," he said.

"I'm not going home tonight," I said.

"We'll come back first thing in the morning."

"I'm not going home tonight," I repeated.

"But there's nowhere for you to sleep."

"I'll sleep in the chair."

He looked at Mom and they had a silent conversation of eye movements and facial furrows I couldn't understand.

"I'm staying here with Mom," I said.

They had another silent chat. "You're decided?" my uncle asked.

"I'm decided."

He gathered his stuff, I gave him a hug, and he left.

"You want me to read you something?" I asked my mom.

She was fading. "That would be nice."

There was no reading material in the room other than some medical paperwork, so I said, "How about I just tell a story?"

"A bedtime fairy tale, perhaps?" she asked, flashing a quick smile as she yawned.

"Alright, a fairy tale."

So I told her about a world where everyone was both real and not real, where everyone knew some things but never all things, where anyone could switch between moments of beauty to moments of supreme awfulness without warning, where both science and magic had their place but it was impossible to tell when to use one and not the other.

It was unclear when my mom went from listening with her eyes closed to being asleep, but eventually I stopped. I picked up the paperwork from the chair my uncle had been sitting in.

What my mom had was called a low-grade astrocytoma tumor. There were a lot of things on the paperwork my uncle hadn't mentioned. My mom had to take a capsule that somehow released a fluorescent dye into her brain. She might need radiotherapy or chemotherapy after the surgery. And each part of the process had its own list of potential side effects.

I wondered if this would all be different if she had just gone in earlier. If she had listened to me. If she hadn't lived in debt because of a system that was flawed. But I knew it was pointless to live in what-ifs. I unfolded a blanket that was laying on the foot of the bed, turned off the lamp, and tried to go to sleep. The chair was uncomfortable—ridiculously so—but I told myself I didn't care. For once, I was where I needed to be.

The Beginning of a New World

Here's what I think of when I think about brain surgery: freak accidents, lobotomies, the living dead, those bizarre self-trepanation cults whose members bore holes in their own skulls to achieve bliss, my mom, my mom.

I felt like I had just closed my eyes when a nurse I'd never seen tapped my shoulder and told me it was time to move to the waiting room. The room was brighter than any room needed to be. My mom was getting helped into a wheelchair. I panicked. "Where are you taking her?" I shouted in a poorly working, creaky morning voice. Everyone stopped what they were doing, too shocked to be amused by how silly I probably sounded.

My mom was the first to speak. "It's okay, Elly," she said, weakly lifting her arms into the vague shape of my body. I walked over and got inside.

"I know it's scary," she said, "but we have to trust that the surgeons know what they're doing. They do this every day." Her voice was calm, almost serene. It was soothing, but also seemed like the type of calm people have in movies when they've accepted death.

I thought about how the more you do something the better you get. But eventually you get so good that you think you can't mess up, and that's when you start to make stupid mistakes. I chose not to bring this up. "I'll try to believe that," I said.

"I love you, El," she said, using her nickname for me from when I was a kid. I hadn't heard it in years.

"I love you too, Mo," I said. She smiled and made a little half-laugh sound with her nose as they wheeled her away.

The nurse I'd never seen led me out, and there was my uncle sitting there all by himself. He raised his arm in an "over here" way, like he was in a crowd and I wouldn't see him otherwise. I couldn't decide if the fact that my family made jokes at this moment meant we were coping or disturbed.

I sat down next to him and he handed me a to-go cup. "Coffee?" he offered.

"Thanks. Why weren't you in there?" I asked.

"I was, but you just slept through the commotion. Your mom sent me out to get coffee. She thought you might need it."

"She was right. I do need it."

I soon questioned this need, though, because with every sip my internal worries became a little more elaborate and probably further from reality. My uncle and I passed the time nervously picking magazines up and putting them down, looking out the window, taking turns going to the bathroom. I walked to get us more coffee, nervously drank most of mine on my walk back, and by the time the head nurse approached us I was so caffeinated I thought my eyeballs were abnormally bulging out of their sockets, pushing against the confines of my skull.

"Are you the family of Susana Fox?" she asked. There was still no one else in the waiting room.

"That's us," my uncle said, his voice shaking in a way only I could hear. I held my breath.

"The procedure is done, and it seems to have gone fine," she said. "The doctor will of course need to do some follow-up tests over the next couple days, but there were no complications. She's just beginning to come to, so I'll come get you as soon as she's fully awake and the doctor's ready to speak with you."

We watched her walk away.

"Did you expect good news?" I asked.

"I never expect good news," he said.

"Really, you're a pessimist? I never knew."

"I try to keep it a secret."

We sat in silence. One that was actually peaceful until we got called back to the room, and the moment ended. My mom's head was shaved and a pile of bandages and gauze covered the right side of it. I gasped under my breath. My uncle put his hand on my shoulder. She didn't seem to notice that we'd entered the room.

"She's still very medicated," the nurse said. "You can talk to her, but she may not be especially responsive. It's normal, though."

I imagined a world where this was normal, where this was my daily reality. People's moms and dads and brothers and sisters and best friends recovering from their heads getting opened up.

"How are you feeling, Mom?" I asked, speaking louder than was probably right or necessary.

She turned her head slowly and stared at me for a while before any hint of recognition showed. I swallowed hard. "I think...pretty odd," she said. "I think I feel...odd."

If I hadn't been worried about my mom being a post-brain surgery zombie, it would have been funny. It was like speaking to someone in another dimension.

Soon after, the surgeon came in and proceeded to tell us everything new we had to worry about. Even though he wasn't worried about major memory loss or change in personality, there could be little details that had gotten lost or would now be more difficult for her to recall. She would have headaches for the next month and might have them for the rest of her life. And then there was the possibility of relapse. That's what we had to really worry about. A tumor could grow back. At any time. When he got done and asked us if we had any questions, I wanted to ask him why he couldn't have just let us be happy for a little bit longer.

He left and my uncle and I looked at each other, trying to come to terms with this new world where Mom was okay but could be not okay at any moment.

Hotcakes

I spent the next week between the hospital and our apartment. My uncle picked up a pile of homework from my teachers. They probably told him about the days I skipped, but he didn't bring it up. Or maybe he knew all along and never said anything. I really couldn't tell if he was letting me off the hook or completely oblivious, but either way I was grateful for it.

My mom was trying not to take any of the serious painkillers so she wouldn't be loopy, but seemed to be going in and out of pain spells because of it. She slept as much as she had before the surgery, maybe more.

When I wasn't sitting by her hospital bed or doing more homework than I'd ever done at one time, I mimicked my mom. I slept for 10 or 11 hours a night. Then during the day I'd take at least a couple naps. I lost track of dates and days of the week. It felt like I was recovering from my own surgery, the removal of something.

My only contact with the outside world was emailing with Claudia. I told her what had happened—Mom's surgery, Ada and the field, Ada and the jail, basically everything. They were stupidly long emails that would have made more sense as phone calls, but at a certain point it would have felt awkward to switch.

Claudia told me what was going on at school, but she didn't mention Maddy and I didn't ask. Time kept moving forward, Halloween came and went without me noticing, and it had suddenly been eleven days since I'd talked to Maddy, which felt like a different kind of scary than any of the scarinesses I'd held for my mom—the idea that my best friend would go on living the same as before but would no longer be in my life.

One day, I spent a few hours at the Original Hotcake House, an all-night restaurant with an old-timey sign in a funny little oblong building two blocks away from our apartment. When we tell people where we live, everyone says, "Oh, by the Hotcake House," and we'll say yes excitedly, as if we were regulars. But my family and I have gone exactly once, when I was nine years old. There's just something about it being right there that makes it harder to actually go than if we lived farther away. Like, on Saturday nights we can hear the parties and fights that break out in the parking lot from our back window and sometimes there are splashes of puke and broken car-window glass when I walk by it on my way to the bus. So it's like it's our charming-but-screwed-up neighbor we feel tenderly about but never want to hang out with.

But for some reason, the whole relationship had recently gotten to me. Like, if I really wanted to have experiences, why didn't I go to the places in my very own neighborhood? Why haven't I seen a show at the Aladdin Theater? Why didn't I stop in at the bookstore that was mostly dusty mass-market paperbacks, used VHS tapes, and old issues of *Playboy*? Places like these are experiences, and I should probably appreciate how weird they are more often.

So I went to the Hotcake House around sundown, ordered a big plate of blueberry pancakes and a cup of coffee, and sat with my book in a mini side booth, reading and watching. I don't know if I saw anything that special, but maybe I had an experience.

When I got home, I pulled my laptop out and wrote Rigby an email. Over the course of the day I'd drafted an email that was long and winding in my head, but when I sat down to write it all of the winding-ness felt unnecessary.

Rigby,
I just want to know how bad or dumb I should feel about Ada and AMF. How do you feel?
Yours,
Elly

After a while, he wrote back.

Elly,
I was introduced to Ada as a genius. My friend Martha told me about the group and said it was led by a "true genius." As you might

know by now, I've lived in Vinton all my life, never went to college, never married. I guess you could say I'm a little sheltered. So I thought "well, I've never met one of those before," and I went. I had the idea that people like that were overwhelmed by thoughts and maybe didn't always make sense to us of average intelligence. And Ada was that. The first time I had coffee with her, she talked about a brain study one minute and invisible lines of energy that run through the globe the next. So she fit my expected image in a way, which I suppose made it easier to get involved in the group.

The group did change at some point. It was gradual, so I didn't really notice. In some ways the fact that I'd had that coffee with her after my first meeting and she'd talked about the more mystical "perception" side of things made the change seem more natural to me than others who had joined earlier. It took other people telling me that the group was once all about combating memory loss with awareness exercises to even realize it was changing.

During my years in AMF, it never really mattered to me what I believed in or didn't believe in, because it was all interesting and it excited my brain just to know there were all these ideas out in the world. Now I can see the possibility that all those ideas, handed out all at once, in such a quickfire way, was a technique to pull the wool over our eyes. And if it was, it worked perfectly on me, but I still like to think there was some sincerity in there. I want to believe that she believed it all.

I've always heard the phrase "power corrupts" and perhaps that's what I believe here: Ada got some bad ideas once she reached a certain number of followers, or financial position, and the brain chemical release of it all hooked her. If that's true, I guess I'm unsure how to feel about her. Should I blame the drug of power, or should I blame the addict of power? I don't know. It seems like people can't figure that question out even when it comes to actual drugs, so I imagine it's even harder to figure out when the addiction is a concept.

The timing of your email is remarkable (I'm still a little stunned by it, in fact), because it just so happens that a small group of us former AMF members are going to Three Rivers Diner tomorrow morning. Would you like to spend another Sunday morning with the old gang?

Best,

Rigby

I'm not sure what they wanted from the day, but I knew I wanted it too. Maybe going would help me stop feeling so dumb, so internally angry. So I said I'd be there.

So We Meet Again

For the first time, I got permission before going to Vinton. As soon as I emailed Rigby back, I walked out to the living room where Uncle was on his couch, among his book stacks. I told him it was pie and coffee and not an official meeting, and he took his time responding, seemingly weighing a lifetime of rule-following against the past month-and-a-half, but finally said okay. Then I texted my mom, telling her the group had ended—even though Uncle almost certainly had already let her know—and that we just wanted to get together. She texted back and said *Sure, just tell me where it takes your mind*, and I said I would.

I hadn't gone anywhere since before the surgery, so the night before I tried on outfits for much too long, finally landing on the simple outfit I started with—a yellow cardigan and a pair of gray pants. I went to bed at nine o'clock, hours before I usually go to sleep, attempting to be properly rested and responsible, but ended up stuck in my head deep into the night. I thought about Eleanor and what she thought about all this. Did her heart break when she found out, or could she see this in some wise way I couldn't? I thought about Ada and AMF and what it all meant, if it meant anything. I woke up exhausted.

When I got to Three Rivers, everyone was already there.

"Oh good, you made it!" a woman I recognized but didn't actually know said. "We weren't sure if you were coming,"

I'd said I was coming and I was on time, so I didn't know what there was to be unsure about. "Well, here I am," I said, trying to sound as cheery as possible. I looked around the table and realized that, other than Rigby, I didn't know a single person's name. The only one I'd even had a partial conversation with was the lady who talked to me on my very first day; now here we were six weeks later and I still didn't know who she was. In my head I'd been part of this group, but maybe I'd just shown up for it without really joining.

"We were just talking about what we're going to do now," Rigby said.

I wondered if this meant they were starting a new group. I didn't know if I was ready for that.

A frail woman answered my silent question in her shaky voice. "What we'll do now that the mind control has been broken."

"Mind control?" I asked. Though Maddy had forced me to consider this possibility, I was surprised to hear it announced so matter-of-factly.

"How else do you explain how we could all be fooled by such a con artist?" a guy with chaotic eyebrows responded. "It's obvious. We're not stupid people. We knew she was powerful, but we believed her power to be something other than what it was. She wasn't helping our memories, she was controlling our minds."

"I mean, I'm pretty angry with Ada too, but I think there could be other explanations," I said.

"Did you get your bank account drained?" a loud man in a cardigan similar to my own asked.

"No," I said. "Did you?" I was just curious, but it came out sounding like an accusation.

He seemed caught off guard. "Well, no." A silence briefly spread across the table before he said, "But Cynthia did!" And everyone murmured in some type of agreement.

I looked around at the group and tried to figure out what that strange hush had meant. I couldn't be certain, but I had the feeling that no one else got their bank account drained. Which maybe didn't change much—it still wouldn't make what Ada did right. But it would mean that none of the people at the table were completely broke because of her. They had just been deceived, paid too much for a flawed product, and got their feelings hurt.

As if he was reading my mind, Rigby said, "I also think there are a lot of possible explanations for what happened. And a lot of reasons to be upset. But for me, it's mostly a trust issue. We put our trust in her and the organization. That trust was betrayed."

For a moment, everyone turned tender and soft, saying how they didn't want to go through life questioning other people, wondering what other intentions people were hiding, how we just wanted community, something to direct our hope toward. I briefly felt my knot of complex feelings untangling inside my gut or maybe my heart or my soul.

Then, the woman from my first meeting turned to me. "Elly, you mentioned being angry earlier. Do you want to talk about that?"

I didn't really want to talk about it, but I had said I was angry and I felt I had to back it up with something. So I picked the only thing I thought would make any sense.

"Well, I joined the group to help my mom." I paused. "She was losing her memory." Some of the ladies made frowny faces; the guys nodded, their heads down. "And I guess I felt kind of betrayed because instead of helping me she just told me I should stop caring about my mom. Maybe disown her? I'm not totally clear on the recommendation now, to be honest, but it was definitely the exact opposite of what I told her I wanted and that just felt wrong."

Before the last word left my mouth, I knew the table was no longer tender. The chaotic eyebrows guy said she should be charged with elder fraud *and* child fraud. Then the loud guy said he wanted to punch Ada in the face and, even though not everyone supported the punching, the conversation devolved into Ada's horribleness, like she was a mythological beast rather than a human woman. I knew my story had started this and they probably thought this was what I wanted, but it all just felt so ugly.

I knew I could have easily kept fueling the fire. I could have told them about the field, the coffee shop, the questionable moments from my internship, my mom's brain surgery. I could have told them about the money she didn't charge me, or the unreasonable amount of hope I'd invested in her.

But I also could have told them how, without Ada's perspective, I wouldn't have considered how the past can get in the way of the present. Wouldn't have thought about the ways forgetting can be interesting instead of scary. Wouldn't have called Rigby brilliant. And I wouldn't have understood how so many people look at life as a competition— wouldn't have seen how short-sighted that is, how sad that is.

There was so much I could have said. And I wanted to say it all. Some of the words even started to leave my mouth a time or two, before louder voices drowned them out.

So I just kept listening and thinking about how this whole conversation came down to the fact that no one wanted to feel stupid. And everyone wanted to be able to believe in people. Part of me was like everyone in this room: I was hurt and I felt stupid. But the other part of me knew it was at least a little more complicated than how they were talking about it. Like, even though I felt messed up by all that had happened, I was glad I could now talk about how memory works and how the brain works and could at least entertain far-out ideas about how we can perceive the world beyond our five senses. Those things made the world feel bigger in a good way—less defined, more open to possibility.

Ada's "teachings" were most likely just everything she'd ever thought was interesting; I could see that now. They weren't coherent or processed or new. It was just a bunch of big ideas thrown together. But I learned from that mess of ideas, and I was still somehow glad I had been a part of all of this, even if it was ultimately some sort of scam. I knew the whole experience wasn't pointless, but everyone else seemed to want to pretend it was. No one was figuring out what to do next; they were all wallowing in a past they couldn't fix. It seemed like everyone wanted to believe we were the victims of elaborate mind control, rather than followers of a manipulative woman who had just enough actual knowledge to get us on board.

When everybody was ready to go, I'd been turning all this stuff over in my head and not saying anything for so long that it was hard to imagine opening my mouth. People were putting on their jackets, paying for their peach pie and drip coffees and Lipton teas with exact change, about to gravitate toward the door. I was missing my chance.

"Hey!" I said, much louder than I intended.

Everybody turned, looking surprised.

I lowered my voice and said, "This just all sounds a little extreme."

No one said anything, but some of the ladies gave me a look that I think meant they were taking pity on me for being so naive. "Look, I put my faith in Ada, too, and she let me down. But maybe everyone is a mix of good and bad things, you know? Like, aren't we all just figuring it out all the time? No matter what age we are? I don't think there are any all-good heroes or all-bad villains. There are just people."

I noticed the eyebrows guy checking his watch. A few people just kept putting on their jackets and digging through their wallets and purses like I wasn't talking at all.

"I'm not saying we should let people off the hook for being jerks, but maybe we can still learn from them. Like, there's still good things we can pull out and use, you know? The ideas are ideas, they're not hers."

I wasn't sure if I was making any sense. Those who were listening were staring at me blankly. "Even Mother Teresa probably did something bad at some point." I seemed to be implying that Ada was like Mother Teresa, which wasn't at all what I wanted to do. This wasn't going well.

I knew Rigby was standing with his little tan Member's Only jacket on, listening to every word, but I couldn't look at him. He'd invited me, and I was making a scene. But I couldn't stop.

"Nobody's perfect, but still we want to believe there are these superhuman saintly people who can do no wrong. But I think we'll always be let down if we keep believing that. Because humans are always going to mess up. I've messed up a bunch lately, and all I want is to be forgiven because I'm not a bad person. So I'm going to start by forgiving people who have messed up. I'm going to forgive Ada, because I think inside she's probably a pretty sad and confused person."

I wiped my face. At some point I'd started crying, yet again, without realizing it. I turned to Rigby. He looked serious but maybe not mad.

"You know, I think you're right," he said, speaking quieter than I'd ever heard him. He didn't say what I was right about and I didn't ask. Everyone stood behind their chairs with their jackets on, fidgeting a little. This wasn't going to be some tender moment where we all came together. It was going to continue being awkward.

"I'm gonna head out," I announced. I gave Rigby a little nod, and I left.

Attempts at Life

I got off the bus and walked into the wind, which sent my hair flying in a variety of directions. I went through the automatic doors of the hospital and tried in vain to smooth it down from its windblown heights while in the elevator. I walked into my mom's room, expecting to see her asleep, but instead found her sitting up and flipping through a magazine in bed.

"Whoa, what's the occasion?" I asked.

She flashed a little smirk. "Does it look like a wild time in here?"

"Yeah, I mean, settle down. You're still recovering."

"Okay, thanks for the reminder. I'll relax," she said, casually tossing her magazine to the floor.

Wide-eyed, I flashed my own smirk. "What's gotten into you? Are you on new meds or what?"

"No new meds." She looked at me, her eyes shiny with excitement. "But they did tell me I'll probably get discharged tomorrow. So I can finally go home."

"Oh, well that is cause for celebration."

"Everything they're doing for me here will have to keep happening at the apartment, so it'll be an adjustment. But I'll be so happy to get out of here."

"I bet you hate doctors and hospitals even more after this."

"It's a bit strange to say, given that I just had brain surgery, but the medical world actually doesn't seem as intimidating as it used to."

"Well, I had nothing against them before this," I said, "but now I think I hate them. So that's even stranger."

She smiled. "Don't get me wrong, I still don't like them. But I'm not scared of them anymore."

"That's a big deal, huh?" I felt like a little kid asking that question, but I didn't know how else to ask it.

"It is a big deal. A bit life-changing, really," she said. "We'll see if I still feel that way when I get billed for whatever insurance doesn't cover, but for the time being I'm just happy it's over. How'd it go in Vinton?"

"I gave a lecture to a bunch of people way older than me."

Her face showed no reaction. "And how was that?"

"Most of them didn't really listen."

"So, not good?"

"I probably shouldn't have done it—you know, they have been around like five times longer than me, I could have shown a little more respect. But they were being kind of ridiculous. It's like they couldn't see anything other than what made their hurt feelings more valid. You know what I mean?"

She nodded, though I couldn't tell if she was actually agreeing or not. "But you could see past your hurt feelings?"

"I think so," I said, now unsure.

She looked off, as if the answer was somewhere in the room. I wondered if I'd gotten my staring-off-while-talking habit from her. "Maybe they had less to fall back on," she finally said.

"How do you mean?"

"Well, you have close friends, family, school, a job, an unwritten future. And they might not have any of that. Maybe the group was all of that to them. Maybe it was their future."

I didn't know what my face was doing, but I must have looked defensive because she quickly added, "I'm not saying their feelings were hurt more than yours. But they just might have lost more from the situation."

A part of me wanted to argue against her. I no longer had my best friend, hadn't seen Claudia or gone to school or my so-called job in weeks, and my family basically lived in this hospital room. But through it all, I'd been able to hold onto the possibility that things would change. I tried to imagine AMF being my only thing, and how I would feel if there was no possibility it would ever come back.

"You might be right," I said.

"Come here." She patted the bed.

I got up on the bed's back corner, keeping my arms at my sides, and just let her hold me. It felt good. Mildly embarrassing, but good.

212

"It's almost your birthday," I said, briefly remembering—without meaning to—that her birthday was the same day as Ada's preliminary hearing.

"That's going to be some birthday party, huh? The birthday girl with a bandaged head, either on pills or having debilitating headaches. I couldn't have imagined looking like this on my 38th birthday. Maybe my 78th birthday, but my 38th?"

"You know what they say, 38 is the new 78."

"And 15 is the new 50."

"So true. They do say that." I stretched and my joints cracked on cue.

"I've always thought I was doing pretty good for my age," she said. "But a craniotomy really slows a person down. I guess now that my head is shaved no one can tell I'm going gray. Maybe I'll keep it like this. How do I look?" She pretended to fluff her bandages.

"Yeah, not everybody can pull it off, but you're really rocking it."

A nurse walked in and announced that it was time for some meds. She didn't seem to notice I was on the bed, she just got on the computer and started typing wildly.

"Well, looks like the party is over," my mom said.

I left and walked around the hospital. I wasn't hungry, but I looked at the food in the cafeteria. I looked at the gifts in the gift shop, the menu board behind the coffee stand. I took the elevator to various floors and walked around, trying to go unnoticed.

There's a guy who wrote a page-turning book where nothing much happens. In it, a whole bunch of characters who live in a small Midwestern town all just go about their daily business. They do their routine, they buy and sell things, have disagreements, make and lose friends, have relationships, often mess up. Against this really simple backdrop, it becomes obvious that all humans need to have something to do, something to keep them busy. And people screw up all the time because we're all just improvising. Anytime we go out into the world, we're going to see or meet somebody trying something out, and our responses are just going to be an attempt to make sense of it. The way we respond is almost never planned; we're all just trying and seeing what happens.

Premeditated Fun

I walked around for longer than I'd planned. When I got back to the room, my mom was asleep and my uncle had appeared, reading in the chair next to the bed. He looked up from his book. His eyes hung down in a way that only happens, I've learned, from working while other people are asleep.

"Long night at work?" I asked.

"It was a double. I think I put in fourteen hours today. I'll probably do another ten tomorrow." He leaned his head back and rested it on the wall, looking up at the ceiling.

"Is this extra work for Mom?" I whispered it, even though I knew she couldn't hear me.

"I feel like our house might need some extra money," he said, talking to the ceiling.

"Maybe I can help you build a blanket-fort room?"

"It might be time. But I'll need some help; I haven't worked construction since I was a teen." He smiled and motioned his head toward the hallway. "Where are you getting back from?"

"I was just wandering around the hospital."

"See anything interesting?"

"I saw some premeditated fun."

"Premeditated fun?"

"There were some people who had gone to visit a little kid with his leg in a cast, and they had decided their visit was going to be fun. There were balloons and everyone was acting goofy, but you could tell the kid totally knew it was insincere."

"So that's different from other kinds of fun?"

"I just don't think you can decide when fun is going to happen. Like as soon as you say 'this is going to be fun,' you've jinxed it and it's definitely not going to be fun."

He looked at me like I'd just recited a poem in Old English or something—somewhat confused but also vaguely impressed.

"So if I understand you correctly, you're hinting that you'd like to plan something fun tonight," he said.

"You understand me so well."

"Great, I've got just the thing," he said.

"Driving home to NPR?" I asked.

"You understand me so well."

On the ride home, I thought about the small-town book and how often the characters would ride around in trucks, just for something to do. I wondered how much you'd have to ride in trucks before you found deeper meaning in it. Like how they say you can become a master of a craft if you practice it for ten thousand hours. I wondered how many hours of practice it takes to find meaning in something simple.

Peace Talk

The next day, I got a text from a number I didn't know. *Hey, I got your # from Maddy a while back. It's Rain. Wanna get coffee?*

I wanted to say no, but I felt like I needed to go through with it for Maddy. She'd given Rain my number, and if Rain was my only connection to Maddy right now, I had to accept that. Maybe it was even a test Maddy was giving me—I doubted it, but I still felt I needed to do the uncomfortable thing regardless.

So a few hours later I was looking at the same bad psychedelic art at the same 24-hour coffee shop where a couple months ago Rain made fun of me for putting a dorky sign in my window. This time she was sitting across from me, though, not looming over me. And she didn't give off the feeling that she was here to harass me.

She looked like the not-gross-but-equally-boring American Apparel ads—a black stretchy shirt tucked into tight blue jeans. I didn't know how we had ever been friends. We sat for a minute fake-sipping our too-hot-to-drink coffees before she asked, "You're like home-schooled now or something?"

"Just on a leave of absence," I said.

"I see. So you'll be back?"

I nodded.

"You had some family shit?"

"Something like that."

I think she saw that I wasn't up for small-talk, because her tone suddenly changed. "Hey, I know this is weird. I don't mean to be all serious like this, but I just feel kinda nuts and I thought that I should talk to you."

"Okay, I feel like I'm missing some piece of information here—did something happen?"

"Maddy told me you think I'm a horrid person." She said it quickly, like the sentence was all one word.

"That's a surprise?"

"I don't know. Maybe. No one has ever said something like that about me. I get that we don't like each other, but that doesn't mean I'm fucking horrid."

"I mean, it isn't that we 'don't like each other.' You've made it clear you basically hate me. I wouldn't have a problem with you if you just left me alone."

"Whatever, I just give you shit. It's all because you get away with whatever you want."

"I'm not getting away with anything."

"You do, and it's super frustrating. You know I can't do what you do, right?" she asked.

It felt like she was talking about somebody else. "Do what?"

"I can't be weird and have it be okay," she said. "Even if I left the house without makeup on people would ask me if I was fucking sick. But you confidently wear sloppy-ass bobby pins in your hair and old-lady glasses and maybe some jocks call you a queer, but ultimately it's okay. Nobody ostracizes you. Nobody kicks your ass. People actually seem to respect you more because you don't give a fuck. But I can't not give a fuck. It's not fair. I guess I've always kinda envied you—in a hate-watch way, of course, but still. I wish I could get away with what you get away with."

"But what exactly do I get away with?"

"Looking like you look and acting like you act, then being confident about it. And then, having that be taken seriously by other people. I don't care whether you think you're a dude or not, because obviously you were raised as one—no girl comes out with that confidence without having some serious issues underneath it."

"You don't think I have issues?"

"No, I really don't."

She was so sincere. Yet she knew I was on leave for "family shit," knew I didn't have a dad—and since everyone seems to think that not having a dad really messes boys up, I figured she'd at least imagine I had *some* issues.

I wanted to yell at her and tell her she was dumb and wrong and judgmental, but then I wondered if maybe she was right. I could check off a bunch of "it's a weird deal" stuff: dead dad, uncle on couch, no grandparents, a mom who ran away from home, existing as some kind of nonsexual being in a world of sexual beings. But I hadn't really felt scarred by any of it before whatever the recent months might have done to me. My family loved me and didn't have a problem showing it, I'd never gone hungry, I'd never experienced abuse, I casually enjoyed the benefits of male privilege without even noticing it most of the time, I'd even somehow avoided ever getting beaten up.

"Well, I have issues now," I finally said. "And maybe it's the first time, I don't know, but it's really hard. I was mostly confident before all this, and I can see how that can be annoying, but you've always been the thing that makes me feel stupid about being positive and trying to like myself. Maybe it's been a good thing—maybe I actually need you to question things I'd otherwise avoid questioning—but it still makes you my bully."

She looked at me in a way she'd never looked at me. Her eyes were doing this thing that made it seem like her jaw was hanging open, even though it wasn't. "*I'm* your bully?"

"One hundred percent."

"Not any of the bros that call you names in the halls?"

"I don't care about them in the least."

"But me?"

"I'm actually shocked you don't see it, but yes: you. You're the only one who says things that are real. I mean, what did you think you were doing?"

"I was just fucking with you."

"And how's that different from bullying?"

"We're the same size, you're a guy—there's no real threat behind it. They're just words."

"Sure, but the words made it so I could never relax; I always had to be on guard if you were around. They made me anxious and self-conscious and just feel generally crappy about myself, for years now."

She didn't say anything, so we just sat there looking at the ceiling or the floor. Occasionally somebody from school would walk by our table with a gym bag over their shoulder or an instrument by their side, but mostly it was just us, sitting alone, not saying anything. I was thinking about how my life had become filled with more uncomfortable silences in the past few months than in all the years that had come before when she said, "Well, sorry."

I never thought I'd hear that from her, but I didn't want to give her too much credit. "Thanks," I said. "Also, I've never worked out a day in my life. You were doing Tae Bo with your mom when we were in elementary school; you totally could kick my ass if you wanted to."

She smiled. "I can't believe you remember how obsessed I got with Tae Bo."

"It was memorable." Against my better judgment, I smiled too.

"We had some good times back then, right?" she said. "Mr. Youngren's class?"

"We did have some good times." Though I'd pushed most of those good times out of my head in the years since then, it was true: our friendship had sometimes been a pretty normal fourth-grade friendship.

"Friends again?" she asked.

"Probably not." We both laughed. "Maybe let's just call it 'not-enemies'?"

"Okay, that seems less drastic." Then she got up and stuck out her hand. I looked at it—*who shakes hands anymore?* I wondered—and eventually shook it.

"Not-enemies," we said, kind of in unison and kind of not.

A Symbol Meaning Happiness

I got home, flopped on my bed, and opened my laptop. My brain couldn't fully process that my first social interaction with someone my own age in two weeks was with Rain Mallory. Even though it had gone mostly well, I felt an overwhelming desire to shut off.

I have a couple of social media accounts—not to post things and show my life off, but just to follow people and stare into these other worlds when I need to escape my own. They aren't real other worlds, but symbols for other worlds. I don't really believe the rose-shaped foam on someone's latte means that person is happy, but it is a symbol for an idea of happiness. It's as if, by posting it, that person is saying, "Hey, I'd really like to be happy." And maybe at the same time asking, "How close does it seem I am?" and then when I give it a heart I am saying, "Pretty close, pretty close. Keep doing what you're doing."

After a sufficient amount of world-escaping and heart-giving, I decided I needed to reach out to Maddy. The talk with Rain had loosened something up inside of me. It wasn't that I felt less fear about potentially losing Maddy, but I just felt like I couldn't keep letting things go unsaid. Given the time I'd let pass, it felt wrong to call or text her—those options seemed both too pushy and too vulnerable. So I started writing her an email.

I'd only ever emailed her funny stuff from the internet, but I tried to channel Rigby. *Be open and unembarrassed*, I keep telling myself. Eventually I settled on something I felt okay about.

Maddy,
Today has been exactly two weeks since the last time we talked, but it feels like two months, two years, and two million light years all at once. I screwed up, and I'm sorry. If you ever want to talk and work

through some of my many wrongs, name the spot and I'll be there.
  Your friend (hopefully still),
  Elly

A few hours passed; it got dark with no response from Maddy. I felt hopeless. I thought about how when my mom was my age, if she had a friend she'd hurt but didn't want to call because calling didn't feel right, she would have had to write a letter and not expect to get a response for days. Why did I feel like I needed a response within a few hours? I should be more patient, I told myself.

Just when I'd come to some sort of half-hearted acceptance of patience, she responded. Just a single line: *Want to come over now?* I looked at the time—9 pm—and emailed back: *I'll start walking.*

One of Many Ways

When I got to Maddy's, she met me at the door. She moved in place slightly, scratching the back of her head, shifting her weight from one leg to the other and back again. Not like she was tired or had to pee, but like she was one of those people who had to work out in some small way all the time so had invented weird exercises for muscles no one else knew existed. I watched her and couldn't help but smile.

She walked to her room and I followed. My eyes went to our collage, like my eyes always do, and I felt overwhelmed by nostalgia, a simpler time before all of this when we could be carefree friends and nothing had ever come between us. My head felt like a bundle of firing synapses.

"I'm sorry I got mad about the whole Rain thing," I said, even though it wasn't what I meant to start with. "I feel so dumb now. Even if you were dating her, it should have still been okay. I just had a difficult time adjusting to the fact that you were suddenly friends with her."

"Thanks, it's good to hear you say that." She paused and I felt her tone change. "Hey, sorry to hear about your friend going to jail."

"How did you know about that?"

"I read it in the paper."

"You read the paper?"

"I mean, usually just the front page. I don't know, it's something I do with my parents." She looked embarrassed. This also made me smile.

"Yeah, things have been nuts," I said.

"So is the quest over then? Or do you have more people to learn stuff from?"

"I guess I don't know if it was even ever a quest," I said. "I just kept going to Vinton."

She nodded confidently, but I think she knew she was missing some part of this equation. "How's your mom?" she asked hesitantly.

"She had brain surgery, but otherwise she's doing pretty good."

Her eyes seemed to bloom. "What?" she asked, cocking her head to get the angle right. "Are you being serious?"

"Yeah. Like I said, things have been nuts."

She started to open her mouth to ask more questions, but I knew this wasn't the order I wanted things to go in.

"Maddy, I'm really sorry I flipped out on you. You should be able to hang out with who you want, or at least I should be able to give you a real reason if I think you shouldn't be friends with someone."

"There's a real reason?"

"Rain's actually the only person who has ever truly bullied me. And she's been doing it for most of my life."

"For real? I didn't know you could be bullied."

"I didn't want you to know."

"I mean, that's pretty crucial information. I just thought Rain was mean in a funny way, but it's not impossible for me to imagine her being mean in an unfunny way. Seriously, you really should have told me. I would have believed you."

"I know." I thought about how we always made fun of shows and movies for creating drama over just one little thing that went unsaid. "Isn't it weird how much just boils down to one person not giving the other person the information they need?"

"It is weird. Like, that's every sitcom plot line ever, right? I can't believe we fell into such a classic trap."

"Do you forgive me for being a jerk and not telling you why?"

She laughed. "Yeah, totally. I forgive you."

"Thanks." I looked at her. I didn't know it until that moment, but I wanted something more. I wanted to know that, if this happened again, I wouldn't lose her.

"Maddy, do you love me?" I blurted out.

"Whoa." The features of her face froze. I'd freaked her out.

"Like family," I said. "You know, like we'll-always-be-friends-no-matter-what kind of love."

"Oh. Well, hell yeah, of course."

"Can you tell me, though?" I didn't know why I was asking this—

it felt like someone else speaking through my body—but my insides were gooey and desperate and seemingly in control of my voice.

"That might be a little much."

"I get that, but I'm kind of flailing here. My mom just had brain surgery, my former mentor is in jail, and everything I've learned over the last few months is supposedly a lie. It seems like I'm not very good at judging the importance or meaning of the things in my life, and I need to know if I'm blowing our friendship out of proportion or if we're in the same boat. Maddy, I love you like nobody's business."

She took a deep breath, tried to look me in the eyes, but settled on some point just to the side of my face and said, "I love you, Elly. You're the coolest."

I unexpectedly felt the sudden desire to lean in and kiss her on the cheek. It was overwhelming and like nothing I'd ever experienced. My own cheeks unexplainably tightened, my whole face seemingly focusing all their energy toward my lips. *Do it*, my brain said, *do it before you think about it a moment longer.*

But I thought about it a moment longer. The feeling faded as quickly as it had come. Nothing happened, and I just sat on the edge of the bed smiling like my brain and face weren't freaking out. Finally she said, "I should probably pretend I'm doing my homework, so my mom doesn't think I'm slacking."

"Yeah, I know. It's late," I said. "And I have a few more cat videos to watch before I go to bed."

"You've always been an overachiever," she said.

"For me, the work day never ends."

I walked out into the night and started walking the twenty-two blocks—we counted one summer—to my apartment. I felt like this is what people meant when they talked about how confusing love is. As soon as I was no longer in her room, I knew not-kissing had been the right thing. It wasn't a romantic or sexual kiss desire—as far as I could tell, I still didn't want to kiss anyone that way. But no one other than my mom and uncle had ever told me they loved me. It's an intense thing to hear, even if you're asking someone to say it. Even if you think the word love is cliché and overused. Even if you maybe don't want to love the same way as other people want to love.

I thought back to the story Ada told me about the guy she followed to Vinton and how their relationship was so much better after they broke up. It made me think that sometimes people get so excited when they feel close to someone that they don't know what to do, and they think that excitement must mean it's sexual. But there's a lot of ways to be close to someone. We forget there are a lot of ways to love.

I got approximately five of those twenty-two blocks and called Maddy. "You ready to hear some stories?" I asked. And she said yes.

Bad Tattoos

Before I was even all the way to the seat next to her, before even saying hello, Maddy asked, "So what do you think now?"

Any other day I would have been grumpy about a random question, one with absolutely no context, first thing in the morning when we'd stayed up way too late. "What do I think of what?" I asked, smiling through a yawn.

"I don't know, I guess about everything," she said. "I mean, okay: I heard the stories, but I went to bed thinking, *What does he* think *about it?* I was so caught up in all the stuff I'd missed, I didn't even think to ask." She was wide-eyed and comically sincere. Somehow, even though we'd gotten off the phone at the same time and most likely slept the exact same short amount of time, she was far more awake than I was.

"I think I get what you're saying, but give me a place to start."

"Alright, so, what about the trippy stuff that came up in the group? Like the powers she was trying to get out of you, the mystical books in the library, and all that?"

"Honestly, I'm a little bummed that medical science turned out to be the answer to my mom's situation. I really wanted it to be some fountain of youth-type memory pool, or at least seriously large doses of fish oil or ginkgo biloba or something."

"But your mom getting her skull opened up is way more hard-core," she said. "And, in its own way, it is pretty trippy."

"I guess I hadn't thought about that, but you're kind of right." I considered all the different medical-science things that were actually pretty bizarre—cataracts surgery, organ donations, blood transfusions—but were so normalized at this point that we no longer noticed how freaky they really were.

"And you know what?" Maddy said. "I bet a gallon of fish oil in a memory pool is actually a real solution for somebody else. Like, somebody without a brain tumor who's just really spacey."

It was so nice to have Maddy back. For the first time in months, I felt like someone understood me.

"But, like, do you have a belief system or something now?" she asked.

I thought about it for a second. "I guess now I just believe that it's a bad idea to believe too much in anything. Like, maybe every philosophy is a little bit right but not all the way right."

"I can see that. But is that really your holy grail answer at the end of the quest?" She smiled, but I could tell she was also serious about the question.

"I mean, like I said, I lost the intention of the quest at some point. Maybe I realized that there's just no end to any quest for knowledge. Or that declaring an end to it, or finding one single answer, is just a way of lying to yourself and making something really complex seem easy and manageable."

She looked at me a little sideways, as she does. "Are you saying that life's a quest?"

I laughed. "Yeah, I guess I am." I felt myself blush a little. "That's pretty cheesy."

"But," she said, dramatically pointing into the air, "sometimes cheesy stuff is true."

"Well in that case, I'll proceed with getting a *life's a quest* tattoo."

"Well if you do that, then I'm getting a *sometimes cheesy stuff is true* tattoo."

"Sounds like the next step in our life quest is to get fake IDs."

She laughed and then her face turned downward in a particular way. "I didn't mean to make fun of your life philosophy," she said. "That was kinda rude."

"No, it was probably asking to be made fun of. But can I have a do-over?"

"Of course, take a do-over."

"I guess I just refuse to believe in absolutes. Good or bad, smart or dumb, winner or loser—it all seems really narrow-minded to me now. And I think that was Ada's downfall: no matter what she tried to tell me or herself, she just thought she was smarter than everyone and thought people who weren't successful in obvious ways were failures. Like, I'm pretty sure some part of her thought everyone in AMF was sort of stupid and deserved to be paying too much for too little. I just don't ever want to think like that again."

"Yeah, you're right. I don't want to be like that either."

"I get that human brains seem to be wired for either/ors, but maybe my philosophy is that those kinds of binaries limit our lives in so many ways and just generally make us less kind and maybe make the world a worse place."

"Damn, Elly, you actually did come out of it with a new belief system."

The bus pulled up to the stop across from the school and my body tensed.

Maddy put her arm around my shoulders and gave me a little squeeze, like she was my cool older brother in an '80s movie. "You ready for this?" she asked.

"I'm trying to be, but I don't think I could ever be ready." In my head, being gone for a couple weeks meant I was going to be a major spectacle. If I was going to be a spectacle because I was the winner of a TV game show, or because I learned some impressive magic tricks and word had spread about my sudden magician status, I'd be okay with it. But I didn't want any of the questions people were bound to ask, and I didn't want to hear the rumors that had been spread about me or my mom or my involvement with a known criminal.

Over the course of the day some people asked where I'd been, a few people gave me hugs, and a couple asked if I was okay, but otherwise it was just another day at school. Math class was math class and English was English. Half of my teachers welcomed me back, but the other half went on with class like I'd been there all along. And no one seemed to know anything about what had happened. I could have been on a luxury cruise for all people knew.

The next day there were a few more askers, but by the third day it was as if I'd never been gone at all. I'd braced myself for what turned out to be, basically, nothing.

Every day when I got home from school, I'd lie around the living room with my mom watching soap operas she'd taped off TV. I think she was just watching them because they were easy on her brain, and it didn't matter whether she paid attention or not. I'd seen soap opera parodies where there were evil twins and characters who die off and come back without any explanation, but I didn't know that type of stuff happened every week on real soap operas. They were so bizarre and fascinating that by the end of the week most of our conversations revolved around them.

Claudia and I met at a show Friday night. The way I'd imagined it, it would be just Claudia and me, out on the town. But when I met her at the haphazard community center where the show was, she already had a circle of people around her. It made the night a little less eventful but also created the pleasant illusion that I had a bigger friend group than I actually do. The bands were all from other high schools and all made a brand of noisy, similar-sounding something-or-other that was both awful and awesome and seemed to make sense with the rainstorm starting outside.

Afterwards, we went to a late-night restaurant in a neighborhood that was both not that far away from where I lived and in a completely unexplored land, where rain drummed on the outdoor seating pop-up tents while heat lamps hummed. It felt both fancy and lawless, like everyone was trying to have a tea party after the apocalypse. I got a drink with lavender in it and listened to conversations about people I didn't know and bands I'd never heard of.

Being back in the world of people my own age was confusing. It was like I didn't know what to talk about anymore, but I also felt like I hadn't really known what to talk about when I was with Ada, or AMF members, or people at the hospital. I wondered if there was a situation where I'd always know what to say, but I doubted it.

I Think I'm Getting the Hang of It

I took a video of the alien children for most of an hour, just to keep them out of trouble. I used the new digital camera their dad had bought and called it "our movie," even though it had no plot or discernible focus. Then we sat on the couch and watched the whole thing. I thought they would get bored, especially since everything in the video had just happened, but they wanted nothing more than to watch themselves move around on a screen doing all the things they had just done.

After lunch, they started asking for ice cream and video games and other things I'm not allowed to give them. So I said, "but we need to start writing the sequel to our movie," and they forgot they had ever wanted anything at all.

Quest Life

That night, Maddy and I had our first movie night in what felt like ages. We decided that, before chipping away at our thematic backlog, we needed a *life's a quest* theme. So we watched *Stand By Me*, *Monty Python and the Holy Grail*, and half of *The Straight Story* before we both fell asleep.

Maddy woke me up before she biked home. I moved from Uncle's couch to my bed, and dreamt I was on a road trip with my mom and Maddy and Ada. We each had something different we were looking for, but all the things could be found on the same path, so we'd decided to carpool. For being a big trip that was supposed to be eventful, all we did was watch the scenery out the window while Maddy played us songs she liked. It was long and boring, just like a real car trip. I never found out where we ended up because I heard my name. I pulled the blanket off my head and saw the fuzzy, before-glasses shape of my mom in my doorway.

"What time is it?" I asked.

"Noon-ish," she said.

"What are you doing up so early?"

I couldn't be sure, but I think she smiled.

"Well, there's a party tomorrow and we need some stuff," she said. "And I think I'm ready to go out into the world. So I thought I'd see if you wanted to take a journey."

"To the grocery store?" I asked.

She nodded, and something in me felt whole.

Today Was Unlike Any Other Day

That night, I wrote an email to Rigby:

Rigby,

Today was unlike any other day. Or else it was exactly like the kind of day I used to have all the time, but I'm just different now so it feels new. I can't tell. I rode on the front of a shopping cart while my best friend pushed me, I sat across the bus aisle from my mom and we pretended like we didn't know each other, I helped prepare fifty deviled eggs, I came up with ridiculous ideas for party games that were rejected by all who heard them. Do you want to celebrate the birthday of some-one you don't know on a Monday night? Tomorrow at 5pm. 3132 SE 9th Ave, Apt. 5.

Elly

The Future Might Suck

Someday, my mom might forget who I am. If she's the one in ten people whose tumor comes back and it doesn't get caught in time, me and everything she knows could disappear with it. In my head, I move that possibility to the distant nightmare world where the second Ice Age, World War III, and the sun exploding are all taking place simultaneously. Because today, my mom's 38th birthday, it feels very distant. She's wearing the high-waisted jeans she likes to wear to parties and beating my uncle and Rigby in the game Claudia and I invented that's a cross between limbo and pin the tail on the donkey. She knows all of her friends' names and all of my friends' names. Our apartment, the one I've lived in my entire life, is a place I feel proud to have not wandered far from.

I look around the room and think about how everyone is like me, how they're all in some way living with the possibility that the future might suck. And to some degree, they're all basing their lives off of it—whether it will or won't, whether the end is distant or near, whether to save or spend money, to make big plans, to have kids, to be nice. And I decide that, given the limitations of memory, I'm going to prioritize remembering this: We're united by the fact that we're all just guessing what the future might look like. So I let myself forget the times it seemed like everyone was disconnected from me, all the times I felt like an island, and instead celebrate the fact that I know just as little as everyone else. I remind myself that we're all just trying. Because trying is all we can do.

Liner Notes

"Why Blue" references the absurdist, posthumously published 1967 novel *The Third Policeman* by Flann O'Brien. It also quotes the then-newly-released 2009 experimental memoir *Bluets* by Maggie Nelson. Both are books Elly chose from Uncle's book stacks.

"What I Have" quotes Paramahansa Yogananda, from his 1946 book *Autobiography of a Yogi*. Uncle's spiritual and metaphysical reading inclinations, though they represent a much smaller percentage of his reading than literary fiction and nonfiction, are alluded to both in this quote and the book he checks out (and Elly reads, in part) about 2012 and the Mayan calendar. It's such a slight part of his life and reading, though, that Elly feels like he has almost no context when organizing the AMF library.

"My Nightmare Over Coffee" mentions the Beverly Cleary character Ramona Quimby and Elly's love of the Ramona book series. Even though Elly's supposedly long aged-out of the earlier books in the series, he still maintains that *Ramona the Pest* is his all-time favorite book.

"In the Kitchen, Learning to Dance" mentions a Stevie Wonder song and the kitchen-dance-party track in question is "Uptight." And, although no recordings were ever released of Mom's high-school band, Makeout Hangover, they were most inspired by the under-sung Seattle band Kill Sybil and covered their song "Deep Sleep" on the cassette tape of demos Elly and Mom dance to.

"The Silent Bus" quotes from the Polaris song "Hey Sandy," best known as the theme song to *The Adventures of Pete & Pete*. Maddy started watching *Pete & Pete* after finding it on the DVD shelves at the Belmont branch of the Multnomah County Library system a few months prior, then the show led her to the Polaris album. She's been meaning to get Elly into both the show and the band, but has yet to do so (in part because, by the time Maddy got fully absorbed in the Pete/Polaris world, Elly's July 25th birthday had come and gone, and the time since has been movie-theme focused). On the bus, she also sang the song's curiously poetic opening line, "Hey smiling strange," but Elly couldn't figure out what she was saying.

"Constraints" mentions the former Portland venue, gallery, and artist studio space, The Artistery, that ran from 2003 to 2011. Their early, pre-Southeast Division Street years are documented on the compilation CD, Live At The Artistery 2003-2005.

"What a Mystery Is" quotes Kate Greenstreet's poem "Great Women of Science" from her book *case sensitive*.

"Not What You Think" is the first mention of the fictional town of Vinton, Oregon, named after famed Oregon claymation artist Will Vinton. (The town's fictional bus routes were created with the assistance of poet and Portland bus expert Cole Cunningham.)

"Welcome to the Working Weekend" borrows its title from the Elvis Costello song "Welcome to the Working Week," a song that Maddy put on a mix CD for Elly the summer before ninth grade. He's tried every other Elvis Costello song since then and has enjoyed none of them.

"Don't Try to Forget" references the 1942 short story "Funes the Memorious" by Jorge Luis Borges, collected in *Ficciones*.

"Brilliance, Redefined" is the first in a series of slight *My So-Called Life* nods, with the Three Rivers Diner (and later Angela's coffee shop). It also references Plato's concept of anamnesis (often referred to as the Doctrine of Recollection or Doctrine of Reminiscence), established in *Phaedo*, the idea that "our learning is simply recollection. . . [which] implies a previous time in which we have learned that which we now recollect."

"Armistice Day" references a compilation of footage from the U.S. and France on November 11th, 1918 showing people celebrating the end of World War I. Maddy began searching Armistice Day to find a movie for their theme because of a Kurt Vonnegut, Jr. quote from his 1973 novel *Breakfast of Champions*:

"It was during that minute in nineteen hundred and eighteen, that millions upon millions of human beings stopped butchering one another. I have talked to old men who were on battlefields during that minute. They have told me in one way or another that the sudden silence was the Voice of God. So we still have among us some men who can remember when God spoke clearly to mankind.

Armistice Day has become Veterans' Day. Armistice Day was sacred. Veterans' Day is not.

So I will throw Veterans' Day over my shoulder. Armistice Day I will keep. I don't want to throw away any sacred things.

What else is sacred? Oh, Romeo and Juliet, for instance.

And all music is."

"Poetry About America" slightly rephrases a line from Matthew Dickman's book *All-American Poem*. "A bus is a diplomat. / It throws us all together, our books, / hats, and umbrellas. I am never more human / than when I'm riding next to someone / who makes me shudder. If my body / touches his body who knows what will happen?"

"The True Meaning of Chess" has Ada borrowing some language from David Shenk's then-recently released book *The Immortal Game: A History of Chess or How 32 Carved Pieces on a Board Illuminated Our Understanding of War, Art, Science, and the Human Brain*. It was the first chess book she'd read in years and activated her interest in how the game could apply to her new life.

"The Intern" refers back to the previously mentioned book about 2012 and the end of civilization, which is now long-out of print and completely lost to time. Other books included in the AMF library are (for better or worse) Rhonda Byrne's *The Secret*, Bruce Lipton's *The Biology of Belief*, Mark Vicente's *What the Bleep Do We Know!?*, Daniel Pinchbeck's *Breaking Open the Head*, Avinash K. Dixit's *The Art of Strategy*, J. Z. Knight's *A Beginner's Guide to Creating Reality*, Emanuel Swedenborg's *Heaven and Hell*, and Jeremy Narby's *The Cosmic Serpent*.

"What We're Not" quotes from the never-released two-part song "Volcano / My Friends" by the Olympia band Kickball. A singalong staple of their post-punk/math-rock era, the song often started and/or ended their shows in the years following their 2007 masterpiece *Everything is a Miracle Nothing is a Miracle Everything is*. Claudia saw them play what she described to Maddy as a "transcendent" house show the previous summer, which led Maddy to the band's MySpace page, and she got hooked on a live recording of the "My Friends" portion of the song. She used the peer-to-peer file-sharing program SoulSeek to track down a studio recording of the song and happened upon an unmastered recording slated for a split LP with French band Clara Clara (which ultimately never came to fruition).

"Nowhere to Hide" references the beloved *George and Martha* picture-book series by James Marshall.

"Edit the Sad Parts" is named after an early Modest Mouse song from 1996's *Interstate 8* EP. This is the final song on Maddy's summer-before-ninth-grade mix CD.

"The Poets Speak of Memory" quotes (in quick succession) from Kate Greenstreet's *case sensitive*, Julio Cortázar's *Hopscotch*, and Claudia Rankine's *Don't Let Me Be Lonely*.

"There Are Worse Things" references The Pica Beats' song "Poor Old Ra," off 2008's *Beating Back the Claws of the Cold*. Maddy would say Elly's interpretation of the song is a bit of a misread, but she would feel forgiving due to the surrounding circumstances. In Rigby's email, he paraphrases the Martin Luther King, Jr. quote, "Life's most persistent and urgent question is, 'What are you doing for others?' which was originally used in a speech, and then put to page in "Three Dimensions of a Complete Life" from his 1963 collection *Strength to Love*.

"Night Drive" quotes Mia Zapata and her lyrics from The Gits song "Seaweed."

"Regarding the Pain of Us" borrows its title from Susan Sontag's 2003 book-length essay, *Regarding the Pain of Others*. Uncle was reading it the previous summer and the title got stuck in Elly's head.

"Attempts at Life" and "Premeditated Fun" both reference Tom Drury's 1994 novel *The End of Vandalism*.

"Today Was Unlike Any Other Day" borrows its title from the zine series of the same name by Ariel Birks.

Acknlowedgements

Michael Schepps at Korza saved this novel from spending eternity in a drawer when he reached out to me about it last year. I'd accepted that this book wouldn't see the light of day and this probably would have held true if he hadn't started a press and remembered the early draft of this manuscript that he, by chance, read years prior. His editorial insight and support changed the shape of the book (and my mindset around the book) in so many needed ways. He's put more hours into this book than seems humanly possible, and I will be forever grateful for his dedication.

I'm equally grateful to Molly E. Simas at Korza, quite possibly the most insightful editor I've worked with. Over the years she's helped me through a wide variety of writing projects, and we've collaborated as co-editors on several projects, so it felt like the right time to finally work together in the long form. If I wasn't so perpetually broke, I would hire her to mark up everything I write until the end of time.

Before this manuscript spent several years in a drawer, the first draft was written over the course of 2013-2017 with the help of the writers Amy Vaniotis, Bharati Kasibhatla, Carly Cohen, Diane Nichol, and Nancy Beaini. Those years together were such a joy, and I learned so much through them. I can't wait for everyone to read the books each of these writers have in the works.

My dear writer-friends Karleigh Frisbie Brogan and Timothy Day both gave much-needed feedback at crucial points in the editing process.

Huge thanks to Fred Thomas for the cover image and for his deep belief in collaboration. I'm such a fan of his collage work, so it was a thrill to work together and to have him tailor a piece to the book's emotional landscape. Also, his songwriting is a true gift and I wouldn't doubt if some of the late-aughts imagery from his brilliant trilogy of albums (*All Are Saved*, *Changer*, *Aftering*) seeped into this text.

Andrew Barton is one of my closest collaborators and it was an honor to have him design the book. The work he did on the cover and interior really completed my vision of what this book should look like and how it should be read. (He also provided a fun history lesson on the cover fonts, Verdana and Belin bold, especially Verdana's connection to the year 2009.)

Endless gratitude and love to my lifer team of writers who have made sure I keep writing and publishing for the past 20 years: Alexis Wolf, Ariel Birks, Cole Cunningham (who also helped create the fictional Vinton bus routes), Craven Rock, Casey Fuller, and the late Craig Oare.

The last big generative portion of this manuscript was written during a Sou'wester Artist Residency in May of 2022. There was a storm my first couple nights and the wind off the ocean dramatically shook the travel trailer I was staying and working in. That's in here somewhere. Big thanks to them (and the wind).

Undying love to my whole family, especially Colleen Jefferson, Carl Amberson, Bob Amberson, and Annah Jefferson, all of whom had to hear about this book for years and years, despite seeing no physical evidence that it even existed as real words on the page. While no characters within are based on my actual family members, some familial structures and small details were borrowed from their lives. (The most prominent of these are Rigby's nightly emails, which were modeled after my grandpa's nightly emails.)

Endless appreciation to The Acknowledgments writing group for renewing my sense of writing community each month.

Thanks to my past roommates over the past nine years (somehow, I've lived with 20+ absolutely lovely people in that time) for letting me be a little stuck on the page at times.

And huge adoration and gratitude to my current apartment-dwelling loved ones: Novie, Sophie, and Rosalie.

A note on the type:

This book was set in Sabon, designed by German-born typographer Jan Tschichold between 1964-1967.

The cover features two common Microsoft typefaces, chosen in part because of their prevelance at the time the story in this book takes place. The title is set in Verdana, by British-born type designer Matthew Carter, released in 1996. The remaining cover text is set in Berlin Sans, based on the first sans serif type ever designed by German-born type designer Lucian Bernhard in the late 1920s and adapted for computer use by American-born type designers David Berlow and Matthew Butterick.

Also by Korza Books

**Is It Just Me Or Are We Nailing This?:
Essays On BoJack Horseman**
Published with Antiquated Future

Joshua James Amberson, Timothy Day, Jessica Fonvergne, Lauren Hobson, Tessa Livingstone, M.L. Schepps, Jourdain Searles, and Molly E. Simas.

Illustrations from: Eileen Chavez, Ross Jackson, Naomi Marshall, and Liz Yerby.

Cover by Sarah Mirk.

Split Aces
M.L. Schepps

Poetry For People: Fifty Years of Writing
Dixie Lubin

Altogether/ Different (Spring 2023)
Brianna Wheeler

Follow Us
@KorzaBooks on Twitter
@Korza_Books on Instagram

Joshua James Amberson writes essays, zines, very short stories, articles about arts and culture, and novels he hides in drawers. His work has appeared in *The Los Angeles Review of Books*, *The Portland Mercury*, *The Seattle Times*, *Vol. 1 Brooklyn*, *Hobart*, and *Tin House*, among others. He's the author of the chapbooks *Everyday Mythologies*, *Slow Motion Heroics*, and *Writing Exercises (And Various Approaches to Life on Earth)*, the zine series *Basic Paper Airplane*, as well as the forthcoming essay collection *Staring Contest: Essays About Eyes*. He lives with a lovely human, an aging Italian greyhound, and an elderly tortoiseshell cat in Portland, Oregon.